Peter Cubed
A Sequel to Peter Squared

Ken Goldberg

Wyndmoor Press
515 Grove Street
Suite 3D
Haddon Heights, NJ 08035
www.wyndmoorpress.com

ISBN:0615671268
ISBN-13:9780615671260

Author's photograph: Steve Sharp, www.stevesharp.net

For Sasha and Matt

NEW YORK

1 PETER

Herb, Anna, and Dave, thought Peter, *three four-letter names.* In his mind, Peter formed the word, HAD, using the first letters of their names. *I HAD to see Herb again. Anna is spelled A-N-N-A. Anna backwards is spelled, A-N-N-A. I never met Dave before. He must have E-V-A-D-ed me.*

YOU IDIOT. HIS NAME IS DAVE, NOT DEDAVE. 72%. NOW DO IT RIGHT.

Peter turned to his left. He could still see Herb, Anna, and Dave as they walked away, Herb and Dave in front, Anna tailing behind.

Two men in front, a woman in the back.

As they walked on, a man who was walking toward Peter obscured his view of Herb.

Two people I just met: visible. One person I knew before: not visible.

A moment later, this person blocked Peter's view of Anna just as another passerby walked in front of Herb.

Two people I've either known or feel like I've met before: not visible. One person I definitely don't know: visible.

Herb's head suddenly emerged between these two passersby leaving Peter's view of only Anna blocked.

Two men: visible. One hot woman: not visible.

HOT!? NO ONE'S HOT FOR YOU. NOW CUT IT OFF.

Peter watched until the three passed out of sight.

Zero friends. One Peter by himself.

***

Peter looked at his watch and saw it was 12:32 p.m. He started eating more quickly, 48% faster, so he could finish lunch in time to get back to work by 1:00 p.m. With his last bite, he looked at his watch again, smiled, seeing it was 12:54 p.m. Holding his head still, Peter pulled his left

1

arm toward his body bringing the watch's day/date screen into focus.

It's still Friday, thought Peter.

***

Peter walked onto the elevator, careful not to brush into the woman who was already standing there. Knowing it was Friday, he stood in the far right corner of the car, as he rearranged the letters of the day – *fir, fry, 'fraid, day, dry, diary, dairy* – broken from his thoughts by the chime that rang indicating he had reached the 4th floor. He walked off the elevator, taking five steps forward, eleven steps to the right, turning right again, standing in front of a door with the sign: Lerner and Branstill, Public Accountants. Peter stopped to think about how things had changed since Carl Schwartz left.

When Carl was here, Peter thought, there were 14 letters in the partners' names: Lerner with 6, Schwartz with 8. Six factors into 2 X 3, eight is 2 X 2 X 2. Six and eight have two as a common factor, and 2 X 2 X 2 X 3 = 24, the lowest common denominator. I have nine letters in my last name. Nine factors into 3 X 3. Three is the only common factor between Lerner and Branstill. Our lowest common denominator is 2 X 3 X 3 = 18. Carl's last name and my last name share four letters: r, a, s, and t. Re-arrange them and put them back together: I'm a star.

YOU'RE NO STAR, PETER BRANSTILL. YOU'RE A GODDAMN DORK! YOU DON'T GET PAID AND YOU'LL NEVER GET LAID!

***

Before leaving the firm last year, Carl secretly plotted to take the clients, assets and staff, leaving Andrew with nothing but Peter and the lease. Peter remembered sitting at his desk, immobile and stone-faced, frozen with fear, as he watched Carl storm out of Andrew's office, shouting ear-splitting invectives and cackling with delight while Andrew quivered and shook, tears rolling down his cheeks. With his gaze fixed firmly on the papers before him, Peter rechecked his work.

Once Carl left, Andrew ran straight to Peter, bawling profusely. Peter tried to look empathic while holding his right hand steady on his calculator repeating the figures as Andrew finally regained his composure and was able to talk.

"Carl's gone. We have no business. We're ruined. I don't know what to do. I'm broke. I can't pay the lease. I can't even pay you. What will I do?"

"If it helps," Peter said. "I'll work for free."

Stunned, Andrew threw his arms around Peter, bawling again now tears of friendship. Peter struggled to keep punching out numbers with his right hand while mentally estimating how badly contaminated he was becoming in contact with Andrew and his tears. Andrew broke his grip and looked at Peter saying, "Thanks, Peter. We're gonna beat him. You're a wonderful friend. I'm making you a partner."

***

Peter's thoughts shifted to second grade as he pictured himself standing on the playground, not far from King George, who was adored by the girls and protected by a posse that roamed the playground, their eyes on the teacher, waiting for her to turn her back so they could punch Peter in the face. Peter would stand motionless, his eyes fixed on the school building, trying to count the bricks on the school building's wall. But now, a partner, Peter could turn around and face the posse, as they quivered with fear, looking Peter's way.

Howdy, Podner, they'd say walking up to Peter, one by one, asking to be his friend.

YOU'RE NO PARTNER. YOU'RE A JERK. WE HATE YOU PETER BRANSTILL.

***

Peter looked at his watch: 4:55 p.m. He placed his papers in the To Do hopper to finish tomorrow. Since Carl left the firm and took the clients, there wasn't any work to do. Peter methodically spent his days checking and re-checking the same calculation, the one he had worked on when Carl walked out, every 5 minutes for 6-1/2 hours (an eight hour day with one hour lunch and two fifteen minute breaks).

Peter recorded in pencil, *76*, the number of times he completed the routine today. He sharpened each of his three pencils before inspecting them carefully. Pencil No. 1 was $\frac{1}{16}$ of an inch shorter than Pencils Nos. 2 and 3. On his To Do pad, he jotted down:

Begin workday with Pencil No. 2

Re-sharpen pencils at 10:00 a.m.

Decide on next pencil.

YOU IDIOT! YOU WROTE THAT WITH PENCIL 2.

The children laughed. Peter pictured Miss Weintraub sitting at her desk, red pen in hand, her expression stern while marking his paper as he trembled in fear.

72%. NOW DO IT RIGHT!

With Pencil No. 3 now slightly longer than Pencil No. 2, Peter carefully erased the number 2 from his To Do pad and changed it, with

Pencil No. 2, to 3.

Peter straightened out his paper clips, tape dispenser and calculator. He opened the stapler and counted: *24 staples left*. Peter fished out a notebook from his pocket and recorded:

May 29: 76 staples used. Pencil No. 3 longest.

Using his ruler again, Peter measured the radius of the roll of tape in the dispenser on his desk – $3/16^{th}$ *of an inch* – unchanged from yesterday having not used tape today.

Peter looked at his watch. It was 5:00 p.m. and time to go. Just as he rose from his seat, Andrew came bounding from his office smiling ear to ear.

"Guess what, Peter!?" he exclaimed. "I just got a call. We've got a tax return to do."

***

Following a brief stop at his favorite peep show, *Private Booths, Sexy Girls*, Peter walked toward the bus where he queued up in line. As the bus pulled up, a matronly woman, 55 years old or so, walked up behind him. Peter stepped to the side and let her pass. She said, "Thank you." Peter felt aroused.

Peter watched while some passengers got off, six in all. The line moved forward. Peter looked in the window realizing it would be a tight squeeze. He felt a rush knowing he'd be pressed flush up against her. He pictured her whispering in his ear, professing her love. She'd invite him home and beg him to undress. With heavy breath, her nipples erect, she'd pull him close and scream with delight. Peter thrust himself deeply inside. Suddenly, the man standing in front of the woman turned around and signaled her ahead. Then, he stopped short and motioned the driver to go on. "I'll take the next bus," he said.

The door closed, and the bus moved on. Peter stood dejected as a group of boisterous young men took their places behind him. One looked like King George. He seemed to look at Peter and say, "I told you man. You should've fucked her then."

Now in a sweat, Peter sprung out of line and hurried uptown. The bus faded from sight, and another appeared. This one was filled with school children who seemed to be laughing at Peter. He quickly dashed into the Barnes and Noble's Bookstore there. Once inside, he looked across the floor and saw that there was a magazine rack on the other side. Peter thought, *They must have hot horses here.*

***

4

Hoping to avoid suspicion, Peter shuffled left and entered an aisle in the TRAVEL section. He picked up *Fodor's United States*. Organized by major cities with their Places of Interest, Arts and Entertainment, Where to Stay, Where to Eat, Where to Shop, Sporting Events and Night Spots, Peter looked for New York. Under night spots, he found adult entertainment. Peter looked for *Private Booths, Sexy Girls* but saw only a general reference to the Times Square section of town.

Peter continued to leaf through the book and came to Washington, D.C. Again, it did not specify *The Capital Girls*, but sent the traveler in its general direction. *I wonder what's in Indianapolis*, Peter thought, wondering if he and Andrew might someday go back there to meet with Harold. Before he could turn the page, Peter sensed another person nearby. He closed the book and looked around, seeing a white-haired woman halfway down the aisle to his left. He tucked the book under his arm and walked out of the Travel Section. Looking back, Peter wondered, *Is she a Capital Girl?*

Peter looked around and saw NATURE AND WILDLIFE to his right. *Wow*, thought Peter. *That's even better than a magazine.* Remembering the old woman nearby, Peter walked to his left, hoping to divert her attention, before cautiously circling back.

Peter quickly came to CHILDREN'S BOOKS where a smiling clown and Sesame Street characters were on display.

Howdy would really like this, he thought. *I'll tell him when I get home.* Peter fished out his notebook and wrote under THINGS TO DO, *Tell Howdy Doody about the children's display at Barnes and Noble.* He returned the notebook to his pocket when, beset with pangs of guilt, he pulled it back out and wrote, *Tell Buffalo Bob and Clarabelle Clown, too.*

Peter then saw the café at the center of the store. People were sitting, talking, and reading books at tables all around.

GO AWAY. YOU CAN'T PLAY. NO ONE WANTS YOU. NO ONE CARES.

Peter looked away and continued on. Soon, he reached four distinct sections: PSYCHOLOGY, SELF-HELP, PERSONAL IMPROVEMENT, and SEX. Sauntering slowly through the aisles, Peter moseyed over to the books on sex. He noticed *The Joy of Sex, Everything You Wanted to Know About Sex, Have Great Sex, Sex for Married Men, Sex and the Single Girl*, and *Sex for Dummies*. Finally, Peter saw a book entitled, *Sex for Accountants*.

Breaking into a sweat, Peter looked to his left, then looked to his right. There, he saw a man standing alone, holding a book. The man noticed Peter and smiled. *He wants me*, thought Peter. Slightly aroused, Peter lowered his right arm bringing *Fodor's United States* near his hips to block the man's view of his crotch, just in time before a full erection formed. Shortly, an attractive woman entered the aisle, approached this man, and said, "Ready?"

"Sure," the man said, flashing the cover of his book her way.

"Got something in mind, big boy?" she asked.

"It has some good ideas," he replied.

"I've got some good ideas, too," she chuckled as she took his arm and led him away.

Peter watched the couple until they left his sight (*One man reading a sex guide. One woman wanting sex. Two people in love. One Peter all alone.*) before removing the book from the shelf and centering its front cover against his copy of *Fodor's United States*. As his erection subsided, Peter pulled his hands back to their original walking-in-a-store-carrying-merchandise position (elbow cocked at a 10^0 angle), and walked on.

Peter next came upon LITERATURE AND FICTION where he saw books sitting in six parallel two-sided books cases (twelve surfaces in all). Each shelf was divided into eight sections, each section with five rows. *12 x 8 x 5 = 480.*

Peter guessed there were 25 books in each section. *480 x 25 = 12,000 books. Wow, that's a lot of books.*

IDIOT! STOP GUESSING! 72%. NOW DO IT RIGHT.

So, Peter looked for the beginning of the alphabet where he found a book by Albert Aaron and proceeded to count the titles until he came to a book which had written on its spine:

Peter Squared * Ken Goldberg

That's familiar, thought Peter as he carefully looked at the spine of the book he was holding in his right hand, its cover still hidden by its position against the travel guide:

Sex for Accountants * Ken Goldberg

Realizing that this novel was written by the same author as the sex-guide he had just picked up, Peter opened the cover and read:

"Peter Branstill is a mathematically and sexually obsessed accountant. He has no friends and he's never gotten laid."

That's me!

Quivering, Peter went on to the reviews.

GREAT BOOK! THIS GUY IS REALLY WEIRD! Literary News.

LAUGHED THE WHOLE READ. HOPE HE GETS LAID IN GOLDBERG'S NEXT BOOK. Literature Today.

I LOVED ANNA, THE NYMPHOMANIAC HASIDIC JEW. I BET SHE'D LIKE PETER. The Best in Books Review.

Anna! recalled Peter, almost calling her name out loud. *The girl in the park today. I've heard of her before.*

Woozy, Peter tucked the book under his arm, haphazardly leaving the Fodor's Guide and *Sex for Accountants* on the shelf, forgetting that he originally wanted a book with pictures of horses, and walked straight to the counter to buy *Peter Squared*. Once outside, Peter raced to the corner and boarded the uptown bus. Trembling and sweaty, he stood near the back, brushing up against no one, and rode home.

2 HERB

By the time they had left Peter's view, Anna was deep in thought as Herb and Dave chattered on.

"Peter? Should I know him?" Dave asked.

"Sure you should. Don't you recall? Petey," Herb replied.

Petey? thought Dave. "No, I don't think I met him."

"I know you never met him. But you sure heard a lot about him, day after day. Every day, that is, until John Waller died."

"You mean that Petey?" Dave questioned. "The big tycoon John used to brag about, his best friend and all that shit?"

"Yup. One and the same."

"How do you know him?" Dave asked

"At Metropolitan. The day John killed himself. He was there a couple a days."

"Petey?! Ya gotta be kiddin'. I thought he was rich," Dave responded with surprise. "What the hell was he doin' in a shit hole like that?"

"The same thing you and me and Anna and all the rest of us nuts do there," Herb answered.

Herb looked at Dave and, seeing a puzzled expression on his face, went on.

"Come on, Dave," Herb explained. "You knew John, what a bullshitter he was. Petey's just an ordinary jerk like the rest of us. Sure, he's got a job, and I give him a lotta credit for that. Other than that, I don't know what to think. John told us he has a gorgeous wife and great kids, but who knows. Maybe, he's just as strange as the rest of us."

As Herb stopped to think and Dave began humming a song that had been stuck in his head all day, Anna walked two steps behind, looking for the entrance to the subway while listening intently to the voices of the girls from her sixth grade Yeshiva class call out in her head.

ONE, TWO. YOU'RE A JEW. THREE, FOUR. YOU'RE A WHORE. FIVE, SIX. YOU SUCK DICK. SEVEN, EIGHT. YOU MASTURBATE.

Seeing the sign for the train, Anna angled to the left until she reached the stairs, and began her descent to the subway platform.

"Bye Anna," Herb called out.

Anna failed to respond as she walked out of view.

ONE, TWO. YOU'RE A JEW. THREE, FOUR. YOU'RE A WHORE. FIVE, SIX. YOU SUCK DICK. SEVEN, EIGHT. YOU MASTURBATE.

"Where's she going?" Dave asked.

"It's Friday. Don't you remember?" Herb replied. "She always leaves early. What about you? Goin' back?"

"Sure," said Dave. "Ain't you?"

"Hell, no. Anna ain't the only one who's got religion."

With that, Herb turned into O'Toole's Bar, saying to Dave as he left, "Shabbot Shalom."

***

Herb walked in the bar and took a seat between two men: to the right, a well-dressed businessman; to the left, a worn and weary 50-or-so-year-old black man, mumbling under his breath, and in sore need of a shave and a bath. Herb turned to his right and stuck out his hand, "Hi there, friend. Herb Whitmore. This your first time here?"

The man looked at Herb, eyed him up and down, and without accepting the offer to shake hands, softly replied, "Yeh," before turning back to his drink.

"Great bunch a people here. You'll like this place," Herb went on. "No pretensions, no affectations. Just ordinary folk like you and me, whatever we do, whoever we are, wherever we live. I've been coming here for years. Hell, we all fart the same. Don't matter one bit. So whatdayou do?"

Herb waited. No answer came.

"I used to be in law," Herb went on. "Got tired of the fuckin' corporate rat race. Couldn't take it. Just decided to work for myself. Take a few cases here and there, the ones I really care about. I suppose ya got a whole stable of lawyers where you work. Right?"

The man picked up his drink, put the glass to his lips, finished, then reached for his wallet and pulled out a ten.

"That's just the type of law I got myself out of. Small practice. It's the only way to go. Here, I'll give ya my card, just in case."

Herb reached in his pocket and pulled out a rumpled and stained business card. He smoothed it out on the bar, and handed it to the man. "Herb Whitmore," he said. "That's me."

The man looked at the card before putting it on the counter along with the ten. After he left, Herb picked up the card and looked at it before returning it to his pocket.

Herbert J. Whitmore
Attorney at Law

For appointment, call
212-637-1000 and ask for Herb in the Day Program

Motto: It's for you, that we sue.

Personal former friend of the Rev. Martin Luther King, Jr.

***

Eight beers later, Herb tried to stand up but he lost his balance and fell to the side, landing on the black man sitting to his left.

"Sorry," Herb called out, adding "bro" at the end when he realized the man was black.

The man's eyes darted to the right. A piercing look, he briefly stared at Herb before turning back. With his head down and his eyes closed, he responded to Herb by saying, "Bro."

"You in Selma, too?" Herb asked.

"Never made it with no Selma?" the man muttered back.

"I was there," Herb boasted. "Sure was. Marched with the great ones: Martin, Ralph, Medger. We believed in something then, didn't we, man?"

"Oh yea, Selma," the man said, his head bopping up and down as he repeated to himself, "Selma, Selma, Selma, Selma ..."

"Right on, bro," Herb added.

Herb motioned the bartender for another beer as he started to sing,

> *We shall overcome. We shall overcome.*
> *We shall overcome some day, some day.*
> *Oh, oh deep in my heart. I do believe.*
> *We shall over ...*

"Fifty cents!" the bartender demanded, as he slapped down the beer, interrupting Herb's song.

Herb reached in his pocket and found nothing there.

"Shit," Herb muttered. "I'll have to pay you tomorrow."

Whisking the beer out of Herb's grip, the bartender poured it down the drain. "See ya tomorrow."

"See ya, man," Herb replied.

He got off the barstool and turned to his new friend with clenched fist salute. The man's head bopped up and down, muttering the name, "Selma."

***

Herb staggered home. He arrived at his apartment and reached in his pants pocket for his key. After four attempts, he looked in his hand and saw a nail clipper there. He reached in his pocket again: *No key.* With a heavy sigh, Herb shifted his coat from one arm to the other so he could reach into the other pocket: *Still, no key.* Herb kicked the door; but it wouldn't budge. He backed away from the door to the other side of the hall. Then, he ran forward, his shoulder down, ramming the door hard. It still wouldn't budge. Herb kicked it again before throwing his coat down and punching the wall. His hand ached with pain. Herb turned around, leaned against the wall, and slumped to the ground. There, he slipped his left hand in his pocket where he felt a metal object: *the key.*

Herb tried to push up with his right hand but collapsed in pain. Switching to his left hand, he pushed himself up, managing to finally rise from the ground. Now standing up, he inserted the key in the lock, turned it right and opened the door. Realizing he didn't have his jacket, Herb stumbled around before seeing it on the floor. He jumped over the jacket to kick it into the apartment, follow it in and lock the door.

Inside, there were dishes piled high, newspapers on the floor, clean and dirty clothes mixed together. Herb pulled a cord that hung in the center of the room turning a 40-watt bulb on. He brushed some bread crumbs off the table to the floor to make room for a bottle of *No Frills Brand Vodka* he removed from the shelf. He looked through the dishes until he found an unbroken glass. He turned it over to let the cigarette fall to the floor, rinsed it, and poured himself a drink.

Herb reached for a dog-eared picture he always kept in the middle of the table of himself as a younger man standing in a three-piece suit with Teri by his side, the children in front.

"Shit!" Herb cried, before launching his half-finished glass of vodka across the room.

You sonofabitch, Herb thought as he stared at this bright, young lawyer with his family and split level home, an associate of Cromwell, Douglas, McDougall, Halperin, Dooley, and Smith.

***

"Some day!" Herb said, exhausted from the march. "Imagine. We met Dr. King himself."

"Shh!" Teri replied. "Daddy's on the phone."

Herb sung while waiting for Teri to get off:

This little light of mine. I'm gonna make it shine.
This little light of mine. I'm gonna make it shine.
This little light of mine. I'm gonna make it shine.
Make it shine. Make it shine. Make it shine.

"Bye, Daddy," Teri said, before hanging up the phone and coming to bed to lay in Herb's arms.

"So, what did he have to say?" Herb asked.

"He wants us back right away. Talked with Phil Douglas. They want to offer you a spot in the firm. I told him it would have to wait. We've got things to do down here."

"Cromwell, Douglas, and Bullshit? No way. I'm not selling out," Herb insisted. Teri just smiled and made love to her man.

***

Herb looked at the picture once more, his mind foggy, trying to recall how, just three months later, he wound up there. He could remember the agonizing lunches he spent with people he didn't respect, quietly nursing his martini as the partners chattered on, seeming to be proud of their wealth, power, and status.

Herb's thoughts shifted to his meeting five years later with Phil Douglas.

"We sent you to rehab," Phil said. "What else could we do?"

Herb pleaded for the job he didn't want. He pictured Teri and the kids, the house, the mortgage. It meant nothing, yet it had become his whole world. He walked from Phil's office, packed up his things and went straight to the bar.

One drink after the other, a familiar scene, he couldn't go home. He staggered out on the street and was approached by a whore. He remembered the room, but not the bed. He never recalled what they did or how he wound up on the street. They told him he was lucky: three floors was high enough.

Teri stuck it out and was there when he came home. But one hospitalization after another was more than she could take. At first, he fought her tooth and nail, dragging her in and out of court to answer meaningless motions. Then one day, he looked at himself sitting in jail, not to fight Jim Crow but to keep from supporting his kids. When he came out, he signed them over to Teri's new man.

Herb tried to pour another drink when he realized the glass was no longer there. Half blind, he walked to the bed and fell in, glad he hadn't made it the morning before.

***

Herb would have slept through the night if not for a loud knock on his door.

"Go away," Herb called out; the knocking continued. He picked up his shoe and threw it hard against the door.

"Fuck you!" Herb screamed, pulling the cover back over his head. Again, there was a loud knock on the door.

"Fuck you!" he screamed again, this time rising from his bed, almost falling before he could stand up. Inured to the large urine stain on his pants, he stumbled to the door and said, "Fuck you! Go away! Who's there?"

"It's me," Malcolm replied.

"Me, too," Dave added.

"Fuck you, Dave, you goddamn traitor. Why'd you call him, you piece of shit?"

"Open up," Malcolm said.

Damn, Herb said to himself as he kicked the bottom of the door. "OK, Hold on."

Herb went to the bathroom, picked up a damp towel, and wiped the front of his pants, the stain still there. He returned to the door and let Dave and Malcolm in.

Malcolm offered Herb his hand. Dave started to explain, "I'm sorry. I saw you go in and ..."

"Forget it man," Herb said. "You did the right thing."

The three men walked to the living room, Malcolm and Dave sitting on the coach, Herb taking a seat on a plastic covered chair to the side. The men sat in silence until Herb spoke up, "I fucked up."

Malcolm nodded his head.

Dave said, "Today's the first day of the rest of your life."

Herb chuckled. "Yea. One day at a time."

A few moments later, Herb reiterated, "I really fucked up."

"You relapsed," Malcolm said.

"No, I fucked up," Herb added. "I relapsed tonight. It's my life that's fucked up. I was married with kids, was educated, had a career."

"You sure did, and you sure lost it all," Malcolm said. "You never failed at what you did. You just never insisted on being who you are."

"I thought I did," Herb said. "We went through the 60s together. We believed in something."

"The same things?"

"No," Herb said. "Not at all. But she sure was a good fuck."

"You owed her amends for what you put her through," Malcolm went on. "But you already did that. She's remarried and has what she wants. The kids are OK. When are you gonna get on with your life?"

Herb started to cry, but then thought about the beer still in the fridge.

"Can you throw that fuckin' can out for me Dave?" he asked. "So, what's left for me?"

Dave responded as cheerful as ever, "The first day of the rest of your life."

"And a stitch in time saves nine," Herb replied. "What the fuck am *I* gonna do?"

"Work your program, one day at a time. Ninety days, ninety meetings. Go to mental health every day. Take your medication. If you feel shaky, call," Malcolm explained.

Herb sneered, "I think I heard that somewhere before."

"And you'll hear it again," Malcolm added, "again and again and again and again, until you get your head straight and go on with your life."

"I know," Herb said. "But this *one day at a time* shit don't work for me. You've got a job, and Dave's as happy as a clam eating chipped beef on toast each Thursday at the Midtown Morons Mentally Healthy Day Center."

"You think I always worked, Herb? You know I fuckin' didn't. I had to pull myself together first. Then, I could have what I wanted. And I don't even have a fuckin' law degree. You still in the bar, ain't you Herb?"

"True. I never lost my license. Even if I was shaking, down to my last dollar, I'd keep up the bar before I'd go to the bar."

Dave and Malcolm smiled.

"Pretty clever," Herb said. "I think I'll write that down."

3 ANNA

Anna descended into New York's underground transit system leaving Herb and Dave and boarded the B train to Brooklyn. She took a seat in the car and looked out the window where she saw G-d. His two piercing eyes followed her home while the sixth grade Yeshiva girls continued their rhyme:

ONE, TWO. YOU'RE A JEW. THREE, FOUR. YOU'RE A WHORE. FIVE, SIX. YOU SUCK DICK. SEVEN, EIGHT. YOU MASTURBATE.

She thought about her father as the train rumbled on, the horrors of Auschwitz, a wife, three children, all perishing in the mire, a pious man made to eat dung, scraps of food, with death all around.

THREE BEFORE, YOU'RE THE WHORE.

Anna stared at the faceless people in the train beside her, their lost humanity, the smell of corpses, death everywhere, an echoing sound as the train sped along.

THREE BEFORE, THERE ARE NOT MORE, ONE OF FOUR, THE ONLY WHORE.

***

Anna walked off the train and down the stairs from the subway that had turned into an elevated line. She continued up 14th Avenue, inured to the people around her, opening the door to take her place behind the others. *Only the prettiest survive,* she thought as she hoped the guards would pick her. *Who would perish? Who would survive?*

THREE BEFORE, HE'LL HAVE NO MORE. ONE OF FOUR, THE ONLY WHORE. THEY'LL MAKE THEIR SELECTION. YOU'LL WIN THE ELECTION. ONE OF FOUR, THE ONLY

WHORE.

"Your selection," Hyman asked, his sharp tone grabbing her attention, bringing her back to the moment. "Anna! What do you want? It's almost Shabbot and I'm about to close."

Anna looked ahead. *It's him, the Butcher of Boro Park.* "Chicken," she answered.

***

Sol entered the apartment and called out to Anna, "Where's dinner?"

In a stupor, lost in thought, standing by the stove holding a fork in the pot, her posture rigid, her hand frozen, Anna failed to notice Sol approach. He looked in the pot, saw the chicken boil, and said, "Chicken?"

When Anna failed to respond, he pulled his hand back to slap her. She still didn't move.

"Idiot," he muttered, holding his punch and leaving the kitchen, to sit in his favorite chair where he began reading the *Hasidic Daily World*.

Anna stirred the pot, turned the flame down, and walked down the hall. She entered the bathroom, locked the door, turned the light off, sat on the toilet, lifted her dress, and pulled her underpants down. The voices grew louder,

ONE, TWO. YOU'RE A JEW. THREE, FOUR. YOU'RE A WHORE. FIVE, SIX. YOU SUCK DICK. SEVEN, EIGHT. YOU MASTURBATE.

Anna listened as G-d joined the Yeshiva girls,

DIE, DIE, DIE.

Anna reached in her pocket and removed a small, single-edged razor. Pulling on the left side of her labia, she carefully inserted the razor into her vagina. She felt no pain as she watched the blood drip on her finger. As always, the sight of blood made the voices stop. Anna could now hear Sol banging on the door screaming, "Where's my dinner?"

Anna put the razor on the counter so she could pull her underpants back up. She washed and dried the razor and returned it to her pocket. With Sol still screaming and pounding, she opened the door. Sol grabbed her by her shoulders and pushed her back, causing her to lose her balance and fall back slightly.

"I'm hungry," he said before returning to the table.

Anna got up. She shook her head and rubbed her back before leaving the bathroom and walking back to the kitchen. When she reached the table, Anna lit the Sabbath candles.

***

After dinner, Sol returned to his chair while Anna cleaned the kitchen. Sol watched her carefully over the top of his prayer book. Once she was done, he got up from his chair, put down his book and motioned her to bed.

"I don't want to," Anna complained.

"It's Friday night," Sol replied.

Reluctantly, Anna walked down the hall and went into the bedroom where she plopped herself on the bed. She pulled up her dress and covered her face with it. Sol removed his trousers and mounted her. Without foreplay, with her underpants still on, Sol slipped inside and climaxed quickly.

Connie smiled now that Anna was no longer there. She pulled the dress off her face and took off her underpants. Showing Sol the blood-stained undergarment from when Anna cut herself before, she said, "Anna's not clean."

As expected, Sol shuddered realizing he had had relations with a woman who was not clean, lowered his head, got out of the bed, and left the room.

Connie smiled as she pictured herself lying on the beach, listening to the rolling waves, feeling the warmth of the sun beating down. She looked up and saw the man she had met at the bench earlier today. As she pictured herself making love to Peter, Anna took out the razor and began to cut again.

***

Anna got out of bed and looked down the hall where she saw Sol's head above the top of the chair, bobbing up and down as he read. Anna walked to the kitchen and lay down on the floor.

Connie looked up and realized they were under the cutlery drawer. She reached up and pulled out a knife as G-d continued to scream at Anna,

DIE, DIE, DIE.

Connie placed the knife lengthwise into her mouth, dull edge against her teeth, sharp edge out, and slowly crawled on all fours until she reached Sol. Engrossed in his prayers, Sol never heard her come. Squatting by the back of the chair, Connie took the knife out of her mouth with her right hand, and sprung to her feet drawing it swiftly across Sol's neck. Like a Kosher-killed chicken, Sol jerked forward before slumping in his chair, his neck gushing blood.

***

Without saying a word, Anna put on a shawl and walked to the door. She looked back and saw Sol in the chair reading his book. She opened the

17

door and walked out the apartment, climbed the stairs up one floor, and continued down the hall until she reached Apartment 435 and knocked on the door.

"What took you so long?" her mother scolded as Anna walked in. "People are coming Sunday and you've got to help. Schlomo won't come. Sadie's got a cold. He'll never leave the house without her. You have to make the chopped liver. I can do the rest. Bring chairs, six will do. Make that eight, Ike and Rachel might come. I hope not. You know I can't stand Ike. He's such a bore."

Anna followed her mother into the kitchen, the voices now screaming at a deafening pitch. Barely able to concentrate, she kept repeating her mother's instructions (*chopped liver, eight chairs*).

"I can't take Rifka," her mother went on. "I'll scream if she talks about her son one more time. He went to NYU: Big deal. He's not the only dentist in the world."

Anna cringed when she noticed her father's davaning sounds.

"He never visits her. He doesn't even fix her teeth. And teeth! She looks like a beaver. I can't believe Nathan married her. A smart man my brother: an accountant, good-looking too. He could have had any of the Yeshiva girls. Why he'd want a buck-toothed monza is beyond me."

Rabbi Pearlman stopped his chant, put his book down on the shelf, walked up to Anna and motioned her back.

"So, let's put this together," Sophie said. "You've got the liver, I'll make the roast. Come early and help me with the vegetables, too?"

Anna followed the rabbi down the hall ...

"Fruit kugel!" Sophie exclaimed quite proud of herself. "We haven't had one for a long time."

...and into the bedroom ...

"So what do you think? Will Schlomo come without Sadie? You're right. He won't be there."

... before he closed the door.

4 THE BOOK

At home, Peter opened *Peter Squared* quickly confirming his original thought that the book was about him. He turned to the back inside jacket and saw a picture of the author, Ken Goldberg, with the words,

Dr. Goldberg, a psychologist and former mathematician, lives with his wife and three children, outside Philadelphia.

Philadelphia, thought Peter. *That's not far.*

Peter went to his file and retrieved a map of Pennsylvania. Since Philadelphia was on the way to DC, Peter figured that he could take the same train he took on his trip to the capital last year. Peter quickly leafed through the book until he found a chapter called, *Washington, D.C.*

Wow! thought Peter. *Even my trip is in here.*

Peter looked at the book again and re-read, *outside Philadelphia*

Returning to the map with a protractor in his hand, Peter placed the point on City Hall, then opened the protractor wide enough to draw a circle that covered the entire city. The radius of this circle was 4½ inches and represented 18 miles, the map scaled 4 miles per inch. Since $A = \pi r^2$ the circle defined an area of 1017 square miles. Peter went to the web and found out that Philadelphia by itself was 135 square miles. *That's 882 square miles outside Philadelphia,* thought Peter.

Since Philadelphia has 1,517,550 people (also found on the web) living it its 135 square miles, or 11,240 people per mile, Peter guessed that about 9,913,680 people lived outside Philadelphia yet 18 miles or less from the center of town. Assuming half are men, Peter figured this would leave 4,956,840 people who might be Ken. If Peter visited these outskirts and systematically asked each man he encountered whether or not he was Ken, the odds were greater than not that he would find Ken by the time he asked the 2,478,420th person, half the male population. Knowing he had a hard time talking to people, Peter figured he would need at least a half hour to muster the courage to approach each person. Peter figured he could find Ken, searching day and night, in 1,239,210 hours, 51634 days or 141½ years.

YOU IDIOT. YOU CAN'T TALK TO ANYONE. YOU WON'T FIND HIM AT ALL. YOU'LL GO TO THE FIRST PEEP SHOW AND JERK OFF.

Knowing he'd never find Ken that way, Peter returned his protractor and ruler to the drawer, and his map to its file. Noticing that pornography just like Pennsylvania began with the letter P, he switched files, returning *Pennsylvania,* removing *Pornography*, and masturbated to a picture of a woman giving a man oral sex.

I wonder if he lives outside Philadelphia, Peter thought, looking at the man in the picture. *Maybe this is Ken.*

***

"You've got mail," Peter heard, drawing his attention to his computer. Seeing an e-message from cuminme@yahoo.com, Peter thought for the moment that she was an old friend, but opened the message and found a standard pornographic internet site.

He next went to the Google search box, where he typed in seven words:

ken goldberg peter squared psychology mathematics masturbate

The Google search returned www.greatauthor.com, Ken Goldberg's personal website. There, he saw words from the book in his hand, Ken's picture, the jacket cover, information about Ken's practice as a psychologist, and an email link.

Wow! Peter thought. *I can reach Ken.*

Feeling queasy, Peter returned to cuminme's website and masturbated once more. Realizing this was his third orgasm since work, he bookmarked the page, knowing he was required to masturbate once more ($2^2 = 4$) before he went to sleep.

***

Peter clicked the Write Mail icon and entered Ken's address kengoldberg@greatauthor.com in the SEND TO box.

His heart racing, Peter typed *A Message from Peter* in the SUBJECT BOX. In the body, he began to write.

Dear Ken,

Peter shuddered. *Too familiar. He'll think I want to have sex with him.* Peter changed the entry to:

Dear Ken:

Can't use a colon, Peter thought. *He'll think I want it up the colon.*

Peter retyped his first salutation – Dear Ken, – and studied it carefully. *Dear,* Peter thought. *It's not the colon. It's Dear that's too familiar.*

To Ken:

Peter began typing:

My name is Peter Branstill. I just bought your book.

Peter looked back at the salutation, To Ken. He returned to the book and re-read the description of Ken,

Dr. Goldberg, a psychologist and former mathematician ...

Peter got out of his seat and went to his file cabinet. There, he found the folder labeled:

PETER BRANSTILL, THE EARLY YEARS, AGES 0-10.

He searched the folder and found records of his treatment with child psychologist, Dr. Richard Kline, with the entry:

Dr. Kline asked me to call him Dr. Richard. He liked to play checkers. I never told him I wanted to play with the horse in the toy chest.

Peter changed the greeting:

To Dr. Ken:

Peter thought about his last session with Dr. Kline as he returned the folder to the drawer.

***

"King me!" he cried, as he continued to build an awesome force. Peter quietly moved his lone checker back to the only square left. Although Dr. Richard could have ended the game on the next move, he postponed the kill to earn one last king.

***

To Dr. Ken:

That was Dr. Kline, Peter thought. *Ken might not like that.*

Peter changed the words:

To Dr. Goldberg:

Peter looked at the greeting again thinking, *That's it. Ken, not Dear was the problem.*

Peter changed his greeting again,

Dear Dr. Goldberg:

Hm, thought Peter. He's a psychologist and a doctor, but this is a book. He's really an author, not a doctor, here. So, Peter changed the greeting again:

Dear Author Goldberg,

Something's wrong, Peter thought.

Dear Arthur Goldberg,

He was a Supreme Court Justice. Maybe he knows the Capital Girls.

Dear Dr. Ken not Arthur, but Author Goldberg:

No. Peter thought. He tried again:

Greetings:

That's good.

Greetings:

My name is Peter Branstill and I just bought your book. In the beginning, it says:

All characters in this book are fictitious. Any resemblance to real persons, living or dead, is strictly coincidental.

But the book seems to be about me. I thought you'd want to know this.

Yours truly,

Peter Branstill

Peter tapped his fingers on the desk, wondering if he should send his message.

YOU IDIOT. IT'S ALL WRONG. 72%. NOW DO IT AGAIN.

Peter grabbed the mouse and blocked the entire text. But, instead of pushing the delete button, his hand slid up and to the right until the pointer landed on the SEND MAIL NOW icon. His hand shaking, trying to bring the mouse back, hoping to delete his words, Peter nevertheless clicked the left button, and sent his message tumbling through cyberspace directly to Ken.

"Oh, God!" Peter screamed out loud. "What have I done?!"

Quickly, Peter wrote and sent another message.

Dear Ken,

Forget my last message.

Peter Branstill

Yikes, Peter thought. *I'm such a fool.*

Peter quickly composed another email hoping he could convince Ken the last emails were jokes written by someone else.

Dear Ken,

Just kidding. Forget the last message.

Harvey Littleberg

BERG! Oh, God! He'll think I'm making fun of him because he's Jewish. And LITTLE. He'll know I have a little penis.

Quickly, Peter sent out another email:

I meant Harvey Bigchristian.

But then, Peter realized there was a bigger problem: the messages were all coming from his email account at work: peter@lernerandbranstill.com.

Ken's smart. He'll know who I am. He'll know I wrote him, and he'll know my penis is small. Four messages. Four stupid messages. What can I do?

YOU KNOW WHAT TO DO. CUT IT OFF!

That's right, Peter thought. *I'll cut it off now.*

Quickly, Peter sprang from his computer and ran to the kitchen. He opened his zipper and pulled his penis out extending it onto the kitchen counter top. Holding it securely with one hand, he opened the top drawer with the other where he kept his butcher's knife. With the knife held high, Peter looked at his outstretched organ and, remembering John's advice, began to count out loud,

"One, two, three, four, five, six, seven, eight, nine, ten."

Peter took a deep breath and put the knife down. He returned to the living room where he sat down, picked up his book, and found the story John told him about the man who did cut it off.

Peter went back to cuminme's website and masturbated once more, knowing that, if he masturbated again tonight, he would have to masturbate four more times to reach 2^3. A thought crossed Peter's mind, *Ken's a mathematician. Maybe, he knows of a number system where five is a power of something.* A rare smile, Peter said to himself, *I'll call it the Base Peter system. Peter Cubed will be five.*

5 THE INSTANT MESSAGE

Saturday morning, Anna waited quietly until Sol left for schul. She put her jacket on and walked out the door, onto the street and toward the train. Afraid to be seen traveling on Shabbot, she continued down the street until the neighborhood changed. She saw three signs:

Dr. Marino, Dentistry
Sal's Italian Bakery
Dom's Pizzeria.

Anna continued to walk to the next entrance of the el. Anna reached in her purse as she climbed the stairs, removed her fare card and put it in the slot. After paying her fare on the Sabbath, the voices began to chant,

ONE, TWO. YOU'RE A JEW. THREE, FOUR. YOU'RE A WHORE. FIVE, SIX. YOU SUCK DICK. SEVEN, EIGHT. YOU MASTURBATE.

Anna walked through the turnstile and onto the platform before boarding the next train. She took a seat and looked straight ahead. G-d peered back through the window, his eyes embedded in the buildings the elevated train passed. Anna squinted with the glistening sunlight, crossing over the Manhattan Bridge before descending underground, G-d screaming all the way,

DIE, DIE, DIE

Anna looked around and saw the vacant faces of the other doomed passengers, locked in the rickety old cattle car, human excrement on the floor, no water or air, the armed guards outside. The train came to a sudden halt, stopped two minutes, then edged slowly ahead until reaching the station. Anna looked at the sign,

TREBLINKA

A voice called out over the loudspeaker.

"Times Square"

Anna rose from her seat and walked forward, the line halting for a woman with three small children as she stopped to gather her things.

Counted and selected, the others will be eliminated, thought Anna as she looked ahead and saw a young man in uniform. *Please take me.*

The man stepped aside to let the passengers out so he could board the train. Anna looked at the woman again. The voices screamed,

YOU'RE NO LADY, KILLED THE BABY. YOU'RE NO LADY, KILLED THE BABY.

***

Anna arrived at the park which was much less populated than it had been the day before.

YOU'RE A FOOL, GO TO SCHUL. YOU'RE NO LADY. KILLED THE BABY.

Although most of the benches were unoccupied, someone was sitting on the one Peter used the day before. Anna walked toward it and stared at Peter while he read his paper and ate his lunch. Peter looked older today, his hair white, with wire-rimmed glasses and a cane propped by the side of the bench. Anna stood across the walkway and placed her heels on the edge of the grass, her toes on the walkway. She gazed at Peter longingly just like she had the day before, Peter lowered his paper, his eyes meeting her, and said with a British accent, "Hello, Miss."

Anna stood motionless, saying nothing, listening to the voices in her head.

ONE, TWO. YOU'RE A JEW. THREE, FOUR. YOU'RE A WHORE. FIVE, SIX. YOU SUCK DICK. SEVEN, EIGHT. YOU MASTURBATE.

Peter smiled as he ate a peanut before raising the paper again and continuing to read. Anna remained in place.

Peter peered above his paper again, this time without smiling, and asked, "Are you OK, Miss? Can I help you with anything?"

Anna remained motionless, still not saying a word. Peter shrugged his shoulders and returned to his paper.

A few minutes later, Peter put the paper down, folded it neatly, stood up and said to Anna, "Let's go."

Connie and Peter walked hand in hand from the park.

"Do you like knishes?" Peter asked Connie.

"Yes, very much," she replied.

"There's a vender across the street. They sell potato knishes. Would you like one?"

Anna smiled. "No thanks. They're not Kosher. You know, I'm Hasidic. I only eat Glatt Kosher."

"Oh," Peter replied. "I didn't know the difference. You know, I'm not Jewish."

Connie laughed. "I didn't think you were."

Peter and Connie chuckled, the inane laughter of people in love.

Peter asked, "Where can I get you a Glatt Kosher knish?"

"I'd rather get a room," Connie replied.

Anna felt herself shake as she and Peter rode the elevator to the 7th floor of the Waldorf Astoria. Peter calmly put the key into the door of room 710 and led her in.

"I'm scared," Anna said.

"Don't be," Peter replied.

Relaxed by his soothing words, Connie opened her arms and gave Peter a hug. Soon, they were lying in bed, undressed. Peter ran his fingers gently through Connie's hair. He pulled her close and kissed her on the lips. Connie purred, offering her tongue in response. When Anna turned over to offer Peter her rear, expecting him to enter the way her father often did, he gently pushed her back and said, "Lie back. This is for you."

Peter warmly caressed Connie's breasts while she lay on her back. He took her firm nipple into his mouth and sucked it gently, a rolling motion. As Connie began to moan, Peter moved his hands slowly along her abdomen, purposefully delaying his approach to tease her and heighten her desire. By the time he touched her vagina, she was trembling with desire. Connie opened her legs to invite Peter in, but he held back, gently separating the folds of her labia and licking her clitoris with the tip of his tongue. Connie screamed while Peter continued to touch her and lick her, pressing slightly harder as she became wet with passion. Having orgasm after orgasm, Connie begged Peter to enter her, but Peter refused, extending the wait, as his tongue darted in and out of her. Finally, he pulled his head up from her vagina and brought his body over hers, kissing her passionately while his hard organ glided in.

***

Anna stood still as an elderly woman, carrying several library books in her hands, approached the bench.

"How are you, Irv?" she asked.

"Fine. Did you get what you wanted?

"No, but I had fun looking at books."

"That's great, love."

"How about you?"

"Couldn't be better. Great weather and the New York Times, a beautiful woman: who could ask for more?"

"Oh, stop it, Irv," she giggled. "We're not children anymore."

"We'll see about that tonight," Irv answered as he got up, took his woman by the arm, and left the park, leaving his paper and bag of peanuts behind.

***

Upon returning from the laundromat, Peter saw two messages in his inbox, both from kengoldberg@greatauthor.com, one with "Your lucky day" on the subject line, the other, "Where the hell are you? I don't have all day." Peter opened the first email which went on to say:

Peter,

Get AOL Instant Messaging.

Ken

Unsure what to do, Peter conducted a Google search for AOL Instant Messaging.

Before long, Peter had an account with the IM screen name: Peter. Within moments, a message flashed on the screen:

The Internet user kengoldberg has sent you an Instant Message. Would you like to Accept?

His hand shaking, Peter moved the cursor and clicked YES.

kengoldberg: Hi Peter. Great job getting IM so quickly. Guess you're not as dumb as everyone thinks. I'd give you an 82% myself. LOL

Peter looked at the screen. Below the message was a box with the word: Respond. Peter clicked the box and wrote in.

Peter: Is that you, Ken Goldberg?

kengoldberg: Did you think it was Santa Claus? LOL. Who else could it be? It's not like you've got friends. Well, I guess it could be one of those pornographic solicitations you often get.

kengoldberg: Hold on. I'll be back in a sec.

Peter sat at his computer waiting for Ken's return. He looked at the first message: *Wow. Eighty-two per cent.* Before long, Peter heard a knock at the door. Not wanting to leave the screen, he called out "Come in."

Peter, you old son-of-a-gun, Ken called out as he walked in the door. *How's it going? Andrew OK? Miss John? Have you screwed Anna yet?*

Peter smiled and shrugged his shoulders, *Not yet, but maybe tonight.*

Ken entered the door again, *Peter, you old son-of-a-gun. How's it going? ...*

For the next three hours, Peter replayed this conversation over and over until he looked at his watch and saw it was time to visit his mother's grave. Peter looked at the screen, which still displayed,

kengoldberg: Hi Peter. Great job getting IM so quickly. Guess you're not as dumb as everyone thinks you are. I'd give you an 82% myself. LOL.

Peter: Is that you, Ken Goldberg?

kengoldberg: Did you think it was Santa Claus? LOL. Who else could it be? It's not like you've got friends. Well, I guess it could be one of those pornographic solicitations you often get.

kengoldberg: Hold on. I'll be back in a sec.
Peter signed off.

.

6 BREAKING FREE

After her shower Sunday morning, Anna opened the bathroom cabinet so she could take her medication. The Lithium kept her stable. The Prozac covered the pain. She also took Thorazine to stop the voices although she often skipped it before visiting her parents, the hallucinations helping her handle her father's assaults.

In July, Anna generally stopped her medication altogether. Before long, she became manic and would leave New York hoping to have sex with a goy. If she timed it right, she could have her tryst before going back on Lithium, stable by Yom Kippur Day. One day of fasting and the guilt went away.

Anna looked at her watch and saw the date: May 30. *Too soon,* Anna said to herself.

Do it, Connie scoffed. *You'll have fun.*

I can't, Anna protested as G-d started to scream in her ears.

Peter's hot. Connie said.

I can't, Anna pleaded. *It's only May. Yom Kippur's months away.*

You'll take an extra Prozac, Connie replied.

That won't work! Anna cried. *I have to confess.*

See a priest, Connie laughed. *You did that before.*

Anna pictured herself sitting in the booth, confessing her sins, a gentle voice on the other side, accepting her as she was, offering G-d's pardon.

I'm a Jew, thought Anna, having vowed she'd never do that again. Connie kept flashing Peter's face in Anna's mind's eye, Peter lying with her in bed, his head between her legs, his strong tongue, just as she imagined him yesterday in the park. Anna picked up her Lithium and slowly turned the bottle over. She recited the *Sh'ma,* as she flushed the pills down the toilet.

Connie placed her hand between Anna's leg, massaged her gently and

29

.

said, *That's good.*

With the razor in her hand, Anna cut herself again.

***

Anna left the bathroom and saw Sol sitting there. He looked up from his book, "Where's breakfast?"

"I'm going out," Anna replied.

Shocked by her defiance, Sol responded, "No, you're not," expecting that Anna would sit down.

Anna walked to the closet and picked out a shawl. She placed it around her shoulders and began for the door. Sol rose from his chair and ran to the door, slamming it shut. Anna looked in Sol's face, his eyes glaring, his face twisted, rage in his eyes. The voices started to scream. For a moment, she thought she'd give in. Yet, she also knew she had crossed a line. For years, she took off quietly, picking up strangers, sometimes on the bus, sometimes in a bar, sometimes a man, sometimes a woman, once Peter's friend, John. But she never stood up to Sol, always taking off in the middle of the night, never telling him what she was doing, never challenging him directly.

"I'm going!" Anna screamed.

"No, you're not!" Sol screamed back, forming a fist with his hand and launching it into Anna's face, punching her in the eye. Sol reared back and hit her again, this time in the jaw. Sol continued to pummel his wife as she fell to the floor. Feeling woozy, she almost passed out.

"I told you, you're not going anywhere," Sol said. Sol kicked her before returning to the kitchen.

Anna rose to her feet, shook her head, and with Sol's back turned, quickly opened the door and ran down the hall. Sol turned to follow her but by then, she was out on the street.

Sure he would call the police (a nutcase, it was always her fault), Anna dashed along the side streets, cutting through an alley, and making her way out of the Jewish quarter until she reached the el and was on her way to the park.

***

The light shined through the torn shade on his bedroom window Sunday morning. Herb pulled the covers back over his head when he heard the phone ring. After eight rings, it stopped. Herb knew it was Malcolm and that he was going to call again. He counted to ten assuming it would take Malcolm that much time. At six, the phone rang again.

He's serious, Herb thought, letting the phone ring five more times before picking it up.

"Where the hell are you?" Herb bellowed out, knowing his words would perfectly match Malcolm's.

"Shit head!" Malcolm screamed back. "I should let you drink yourself to death, you fucking jerk."

"Don't worry. I haven't slipped. I'm going to the one o'clock meeting," Herb said.

Not easily deterred, Malcolm went on. "I waited for you. You should've been there this morning. Hey, it's your life. You want to fuck up, go ahead. Why should I give a damn? There's lots of guys I can sponsor. I don't need to waste my fucking time on a fucking loser like you."

"Cool it, Malcolm. Take your own inventory, not mine."

Herb hung up the phone thinking, *Whew. That was close. I'm lucky he called.*

Herb went to the refrigerator and removed a half-filled container of orange juice, the only thing there. Sitting at the kitchen table, he drank from the container and looked around, *What a mess! I should move.*

Or clean it? he wondered. *Clean it. There's a novel idea.*

Herb found a garbage bag and began filling it with week-old refuse. A half hour later, he looked around. The dishes were washed, some garbage thrown out, and the broken glass gone.

Herb then looked at his desk, piled high with papers. He started to sort through the stash. There were unpaid bills, an unopened letter from his sister and several applications to law firms that he never sent out.

He opened one, read it and said out loud, "Bullshit!" He turned the letter over and on the back side revised it:

Dear Mr. Randall:

I am applying for a position with your firm. Enclosed is my resume.

As you will see, I am an experienced lawyer who started my career in the 60s fighting for social justice. I worked briefly as an activist after passing the bar until my wife railroaded me into a position with her father's lawyer's firm, Cromwell, Douglas, and Bullshit. Although it was a great opportunity, I felt like shit. Alcohol proved invaluable helping me tolerate the bullshit. Cocaine sharpened my thinking so that I could eventually explain my discontent to Art Cromwell, knocking him to the ground. Before long, my wife left me for her dentist and I was admitted to the psychiatric ward at Bellevue Medical Center. For many years, I have actively ruminated about the career I never had, and have continuously spun complex, well-reasoned legal arguments in support of meaningless causes. I will readily bring the fruits of my research with me to your firm.

Among my most celebrated legal treatises are:

- An analysis of why you can assault a hot dog vender for putting

too much ketchup on your dog.
- A brief challenging a city ordinance that prohibits public urination (an equal protection argument based on police practices that allow vagrants to pee under the 2nd Avenue Bridge while not affording the same rights to citizens of Park Avenue).
- A friend of the court brief arguing that salt and pepper shakers lie in the public domain in support of a friend arrested for taking them from a restaurant.

I hope that you find my background and experience compatible with your firm's needs. If not, you can kiss my ass.

Sincerely,

Herbert Whitmore, Esquire

Satisfied with his letter, Herb placed it in an envelope with his resume and walked out the door.

***

Anna reached the park and walked to Peter's bench. No one was there. Just as she did the day before, she stood with her feet half on the pathway, half on the grass, staring blankly at the bench. Before long, Herb came walking through the park, saw her and called out,

"Anna. Whatcha doing here? Thought you lived in Brooklyn."

"I do," Anna replied.

"This is great. I never see you outside the program. You know, the staff is great but they don't mean half as much to me as you, Dave, and everyone else. You're like family."

When Anna failed to respond, Herb looked at his watch and said, "It's early. I could use a rest. Let's sit down."

Herb sat on the right side of the empty bench. When Anna didn't follow, he motioned with his hand for her to sit down.

"I'm not clean," she told him.

"Not clean? Bullshit! You look clean as a whistle. Come on and sit down."

Anna remained standing.

Herb sat there perplexed for a few minutes when he looked up, "You mean your monthly? Shit, that don't mean nothing at all. It's not like we're fucking, and frankly, I wouldn't care even if we were. Now, sit down already."

After Anna sat, Herb said, "Listen. I'm sorry about what I said. I didn't mean to put it that way."

"It's OK," Anna replied.

"So, how are you?"

"Fine. And you?"

"I think I'm OK," Herb said. "Had a bad weekend. Dave and Malcolm helped me through. You know, I've got to get off this shit. I'm on my way to a meeting over there," he said pointing to a church across the park. "I was gonna get there early. Then, I lucked into seeing you. What brings you out here today?"

"I'm meeting someone."

"Anyone I know?"

"Kinda."

"Wanna tell me."

When Anna didn't respond, Herb stopped his questions remembering that Anna was married. Hoping to break the awkward silence, Herb spoke up, "Know what today is?"

When Anna failed to respond he said, "It's the first day of the rest of my life."

Herb went on to tell Anna about his struggle to stop drinking. He failed to see Peter approach. *Peter smiled at Anna and said, "I've got the room."*

Connie got up and placed her hand on Peter's arm just as she did the other day. Anna continued listening to Herb's story while *Connie shivered with anticipation accompanying Peter to the hotel.* Herb told Anna all about his broken marriage with Teri.

Connie glowed with love as she and Peter exited the elevator. Herb described how much he hated corporate law while Anna sat quietly by his side. *Connie disrobed watching Peter's organ grow.* Herb told Anna he was resolved to find himself again.

Connie gasped with delight feeling Peter's hot penis inside her as Herb ended saying, "Anna. I'm gonna practice law again someday. Mark my words. But as Malcolm always says, it's one day at a time. Hey, this was a real pleasure meeting you this way. Sorry I have to go, but the meeting's about to begin."

7 PETER CUBED

On Sunday evening, Peter logged onto the internet, an instant message immediately popping up.

kengoldberg: Hey, Peter. What happened? You weren't on when I got back to my computer.

Peter stared at the message, not knowing what to say.

kengoldberg: Peter, it's me, Ken Goldberg. Don't tell me you forgot already. You can't be that dumb.

Still awed by the fact that he was talking with Ken, Peter failed to recognize the put down, clicked RESPOND and typed *Wow*."

WOW? WHAT A DORK.

Peter changed his message to "Hi," then "Hello," before sending it out.

kengoldberg: And a hearty hello to you. Glad to talk with you. You've been a great friend. Gee, you've been climaxing all over my keyboard for years. LOL. I had to buy a new one, the keys got so sticky. ROFLMAO. Just kidding. So, how you doing?

Peter: Glad to hear from you, too. Sorry you're having problems with your computer.

kengoldberg: LOL. Nothing a little elbow grease can't solve. I guess you're the master at greasing an elbow, aren't you? Anyway, how do you like the way I described you in *Peter Squared*?

Peter: I don't know. I can't remember many of the things you said, like that thing about my parents having trouble conceiving me and Dr. Kelly helping them out by teaching them how to ... you know what I mean.

kengoldberg: Hahaha. Yes indeedy I do. What a master stroke the Dr. Kelly bit! You're right. It never happened. I just made it up. It was one of my better ideas. Of course everything I wrote was good. Wish someone would tell that to the damn New York Times.

Peter: But you did get some great reviews. I saw them in the book.

kengoldberg: LOL, I made those up, too. I wrote the Literary News review. My wife did Literature Today. Our cat's the publisher for Best in Books. ROFLMAO.

kengoldberg: Anyway, you should've seen Dr. Kelly in the first draft. I wrote him in a lot of intricate, sadistic detail. My editor watered it down, the jerk. Lost one helluva funny story. Remind me someday. I'll find the original draft and share it with you. So, how are you doing?

Peter: Fine.

kengoldberg: Come on Peter, you can say more than that. I'm not one of those people in your life that scare you so much. I'm Ken Goldberg, your author. You can tell me anything (after all, I probably wrote whatever you have to say in the first place). LOL.

Peter: Well, there was something I was wondering. The book jacket says you're a mathematician, too?

kengoldberg: Yeah. That was a long time ago. I was really good if you don't mind me bragging. Did I ever tell you about fixed point theorems?

As Ken pontificated about mathematics, Peter visited a pornographic website and masturbated to pictures of men and women having group sex. As he climaxed, Ken finished his lecture and wrote,

kengoldberg: So what's your question already? I have a lot to do so make it quick.

Peter: I was just wondering if it's possible to have a number system where the third power of something is five.

kengoldberg: You mean where $X^3=5$, for some number X belonging to the system.

Peter: Yes.

kengoldberg: That would be the Base Peter system where Peter Cubed equals five and you can jerk off five times without feeling guilty.

Peter: Exactly. How did you know that's what I was thinking?

kengoldberg: Hello dork. Come back from outer space. Did you forget? I'm writing this story.

Peter lowered his head in shame. Failing to reply, he sat quietly while Ken sent a succession of messages.

kengoldberg: $Peter^3 = 5$. OK. If Peter Cubed is 5, that means the system has letters and numbers in it. Peter could be the combination of five letters, p, e, t, and r, using e twice, or Peter could be a mathematical entity in itself. If Peter is a mathematical expression involving five letters, then there are 36 characters in your system, 0 through 9 and a through z. If Peter is a character itself, then you have virtually infinite characters in your system, unless there is some rule that restricts which English words can be used as characters (names only, first names only, names of people who jerk off too much. LOL).

kengoldberg: If Peter is a character, then you'd have to find ways to add Peter to Joe, John, Bob, Ted, and Felix. Your calculations have to adhere to associative and commutative laws.

kengoldberg: That means Peter plus Joe has to equal something, say Ralph. And maybe Joe and John equals Paul. To be associative, then (Peter + Joe) + (John) = Peter + (Joe + John). So Ralph + John would have to equal Peter + Paul which we'll call Tommy. So, let's see what we have.

Ralph + John = Peter + Paul = Tommy.

kengoldberg: We can also say that:

Ralph + Paul = (Peter + Joe) + (Joe + John) = (Peter + Joe + John) + Joe = Tommy + Joe.

kengoldberg: The commutative laws are a lot simpler, but I should mention them anyway. Commutative laws mean that $a + b = b + a$. Everyone knows that $1 + 2 = 3$ just like $2 + 1 = 3$. In the example I gave you before, Ralph + John = John + Ralph = Peter + Paul = Paul + Peter. You know what Ralph + John + Mary equals don't you?

kengoldberg: Peter, Paul and Mary! ROFLMAO.

kengoldberg: On the other hand, if Peter is an expression where the alphabet is added to the usual digits, then Peter means that P is in the 10,000th place, E (I'm not going to distinguish capital and small letters here. If I did, that would mean 52 plus 10 numbers equal 62 characters) is in the 1000th place, T in the 100th place, E in the 10s place and R in the 1s place so,

Peter = P(10,000) + E (1,000) + T (100) + E(10) + R

kengoldberg: This reminds me of Abstract Algebra. I took that in graduate school. There are several types of numbering systems depending on the operations you want them to have.

kengoldberg: It's been a long time but I think they were called rings, groups, and fields. There may have been others, but I'm not sure. Whatever, keep your mouth shut and don't give me any grief about it. You know I'm a lot brighter than you are.

kengoldberg: Oops, I forgot. We've got to consider distributive laws, identities and inverses, too.

kengoldberg: In the real number system, multiplication distributes over addition.

2(3+4) = 2X7 = 14 is the same as

2X3 + 2X4 = 6+8 = 14

kengoldberg: Addition has zero as its identity, -x is the inverse of x.

0+10=10 Identity

10 + ‾10 = 0 Inverse

kengoldberg: One is the multiplicative identity and $1/x$ the inverse.

1X10=10 Identity

1X $^1/_{10}$ = 1 Inverse

kengoldberg: Now for your system, you want Peter Cubed equal to 5 so you can jerk off five times without feeling guilty. Frankly, if you don't want to feel guilty, find yourself a shrink. Don't ask me these ridiculous math questions.

kengoldberg: If you want to see me, I have an opening next week on Tuesday at 11. LOL. Cash only and I charge if you miss your appointment. ROFLMAO.

kengoldberg: Anyway, I've got to go. The kids are out and my wife's upstairs all by herself. I figure at least one of us ought to get some action. LOL. And if history repeats itself, it sure *ain't* (Pardon the use of slang. Even a great writer like me has to sometimes resort to crude language to emphasize a point) gonna be you. ROFLMAO.

After Ken's messages stopped coming in, Peter typed in his own message,

Peter: So, do you think the Base Peter system will work?

Peter clicked SEND. The screen displayed the message,

kengoldberg is no longer logged in.

8 THE CONSULTANT

Peter was just finishing his standard calculation the 17th time Monday morning when he heard Andrew slam the door to his office behind him.

"Goddamnit," Andrew bellowed. "We are truly fucked up. Damn, damn, damn, and double damn. One lousy appointment to do a late tax return and the goddamn client doesn't even show up. So, I call him up: goddamn humiliating, no other accountant who is really in business would ever do that. He tells me he's decided to wait.

"Wait! He's a goddamn deadbeat. Can't do his taxes on time, then cancels his appointment to actually get them done. I should goddamn call the IRS and report him, that's what I'm gonna do.

"So, what do you think, Peter. Perfect score? No taxes during tax season, none afterwards."

Peter quickly put his prior calculations aside and on another sheet of paper neatly wrote,

Season	No. of Tax Returns Completed
Tax season	0
After tax season	0
Total tax returns done	0

Peter pondered to himself whether a perfectly negative score was the same as a perfectly positive score.

***

While Andrew continued to talk, questioning how he would survive, Peter reflected on his own circumstance, managing easily without an income. A methodical saver, Peter spent only 72% of his pay before Carl left. Along with the money Aunt Cindy left him, Peter knew he could continue to survive at a constant rate of consumption as long as he lived to no more than 98 years. Peter remembered the day Aunt Cindy told him he'd be her sole heir.

"Peter, you're the only one left who's such a schmuck you won't spend my money once I put it in your name. Otto would send me off to a Medicaid dive and give it to that two-bit whore he calls his wife. For God's sake, don't let him do it. If I have to go to a home, make sure there are staff who can still get it up. I won't be stuck with no old codger with alligator skin and a shriveled dick, who beats himself off."

With that, Cindy leaned close to Peter and whispered in his ear the locations and numbers of her various accounts, sure that Otto had bugged her place. Seeing a bulge in his pants, she stroked Peter's hair, blew in his ear, then pulled back and yelled, "Flick that goddamn thing down. What the hell are you doing? You're no Otto."

***

Peter broke from his memory when Andrew asked him, "Really Peter, what do you think we should do?"

"Get some more clients?" Peter responded.

"Great. You're really on top of things, Peter. Any ideas where we're going to get these clients?"

"Didn't we have clients before Carl left?" Peter asked.

"Sure. So, what's your point?"

"Could we ask if some of them would come back? It's only fair that Carl share them with us."

"Thanks, Peter. That's a big help." Andrew said as he walked back to his office mumbling loud enough for Peter to hear, "Maybe he's got the clients. At least he left me one of the great minds in the world of accounting."

Pleased with Andrew's compliment, Peter decided to start intermixing his two calculations, the one he had done all day every day since Carl left and today's calculation:

$$0 + 0 = 0.$$

***

Peter arrived at the park at 12:05 p.m. to find his bench unoccupied. There were crumbs in the middle where he had planned to sit. The right side of the bench was perfectly clean. Peter fished out his notebook to record the change as he took the right seat. He opened his lunch bag and pulled out a sandwich. With his teeth, he carefully separated a parallelogram that he had pre-cut in the bread from the rest of the sandwich. While chewing, he looked up and saw Anna standing in front across the walkway, her heels on the grass, her toes on the sidewalk, her left foot pointed directly at Peter. Her right foot was turned about 10 degrees, seeming to mark a line from Anna to a tree behind the bench. Anna looked in Peter's direction with a vacant stare. Peter took a second bite of his sandwich, this time separating a trapezoid while trying to look away from Anna. Making no more eye contact, Peter continued to eat.

As Peter bit into a triangular piece of sandwich, it felt like a person was sitting to his right. He looked ahead and realized that Anna was no longer there.

Peter continued to eat when he felt Anna reach for his pants and unfasten his fly. On her knees, she grabbed his erect penis and placed it in her mouth. Peter felt his organ throb until it finally exploded spilling semen into a plastic bag he had taped around his penis and secured to the air conditioner filter he kept inside his pants. Peter turned to his right and saw Anna sitting on the bench, staring straight ahead.

A moment later, Anna turned her head left, slowly and steadily, toward Peter, until she returned his glance. Peter quickly looked forward to avert her gaze and continued to eat his sandwich.

Connie reached for Peter's hand and led him off the bench, down the street, and back to the Waldorf Astoria. Once again, they made passionate love until Peter looked at his watch, saw it was 12:55, p.m. and stood up. Anna returned to the bench to see Peter standing by the refuse container, dropping his neatly folded lunch bag directly in the center.

***

After pausing briefly at the door to the office to redo his standard calculation of the common multipliers and divisors formed respectively by Carl's and Peter's names with Andrew's, Peter opened the door and walked in to see Andrew standing there, grinning broadly.

"You're a genius! I can't believe it. The solution was right under our noses all the time, but I didn't see it. Great job, Peter!"

Holding his face straight, Peter looked down and turned his eyes in, hoping he could see what Andrew thought was there. Peter shuddered as he remembered the day Simon Minsky's nose dribbled in second grade creating a long, unwiped string of mucous that practically reached the floor.

"You were right all along," Andrew continued. "Get some clients back. I followed your advice and called Harold in Indianapolis. He didn't exactly jump for joy but he was willing to listen. We're meeting him next Monday, a week from today."

Peter looked around. With no staff but Andrew and he, Peter

wondered who would do his calculation while they were away.

"I'm flying out this weekend. I've got friends there I'd like to see. I'll meet with Harold Monday morning. I need for you to join us in the afternoon. It's very important that you get there. You are the key."

Quietly, Peter slipped his hand into his right pocket: *My keys are still here.*

"I hope you don't mind, but I did kind of lie to him. Not a big one, just a little white lie. I knew we had to offer something different and new, more than Carl can do. I told him we now offer full service accounting along with high-powered business consultation services. I know he plans to expand his operation. I insisted we were the guys who could help him on his way."

As Andrew smiled, proud of his coup, Peter pondered his words and finally said, "I didn't know we do that."

"Well, we don't. I guess I got so excited the words just sneaked out on their own while we were talking. I didn't actually plan to say that, but once I did, there was no way back."

"How are we going to do this?" Peter asked. "Who's the consultant?"

"Great point!" Andrew bellowed. "I knew you'd be on top of things. Can't get anything past you, that's what I've always said. You're right. Can't do consulting without a consultant, and that's exactly the question Harold asked me. Who's your consultant? That's just what he said."

Andrew stopped for a moment, a confident smile on his face.

"So, what did you say?"

"You!" Andrew exclaimed. "That's what I told him. He asked who our consultant was and I blurted out, Peter Branstill." Andrew slapped himself hard on the side of his legs.

"As soon as I mentioned your name, everything changed. Remember how impressed Andrew was when he first met you? We were working like dogs and you got up, out of the blue, and started off to lunch, quiet and calm just like everything you do. He got the point. Now, he says everyone takes lunch and productivity's up eight percent."

Andrew paused, then said, "So, what's it like being a high-powered consultant?"

Peter failed to answer Andrew's question. Andrew slapped him on his back before walking back to his own office saying, "That's what I love about you, Peter. Always thinking. No small talk."

9 NO MORE

After dinner, Peter turned his computer on. In minutes, he was back on line. On the screen, a message popped up:

You have an Instant message from kengoldberg. Do you choose to accept it?

Peter clicked YES.

kengoldberg: Hi, Peter. What's up?

Peter: Nothing.

kengoldberg: Come on. Talk to me. Something's up. The sky's up The sun is up. And I'm sure later tonight, you'll be up. LOL. Tell me what's happening, Peter.

Hesitantly, Peter typed an answer.

Peter: Andrew told Harold I'm a consultant. I don't know what to do?

kengoldberg: Oh. That consultant thing. I thought I edited it out. Hold on a second.

Peter waited a few minutes before another IM came through.

kengoldberg: I did leave it in. Sorry, Peter. You are in trouble.

Peter: What should I do?

kengoldberg: Come on, Peter. Don't get all jerky on me. Trust me. I'll figure something out.

kengoldberg: HAHAHA. What a dork you are. Of course I've got it worked out. I just can't tell you. It would ruin things for the reader. Actually, it's one of my better ideas if I don't say so myself. So, anything else up?

Peter: Actually there is. I'm reading your book and some things don't make sense.

kengoldberg: Believe me. It all makes sense. I'm too good of a writer for it not to. What's your question?

Peter: It's my father. I was hoping I could learn more about him from the book, but there isn't much there except what I already know.

kengoldberg: I know what you mean. It's just like the Dr. Kelly thing. I wrote a great story about your Dad and the goddamn editor slashed that one, too. I guess that what happens when you're a great author like me. You write so much great stuff, at some point you've got to pare it down and tighten the story. Frankly, I thought he was wrong, but who gives a damn as long as the book sells.

kengoldberg: Originally, *Peter Squared* started at your Mom's and Dad's wedding. Then, I described your birth and early childhood. I didn't get to your present life until much later. Some of those early bits were very funny. But the editor thought I should start with you as an adult about to go mad, calculating and masturbating, all the time. I tried to weave in your childhood through a series of dreams, fantasies, and flashbacks. That worked well for most of the story. But I couldn't get that stuff in about your Dad.

kengoldberg: Your Dad died when you were seven, so I didn't think you would remember much about him, so it was hard to give you memories. All you'd know was what Aunt Cindy told you about him. You know, most people can't remember anything that happened before seven, particularly if they have been abused the way you were.

Peter: So what was my father like?

kengoldberg: A boring dolt, just like you.

Ken cackled with laughter at home while Peter listened to children scream in his ear.

PETER BRANSTILL IS A BORE. PETER BRANSTILL NEEDS A WHORE. COME ON PETER, JERK OFF MORE.

Peter pictured himself slicing his penis with a steak knife as he counted: *One, two, three, four, five, six, seven, eight, nine, ten.* He repeated the numbers until Ken's next message appeared on the screen.

kengoldberg: Sorry, Peter. I shouldn't have said that. If there's anyone who should know better than to tease you, it's me. Anyway, what did you want to know about your father?

Peter: What was in the section?

kengoldberg: Oh, I don't remember Peter. Stop asking such ridiculous questions. What do you want me to do? Go back to my files and look up the old text. You know, I've got more important things to do than to keep answering your dumb questions and going back to things I wrote years ago. Geez. It's been edited out. It's history. I don't have it anymore. Don't you get it?

kengoldberg: Oops. Here it is. I just found it. Hold on and I'll send it to you.

A few minutes later, the next message appeared.

kengoldberg: All done. Check your email. I'll hold on.

Peter went to his mailbox where he saw, as Ken promised, an email from kengoldberg@greatauthor.com with an attached file. Peter downloaded the file, then opened it up. To his surprise, Ken sent Peter a pornographic video clip, no text at all.

What should I do? thought Peter. *I can't let Ken know I'm looking at porn instead of the file he sent me.*

Peter quickly typed his reply.

Peter: Thanks for the file, Ken. I'll read it later.

kengoldberg: Hahaha, you dork. I didn't send the file. I sent you porn. LOL.

kengoldberg: Now, forget the first draft. It wasn't any good anyway. I'll tell you about your father now.

kengoldberg: Oops. The kids are out and my wife just pulled into the driveway. If I rush out quickly and put the groceries away, she'll be in a good mood and I just might get lucky. HO! HO! HO!

kengoldberg: Talk to you soon. Why don't you think about us doing it while you jerk off tonight.

kengoldberg: Or use those pictures I just sent you. Trust me, they're really good. Used them myself (the rare times I don't get it the right way and have to do it your way, the loser way).

kengoldberg: Bye. Your friend, and world renowned author. Ken (the great, brilliant, superb) Goldberg.

***

Anna sat in the kitchen, listening to Sol's footsteps, hearing him walk out the door slamming it shut behind him. She cringed as she pictured him pounding her with his prayer book when she returned Sunday night. She waited several minutes to make sure he wasn't coming back, then pulled her dress up and her underpants down. With a razor in her left hand, right fingers spreading the lips of her vagina, she stopped and thought: *Why am I doing this?* Anna put the razor down and her elbow on the table so she could rest her chin in her left hand.

For seven years, life had been strange: Rape, beatings, hallucinations, annual promiscuity, hospitals, medications. It wasn't like that before. Anna could just barely remember a time of happiness and joyful celebrations, reveling in her rich heritage, telling stories, visiting people, laughing, dancing – crying, too, but tears of life not tears of shame. Each year, she'd go off her pills, knowing it pleased the doctors and her family, not her, when she took them.

Transporting herself to one hospital stay, she remembered Dr. Brown leading a group of residents into her room, asking if she'd let them meet with her: *Why not?* She was so heavily drugged she'd agree to anything.

***

"This is classic Manic-Depressive Syndrome, now known as Bi-Polar Disorder. It highlights how far we've come with psychopharmacology. Yet, nothing works unless we gain the confidence of the patient and form a partnership with her. With medication, Anna is stable; without it, she is manic. For ten months of the year, her life is good, thanks to our modern interventions. Two months of the year, like clockwork, she breaks down with disastrous results. It's not her fault, gentlemen. The era of blaming the patient is over. It's on us. We have to gain her trust and teach her to identify the early warning signs. We have to earn her confidence so that she tells us what's happening in the midst of agitation and paranoia.

"Last month, we found her in Nebraska, traveling with another patient, an odd, psychopathic man who later killed himself. It's her illness, not her fault.

"Anna, it's clear you know now that you need to stay on your medication. Please, tell us what happens when you stop taking your pills. Surely, you must feel it is out of your control."

I want to be loved by someone who won't beat me up. I want to have relations with someone other than my husband and father.

Anna squashed her thoughts, instead saying meekly, "I don't know."

"INSIGHT!" pounced Dr. Brown. "That's the key. If patients have insight, they get well.

"'I don't know,'" Dr. Brown repeated softly. "How poignant yet telling. A plea for help, a wish to know, looking to us for a way out of the darkness.

"All I can say, Anna, is: I'm sorry. We'll try our best to help you work this out."

As Dr. Brown led his charge out of the room, one of the residents turned to another and whispered, loud enough for Anna to hear, "She's reminds me of this gal in high school. Great head."

***

Anna's thoughts were broken by a loud knock on the door. She quickly put her razor out of sight and walked toward the door. From across the room, she called out, "Who's there?", unheard by the visitor who by now was banging loudly on the door. Even when Anna reached the door, she could still not be heard over the furious pounding and screeching sounds. Anna looked through the peep hole, the image distorted by the vibrating door. Finally she recognized her mother's contorted, rageful face and let her in.

"You bitch!" Sophie Pearlman cried out. "Where the hell have you been? What do you think you're doing?"

"Nothing, Mom," Anna protested. "I'm just here by myself."

"By yourself? You leave me with the beast."

"Mom, he's your husband. Why do you do this to me?"

"Husband, you say. He's a dirty old man who thinks his faith makes a difference. He's a wolf in rabbinical clothes. He's disgusting Anna, and you leave me with him. How could you do that?"

"I'm not doing it, Mom. He's your husband not mine. I'm not doing it anymore."

"You're what!" Sophie screamed. "Where the hell do you think you get off? He needs it and he sure as hell isn't getting it from me."

"You're crazy, Mom. You and Dad are crazy. He's a rabbi and I'm his daughter. I'm not doing this anymore."

"You're sick, Anna. You're a sick girl. I'm putting you away."

"You're not, Mom. I'm telling the truth. They won't put me away."

"They won't believe you. You're a nut, Anna. You always were and you always will be. You're coming with me now."

Sophie Pearlman grabbed her daughter's arm. Anna pulled away. With rage in her eyes, Sophie looked around and spotted the umbrella stand on the floor. She picked up an umbrella and began swinging it at Anna. Anna tried to grab the weapon but it nicked her finger causing her to cry in pain. In full control of the tool, Sophie swung strongly at Anna, crashing the side of the umbrella across her face. She began stabbing the point at Anna's face, hoping to impale Anna's eye. Anna held her hands to her face to protect herself. Her mother stabbed at her body, causing her to move her hands away from her face. Her face exposed, Sophie tried once more to put her eye out. Anna turned and the umbrella dug into her left temple.

As the melee ensued, Mrs. Feingold came out of her apartment to see Anna and Sophie wrestling on the floor. "Sid," she cried out. "Anna's sick again."

Sid ran to the phone and dialed 911 while Mrs. Feingold and another neighbor rushed inside and tried to pull Anna away.

"You're a sick girl," Mrs. Feingold screamed "They should put you away for good. You should be ashamed of yourself, treating your mother like this."

Sirens wailed from outside as the two women and their husbands watched the fight. Soon, the police arrived and whisked Anna away, rushing her to the Emergency Room of Kings County Hospital.

10 NEW FRIENDS

Peter smiled broadly as he went through his morning routines, urinating at a 45° angle, showering with $1/7$ of a bar of soap, drying the four quadrants of his body with his towel, and dressing in his standard suit, shirt, tie, socks and shoes. Throughout, he kept repeating Ken's words:

Your friend, and world renowned author. Ken (the great, brilliant, superb) Goldberg.

Friend, thought Peter. *Another friend.*

Peter went to F in his cabinet to find his file on FRIENDS. He removed a copy of the Graduated Friends Rating Scale (GFRS) Worksheet and rated Ken.

Peter rated friends on six variables: size, color, discoloration, symmetry, odor and texture, assigning values 1 to 5 for each and weighting the scores respectively 3, 2, 4, 1, 5, 5. This led to a scale from 20 to 100 on which Peter could measure the quality of a friend. With Ken, Peter now had five friends, John, Howdy Doody, Buffalo Bob, and Clarabelle Clown the other four. In general, Peter preferred large friends over small ones, friends with good symmetry, ones that did not smell at all (good or bad), and friends with smooth skin. Color was quite complicated to rate since Peter tried to avoid the impression of racial bias. For each race, Peter identified a sample skin color that he then viewed as ideal. Color ratings were made according to how different the person's color was from the color of the identified standard. Discoloration, of course, was undesirable regardless of racial group.

With nothing but Ken's picture, Peter knew he could only estimate Ken's value as a friend. For sure, he had no idea how Ken smelled, even after he held the book close to his nose and inhaled deeply. Pictures are deceptive for rating size, particularly when they are taken by professionals intent on making the person look thinner. Using what else he could glean from the picture, Peter completed the GFRS Worksheet and rated Ken, 49. This placed Ken, among Peter's friends, behind John, but ahead of Howdy, Buffalo Bob, and Clarabelle Clown, mostly because they were small puppets.

Graduated Friend Rating Scale Worksheet

Friend's Name: Ken Goldberg

Date: June 2, 2002

Factor	Score	Weight	Wt Score	Comment
Size	3	3	9	No info
Color	3	2	6	Ave white man
Discoloration	2	4	8	Mottled skin
Symmetry	1	1	1	Nose off axis
Odor	3	5	15	No info
Texture	2	5	10	Some acne
Total			49	

Peter placed Ken's completed GFRS sheet back in its folder which he returned to the file. As he began to close the drawer, he noticed another folder: Fillies. Peter removed the folder and masturbated to the contents inside.

***

At 12:10 p.m., Peter arrived at his bench, this time taking a seat to the left. As he opened his lunch bag, Herb came bounding across the park and called out, "Hey Peter. Or should I say Petey?"

Aware Herb was using John's old salutation, Peter smiled and thought, *Herb's my friend, too.* Peter quickly calculated Herb's value as a friend, arriving at the number 51, ahead of Ken but still behind John.

"So, how you doin'?" Herb asked.

Peter continued to chew his sandwich, two bites on the right side of his mouth, one on the left, one bite on the right side of his mouth, two final bites on the left.

"I'm glad we finally got together after all this time. I wanted to talk with you about John," Herb said.

Peter listened intently while he counted to 60 to insure a one-minute interval before eating again.

"It's funny," Herb went on, "But now that I'm sober, he doesn't seem so strange. It's weird. I had a dream last night that we were at Shea stadium watching the game. John was clean, clear-thinking, quite funny. I thought he was a client of the firm, some big tycoon fighting a product liability suit. We watched the Mets lose, a close game spoiled by an awful play. He took me home in his limousine. I swear, the dream seemed real. For a while, I thought I knew John somehow from the past. It took me a while to realize I was just having a dream."

As Peter continued to eat his sandwich, Herb went on to tell him about his past life as a civil rights protester and activist lawyer, who later compromised himself going into corporate law. "Hell, I was proud working with Marty. I'll never forget the day he came to me and asked what I thought about his *I Have a Thought* speech.

"I told him, 'Marty. People don't care what you think. They want to know what you feel, what you love, what you dream.'

"You shoulda seen his face light up, like a lightning bolt: DREAM. He was happier than all get out. Before long, he revised the speech. I was the first one to see it. No more *I had a thought that black and white children can play together*. He was having dreams, man. It was great."

Peter wondered if he should tell Herb about the dream he had last night. In his dream, Peter imagined that he was a folder, in the F drawer, filed behind Friends. As Ken closed the drawer, Peter called out, his voice fading as the drawer kept closing, *I'm ahead of Fillies. My name is Feter. Fe before Fi.*

Ken laughed and slammed the drawer shut. "You're a *fucking* idiot."

When Peter finished his sandwich, he got up to leave but was stopped by Herb who called out, "Whatcha doing tonight?"

Peter imagined himself leaving the office, walking to *Private Booths, Sexy Girls*, jerking off, going home, having dinner by himself, jerking off again, then getting on line to see if Ken was there. He would then jerk off twice more before bed, six times if particularly horny, three times if Ken had an answer for the Base Peter system.

"Nothing," Peter replied.

"Great! Let's do dinner tonight."

Peter did not know what to say so he answered in a mumble hoping

Herb would let it go.

"Oh, shit!" Herb said. "I forgot. I've got a meeting tonight."

Herb pulled out his AA meeting guide and asked Peter, "Where do you live?"

With shivers down his spine, a plethora of different places rushed through his mind: *Brooklyn, LA, Tokyo, Afghanistan, Mars.*

"88th Street," Peter answered.

Scanning his meeting list, Herb found one at a church on 87th Street.

"Great. There's a meeting at 5:30 right near your house. It won't last too long. Let's say your place at 7?"

"OK," Peter reluctantly replied.

Herb then asked Peter for his address which he wrote on his hand with a ball point pen.

"This is great. I'll be there by seven and we'll find some place to eat. Unless of course, the Mrs. has something scrumptious planned tonight."

11 THE VISIT

Anna sat in her room at Kings County Hospital, her mind racing trying to figure out what to do. *Peter's out there and I'm here. I've got to get out.*

Anna replayed the years of her father's abuse. With each thought, Connie popped out, her big smile, heavy makeup, red hair, Irish eyes. Anna shivered as she tried to shake Connie out of her mind. *No more,* Anna said to herself. *I'm not doing it anymore. I won't run away from the pain.* Each time Connie tried to make it right, Anna forced herself to picture her father, standing behind her, his organ up her behind. *Never again,* Anna said to herself. *This story must be told. I can't look away. It happens and it's real.*

I've gotta get out of here, Anna said to herself. *They think I'm sick. They're gonna quiet me with their medications. I won't be strong if they put me to sleep. I've gotta stay clear. I can never turn my eyes away and let this happen again.*

***

Peter paced nervously in his apartment waiting for Herb who knocked on his door twenty-five minutes late. Peter quickly went to his desk and, remembering the last time Sammy Pietrowski was at his house, wrote down on paper,

Year	Mo	Day	Hr	Min
2002	06	02	19	25
1961	10	17	15	46
0040	07	15	03	39

Forty years, seven months, fifteen days, three hours and thirty-nine minutes since someone last came over.

Peter then double-checked the glass of milk and plate of chocolate chip cookies he had set on the table for Herb, just like his mother used to do for Sammy, before answering the door.

"Hi, Peter," Herb bellowed as he looked around. "Pretty nice pad."

Herb handed Peter his jacket and hat and asked, "So, is the Mrs. home?"

Peter looked down. "It's OK. I'll meet her next time."

"Well. I'm not actually married," Peter hesitantly admitted.

"Not married," Herb laughed. "So you're a goddamn bachelor. Not bad. The best of both worlds. All the freedom you want and a honey to love you, too. So, is your *significant other* here?"

"I, uh, live by myself," Peter added, his voice even softer than before.

"Nothing wrong with that," Herb bellowed again. "Just like me. So, did you want to go out to eat or just stir up some grub here."

Peter didn't want to do either. He just wished that Herb would go.

"You're right. Let's eat in," Herb decided.

Herb opened the refrigerator. "Oh? You're in AA, too. No beer?"

When Peter didn't answer, Herb gathered food from Peter's refrigerator and shelves himself.

"Not too much here?" Herb commented, "Didn't get a chance to shop."

"I stopped by the store on my way home from work," Peter answered reflecting his long-standing practice of purchasing food each day so he could consume it within 24 hours, staying safe from spoilage and disease.

"Well, you don't have much in reserve, do you?

"It looks like we have one chicken dinner, one breakfast, and a sandwich for lunch. Which do you want?"

Peter hung his head and quietly said, "I usually have chicken."

"Then, it's time to let loose and get out of your rut. I'll have the chicken. You're having breakfast."

With that, Herb looked for Peter's cooking ware, clanging pots and pans together that, for years, had been carefully protected from ever having contact with each other. Herb broke a dish, too.

"Oops. Don't worry. I'll take care of that," Herb said as he swept the debris with the bottom of his shoe into the opening under the stove. "Clean as a whistle."

In minutes, Peter found himself sitting at the table with Herb, his breakfast in front of him while Herb ate his dinner.

***

After dinner, Herb invited Peter to the living room, refusing to let him clear the table.

"You've got to relax, Peter. You can always do that tomorrow after I'm gone."

Herb sat on the couch and lit up a cigarette. The ash had grown long when Herb realized there were no ashtrays there. Quickly, he got up and rushed to the kitchen where he picked up the plate with his leftover chicken. He brought the plate back and placed it in the middle of the couch, too late to catch the ash before it fell to the floor. Seeing it perched on the carpet, Herb got up and said, "Don't worry. I've got it."

With his mud clad work boots, Herb ground the ash in. He returned to the couch, sat down, put his feet on the coffee table, and, now noticing *Peter Squared* picked it up, commenting, "Interesting cover. Something you're reading?"

"Yes," Peter answered.

"Any good?"

Peter wasn't sure if he should tell Herb it was a book about himself.

Herb said, "Tell you what. Don't spoil the ending. I'm a fast reader. Let me borrow it. I'll have it back to you in a day or two."

***

That evening, Sophie came to Kings County Hospital to see Anna. She went directly to Anna's room and railed against her.

"You're selfish," she said. "You're goddamn selfish. That man has cared for you with all his heart ever since you were born. And this is what you do to him? This is the kind of daughter you turned out to be? No. Not my Anna. You weren't raised this way. It's written. 'Honor your mother and father.' You disgrace us. You're sick, Anna. You're goddamn sick."

Anna looked at her Mom, then at the chair in the room. She imagined herself picking the chair up and smashing it over her mother's head. *Calm down,* Anna said to herself. *You've gotta get out.*

"I'll do him, Mom," Anna said. "Get me out and I'll take care of him."

Sophie stopped short not sure she heard what Anna said, "You'll what?"

"I'll take care of Dad. Get me out tonight and I'll do it."

Sophie quickly left the room and went to the desk. Intent on keeping her horny husband away, she demanded Anna's release.

"The doctor is not in, Mrs. Pearlman. You can call him tomorrow."

Not willing to leave and be home alone with the rabbi, Sophie parked herself in the hall outside the psych ward and slept on the floor, waiting for the doctor to come in.

***

After Herb left, Peter went on line. He quickly received another IM

53

from Ken.

kengoldberg: Wow! I'll bet that's the first visitor you've had since Sammy used to come over.

Peter: I know. It's been a long time: forty years, seven months, fifteen days, three hours and thirty-nine minutes.

kengoldberg: LOL. Leave it to you to figure that out. How did it go?

Peter: OK, I guess. I wasn't really expecting him and he is awfully messy.

kengoldberg: That's for sure. You should see his apartment. Did he leave you much to clean-up.

Peter: I don't think I can clean it up. I may have to buy new dishes, carpeting and a couch.

kengoldberg: That bad? I know you hate messes and probably think the place can't be repaired. But think it over. It might be salvageable. I have a great cleaning lady here who does our place (and gives me a little you-know-what on the side, too). Maybe, she could help you out.

Shocked by Ken's offer, Peter wrote back,

Peter: You'd really do that for me, Ken? Wow.

kengoldberg: Are you kidding? I'm not doing anything for you. Where's your head at anyway. You live in New York, and I'm here in Philadelphia. You should get a life. Go hire someone yourself. You can't keep thinking I'm gonna pick up the pieces for you just because I'm a great writer. Geez.

Peter: Sorry.

kengoldberg: Don't be sorry. I'm just teasing you. God. You really can't take a joke. Anyway, do whatever you want. Just don't bother me with your petty problems.

kengoldberg: So tell me. Anything else happen during the visit. Did you have a good time? What did you guys do?

Peter: We ate, sort of. I never have much food around. He ate my dinner.

kengoldberg: LOL. You'd better start having more provisions on hand if you're planning to be a social butterfly. LOLOL. The host with the most. ROFLMAO.

kengoldberg: What else happened?

Peter: Not too much. He smoked a cigarette, the first one ever since I took over the apartment. Oh yes, he also borrowed your book.

kengoldberg: He what?

Peter: He took the book. I had it out on the table. I wasn't even done reading it. He just saw it and took it. Promised to bring it back in a day or two.

kengoldberg: Let me get this right, Peter. Herb came over to your house and took your book. He didn't buy one for himself? Is that right?

Peter: Yes. That's what he did.

kengoldberg: Now tell me something, Peter. How the *hell* do you expect me to earn any money off of this book if you keep giving it away left and right to any Tom, Dick, or Harry who wants it. I don't make money when people read the book. I make money when they BUY the book. You understand, BUY, B-U-Y, the bleeping book. I don't get a royalty unless they purchase the book.

kengoldberg: What the hell do you think it's going to do for me if Herb reads your copy of my book. You know, he's a loser. It's not like when some college professor reads the book and assigns it to the class to read. Hell, I'd give those jerks all the free books they want. I'd give it away to a celebrity who's respected by lots of people. Invite Oprah over to your house and I'll give you a free copy to give her.

kengoldberg: Or have someone over who has lots of friends and a giant Christmas list. But Herb. You've got to be kidding. You give my book to one lousy mental patient who is going to slobber all over it and give it back to you after reading it only halfway. No commission for me, not a damn thing to help my kids with their college tuitions. And all because you decided to give him your copy of my book. So what do you have to say for yourself, Peter?

Peter: Gee whiz. I'm sorry.

kengoldberg: Sorry. Well, I hate to tell you but sorry doesn't get my kids through college.

Peter: Do you really think he'll slobber on the book?

kengoldberg: LOL. You're right. What was I thinking? Of course, he'll slobber on the book and you'll have to buy another copy. ROFLMAO.

kengoldberg: That's it, Peter. You replace the copy you gave him and I'll get another commission. LOL.

kengoldberg: Anyway, talking about slobs, I thought you wanted to know more about your father. There was a slob for you. He ate just like a dog right out of the bowl. Dripped gravy all over his shirt.

Peter: I know. I read about it in the book. But, I don't actually remember him being that way. Was there anything else about him in that first version?

kengoldberg: Forget the first draft already Peter. God. You have a way of needling a guy. It wasn't very good. And stop asking me questions about what I wrote about your father before. He was a slob. Got that. Don't go remembering him any other way.

Peter: I'm sorry, Ken. I just thought you said it was some of your best writing.

kengoldberg: Well, it was. But that's no reason to be a pest. Now, if you really want to hear about fathers, let me tell you about my Dad.

kengoldberg: My Dad was a great guy. He was really bright, a doctor, top notch researcher, medical school professor, excellent surgeon, developed many innovative techniques. Saved thousands of lives in the course of his own. Had a great sense of humor and was a world-class bridge player, too. Oh, I just remembered something funny about him. Let me tell you.

To Peter's chagrin, Ken went on with story after story about his own father, never answering Peter's question. Peter dutifully sat by his computer, reading Ken's messages until Ken ended saying,

kengoldberg: Oops. Didn't realize how late it was. 10:00 and time for *Law and Order.* Sorry to sign off before I can tell you about your own father. I just don't want to miss the theme song. You've heard it, haven't you? Da-da. Da-da-da, da, da.

Peter waited a half hour before realizing that Ken had stopped sending messages. Finally, he typed,

Peter: Enjoy your show.

In response, the screen displayed,

kengoldberg is no longer logged on.

12 SANDY

At noon Wednesday, Peter left work to have lunch at the park. When he arrived at his bench, Herb was already there, holding *Peter Squared* in his hands, open to about the middle.

"This is a great book!" Herb said as Peter arrived. "I can't put it down. I even took it to the bathroom and read while I peed."

Herb sheepishly showed Peter a stain on the bottom edge.

"Sorry. I missed," he said shrugging his shoulders.

"Sorry, too, about the mess I made last night. I've gotten far enough into the book to realize it's about you, and what a neat freak you are. If you want, I'll come over tonight and help clean up."

"That's OK," Peter quickly said. "You don't have to."

"Fine. Anyway, we've got more important things to talk about. You know all those things I said about you having a Mrs. or a honey. It says here that you don't. In fact, this book suggests that you're a ..." Herb cuffed his mouth with his right hand and leaned over to Peter's ear so he could whisper, "fuckin' virgin."

Peter's face turned slightly red. Herb continued, "Listen. It's nothing to be ashamed of. Not everyone gets it. Not everyone even wants it. There was this guy, Joey Connor. He lived down the block from me in Bay Ridge. Wanted to be a priest. What can you say? The kid was such a nerd, he wasn't gonna get it anyway. Why not make a religion out of it? We used to tease him a lot, but some of the guys felt bad for him. When we graduated from high school and were going different ways ...

"Oh, did I tell you? I went to college. I'm a lawyer. Really, No shit. I protested the war, and did the civil rights thing. Was real close to Marty. Then I got married, had some kids and got railroaded into corporate law. It's a long story. I'll tell you some time.

"Anyway, Joey was going to priest school, and we all started feeling sorry for him. I thought he should get laid before it was too late. There was this girl, Amy, who ran with our crowd. Busted her cherry long before the other girls. A fuckin' nymphomaniac, but a good kid, too. Laid down for everyone.

"I think I was the best," Herb added grinning ear to ear.

"Anyway, I'm balling her one night and say, 'Hey Amy. Did you ever do, Joey?' I think I picked the wrong time. She got kinda pissy. She sneered at me and said, 'Joey. You've gotta be kiddin'. He's a virgin.'

"I asked her if she wanted to and she said, 'Not really.' So, I asked if she'd do it for me and she said, 'OK.' Amy was always a good sport.

"You shoulda seen Joey. He was scared shitless, but I think he enjoyed it. The first time just don't come easy for everyone. Look at him now. I hear he's done real well in the church, a bishop or a cardinal. He might be the fuckin' pope for all I know. Whatever, I hear he gets laid more than any of us now."

As Herb talked a woman in her thirties walked by the bench and stopped to blow her nose. Thinking it was Anna, Peter stood up and took her by the hand. *Anna smiled, took Peter's hand and threw her tissue on the ground. Peter led her to a spot on the grass, 20 feet behind the bench, 25 feet from the volleyball net. Naked, entwined in each other's arms, Peter let his long, erect penis slide comfortably in and out of Anna's vagina. As they rhythmically made love, the volleyball players stopped their game to watch Peter climax and Anna contort with pleasure. They applauded loudly, congratulating the couple.*

***

Peter finished his sandwich and started to leave when Herb blurted out, "Wait! Do you have to go back to work, now?"

"I'm supposed to. I have some calculations to do," Peter answered.

"What would happen if you took the rest of the day off?"

Peter tried to picture the consequences. The voices would get louder. He'd have to take another afternoon off toward the end of July to keep his absences symmetrical. He might have to backtrack to the office before going home to insure that he reached *Private Booths, Sexy Girls* and arrived at the bus following his usual path. Since he always did the same calculation, taking off would not truly interfere with work.

"Nothing really," Peter said.

"Great," Herb declared. "Then, you're coming with me. Today's the day that you finally get laid."

With that, Herb led Peter to 42nd Street.

Peter looked longingly at *Private Booths, Sexy Girls* as they passed without stopping in. Six doors further down, Herb turned into 198 West 42nd Street, an inconspicuous looking building with peeling paint, and a sign declaring, in barely readable print, *Rooms for Rent*. Peter followed Herb, holding his shoulder tightly in, hoping he could ascend the stairs without making contact with the dirty walls.

Herb continued up swiftly with Peter following close behind. On the second floor, they stopped at the front desk where a short, balding man was sitting in a wheelchair behind a wire-reinforced glass partition with one small opening to let money pass between the customers and him. Taped to the glass, a hand-written sign declared,

Rume raytz – 2 dolar quartr hour.

"Is Sandy free?" Herb asked.

"In 5 minutes," the man replied.

Herb reached in his pocket to offer Peter an unwrapped piece of gum while saying, "Sandy's good, especially with beginners. You'll like her."

A minute later, a man wearing an Oscar DeLaurent sweater and cardigan tasseled shoes, holding his hat in front of his face, rushed down the stairs past Peter and Herb.

"She's free," the man said.

"We'll need a half hour," Herb replied.

Herb directed Peter to give the man $4.00. "That's for the room. We pay Sandy separately."

Herb led Peter up the next flight of stairs. Once inside, Sandy smirked, "A twosome. I can use the extra cash."

Herb laughed, "Sorry sweetheart. I'm not here for me. It's my friend, Peter. Can you do him?"

"No problem," Sandy replied. "A friend in need is a friend indeed. Twenty bucks and he wears a bag."

Herb leaned over and whispered, "He's a virgin, Sandy. Do him bare back. Just this once."

"Listen, I ain't taking no chances. I've heard that virgin line before. How do I know it's true."

"Here," Herb said, holding out his urine-stained copy of *Peter Squared*. "It's in this book."

"*Peter Squared!*" Sandy exclaimed. "I read it. That's a great book and those characters are out of sight. Can you imagine anything weirder? But what does that have to do with your friend, Peter."

Sandy stopped suddenly, her eyes opening wide. "Peter? No, that's a story. Get outta here."

"No," Herb said, now talking even more softly than before. "This is Peter. I know it's weird, but the story is true. I don't know what the hell to make of it either. But somehow, this character just popped out of the book, something like Pinocchio becoming a real boy. I hate to tell you, but I think you and I are characters in the next book."

Sandy stopped and thought. "You know, that really helps me

understand why I feel so unreal all the time. I thought it was just fucking anyone who came in with a twenty. Maybe all us girls are just characters in novels, nothing more. All I can say is that's one for the books." While Sandy chuckled over her joke, Herb went on to plea,

"Come on Sandy. Do it bareback this one time for Peter."

"OK. But it's going to cost you. Double. Forty bucks."

"You drive a hard bargain, but it's worth it. Peter, give her $40.00."

Peter reached in his wallet and pulled out his Master Card. Sandy and Herb laughed. Herb quipped, "Getting laid: Priceless."

Sandy guffawed and said, "Now, I know he's a virgin. OK. What have you got, cowboy?"

"$25.00," Peter answered.

"I won't fuck him, but I'll give him a blow job. That's my final offer."

Herb turned to Peter and said, "I'm only halfway through the book. Have you ever had a blow job?"

"No," Peter meekly replied.

"OK, Sandy. You've got yourself a deal."

After Peter handed Sandy the money and she counted it, placing it securely in her bosom, she directed Peter to a chair. Before he could object (with just a glance, Peter knew it was covered with a lot of dirt), Sandy pushed Peter to the chair, got on her knees and reached for his crotch. Peter held his legs tightly together as Sandy tried to undo his zipper. It took several minutes before she could finally pry it open. Trying to be gentle, Sandy smiled and looked sweetly at Peter as she placed her hand inside, reaching Peter's outer underwear. Pushing passed this first layer of protection, Sandy grimaced slightly as she felt the next undergarment: an odd texture. Pulling tightly, a piece of Peter's air conditioning filter separated from the rest and came out in Sandy's hands. Sandy laughed out loud as she reached back in. By now hysterical, Sandy struggled to spurt out the words, "He's got more underwear in there."

Sandy got up, put her hands on her hips, and said, "I can't do this. Three layers between his pants and his cock."

Dejected, Herb said, "OK. Give him his money back."

"Money back?" Sandy balked. "Since when did you think there were refunds in a whorehouse? He gives me a credit card and you want a refund. What do you think this is, Macys?"

Herb stumbled trying to find something to say when Sandy added, "OK. I provide a service. I'm a professional. I won't take your money without doing something. Herb, sit down."

Herb sat on the chair next to Peter. Sandy got on her knees and gave him oral sex. Peter reached in his pocket, retrieved his calculator and completed the calculation he would have done had he returned to the office.

***

Peter and Herb left the whorehouse, Herb keeping his shirt open to display the cum-stain on his pants. They reached the door and walked onto the street. As Peter and Herb talked, Anna jumped out of nowhere and grabbed Herb by the shirt.

"Help me, Herb. You've gotta protect me."

"What's wrong, Anna? And where have you been? Everyone missed you in the program."

"My Dad wants to rape me. Sol's gonna kill me."

"You're talking crazy, Anna. You need help. Let's go back to the program and talk with Dr. Brown."

"No!" Anna shouted. She took a deep breath to compose herself knowing she had to appear sane if she was going to get helped.

"It's not what you think, Herb," Anna said much more calmly now. "A lot's happened that I never shared with anyone. It's too much to say now except you gotta believe me, my family's really crazy. I just got out of Kings County. As soon as we hit the street, I took off. I know they're coming after me. I know it looks like I'm crazy, but it's really not that way. I don't need a doctor, Herb. I need a place to stay."

Herb took a long look at Anna trying to decide whether she was telling the truth or if this was part of her illness. He wasn't convinced, but he never liked the way the doctors act as if they know better than the patients, so he took a chance and said, "OK. You can stay with me."

Peter, who had drifted from the interaction and was adding the address numbers from the fronts of the stores, was jarred from his thoughts when he heard Anna demand, "No. I want to stay with Peter. I'll be safer there. No one knows him."

"Your choice," Herb replied. "Just be warned. He doesn't have much to eat."

After reassuring Anna that he'd come back to the park tomorrow and check up on her, Herb took off.

"Be good," he winked at Peter. "Don't do anything I wouldn't do."

***

Peter shook as he looked at Anna, quickly calculating the number of days since a woman stayed in his apartment. *Mom died, March 3, 1992. It was late at night. They didn't actually remove her body until March 4, 1992. That's ten years, two months, twenty-nine days until today, June 3, 2002.*

Suddenly, a familiar voice bellowed out across the street, "Peter. Where the hell have you been?"

Peter cringed as he saw Andrew crossing the street, catching up with him in front of the whorehouse.

"I thought you'd be in the park, not here," Andrew said. "It's 3:00. Kind of a long lunch. Where have you been?"

When Peter failed to reply, Andrew went on, "I wouldn't normally care but Harold called. He wanted to cancel our meeting Monday. I worked my tail off talking him out of it. Now, he wants tentative ideas. You've gotta come back and put something together for him right away."

Looking mournful, Peter shrugged his shoulders and said, "I don't know what to do. I'm not really a ..."

Before Peter could finish his sentence, Andrew took notice of Anna and interrupted Peter with a smile, "Oh. You didn't introduce me to your friend."

Peter looked around to see if either Ken or Herb were there.

"My friend?" he puzzled.

"Well, unless you're more than just friends," Andrew said with a wink. "Come on, Peter. Be polite and introduce me to the lucky lady."

Realizing that Andrew was referring to Anna who seemed quite agitated looking all about afraid her family would suddenly appear, Peter replied, "Anna."

"Hello Anna. I'm Andrew. Peter and I work together. Glad to meet you."

When Andrew held his hand out, Anna jumped back two feet screaming, "Eek!" not used to men offering women handshakes in her Hasidic community.

"Oops! Sorry to scare you Miss," Andrew said.

Without further notice of Anna's strange behavior, Andrew continued to talk with Peter, insisting they go back to the office. Anna followed behind, constantly looking around to make sure she was safe.

The group took the elevator up to the fourth floor. There, they got off and walked through the front door of Lerner and Branstill, Public Accountants.

Once inside, Andrew offered Anna a seat at the front station while he and Peter met in his office. Fascinated by the setup and no longer afraid she'd run into her family, Anna picked up the telephones and started having imaginary conversations with make believe clients.

***

"Peter, I really fucked up," Andrew said.

Holding his thumb and index finger on his right hand one inch apart, he went on, "He was this close. Harold doesn't like Carl at all. He's just not sure we have the operation to pull this off. I had him just about there when I got this ridiculous idea that consulting would nail the thing down. I had him without it. Now, all he can think about is how we're going to make a ton of money for him. And if we don't, we lose him. Do you have any ideas?"

Peter had lots of ideas. He was particularly proud of his scales for rating dirt and friends, and his procedure to measuring the orgastic value of an X-rated magazine. He had recently created his own Best Places to Live in America Scale as the logarithm of the ratio between peep shows and EPA environmental hazard scores, the value going up with each peep show, down with each toxin. Peter had the recent idea to buy new carpets for his apartment since Herb's cigarette ash fell on the floor.

Peter also thought that Blockbuster's would do better if they changed their name to Videolender's, communicating more accurately the nature of their business, without changing the number of letters in the name (although he was still trying to resolve the problem of having an extra two vowels in the name).

Finally, Peter was particularly proud of his idea that there could be a comprehensive family entertainment center where men would masturbate to girls and dancing horses while their wives and children bowled nearby.

"No," Peter replied.

"Well, we'd better get one and get one fast 'cause Harold is waiting for a call right now."

"Do you know what type of idea he's looking for?" Peter asked.

"No. All I know is that he has a ton of money and the feds want to tax the hell out of it. He was going to expand his own business operations when Congress passed this ridiculous Heartlands Economic Recovery Option. They call it HERO. The write-offs are unbelievable. Obviously, there's some two-bit farmer-congressman with a ton of clout or a stable full of gorgeous girls who pushed this one through."

As Andrew cackled over his quip, Congressman Peter Branstill donning a straw hat, overalls, work boots, and bright red suspenders, announced to his legislator brethren that the horses were here.

"It's strange because the best thing for Harold and the country is for him to invest the money the way he planned. He can't lose now as long as he puts his money in some, ridiculous rural venture.

"So, that's where we come in. He needs a good, innovative, business plan."

Peter stroked his chin as he pictured himself, standing by a field of corn as he received the Congressional Medal of Honor, the proud owner, now in front of his new business, Peter Branstill's Peep and Bowl.

"So what do you think?" Andrew asked.

"Entertainment," Peter quietly replied.

***

Andrew followed Peter out of his office to see Anna handle three phone calls at a time, put people on hold, take messages, and give information, pleased with her chance to play receptionist. Engrossed in her work, she failed to notice Andrew and Peter approach from behind.

"Peter, you didn't tell me about your friend. She's quite a secretary. Even Mary couldn't manage the phones with this much pizzazz. Damnit, Peter. I'll never figure you out. You have these great ideas, yet you're so laid back about everything. You're absolutely right. How did I think we'd function without someone on the phones? Here I am thinking there are no clients. We're just not answering the damn phone. And the way you do it really kills me. Surprising me by conducting your interviews on the street. I'd say she looks damn good. Let's see what we've got here."

Andrew walked to the desk and picked up 35 messages Anna wrote with the names and telephone numbers of imaginary clients.

"Hot dog, Peter. We're in business now. Forget about Harold's proposal. You start returning these calls. I'll tell him you're too busy to write it up now, but it's in entertainment and it's really good. Hell, he'd have to be a fool not to see that even our hard-working friends on the farm need something to unwind to."

13 IT'S HOWDY DOODY TIME

On Wednesday night, Peter logged onto his computer, again to receive a message from Ken.

kengoldberg: Hi, Peter. Did you buy another copy of *Peter Squared* yet.

Peter: Yes.

kengoldberg: Hold on a moment.

A few minutes later, Peter saw:

kengoldberg: Sorry. Just wanted to enter it on my spreadsheet. That's how I keep track of commissions. Thank God you're so nutty about dirt. I can't stand it when people lend out their copies. Have them buy their own books. Or put them on your Christmas list and get them a copy.

kengoldberg: By the way, did you buy one for Howdy yet? LOL

Peter: I don't think Howdy reads.

kengoldberg: Good point, Peter. You're always on the ball.

kengoldberg: Wait a second. Maybe, you're onto something. A children's version.

kengoldberg: Look Jane look. See Peter peep.

kengoldberg: So, what page are you on now.

Peter: I'm on page 183.

kengoldberg: Hold on.

After another pause, the screen flashed,

kengoldberg: I just checked it out. They just kicked you out of the bowling alley.

Peter: Yes. The next chapter is called *Curly*.

kengoldberg: That's a great chapter. I think I outdid myself on that one. Imagine Peter, an ordinary psychologist like me who never wrote a book before ends up creating one of the greatest novels ever written. I never even studied literature in college. I was a math major, and a real good one, too. Hate to tell you, buddy, but I was ten times the mathematician you are. You think those calculations you did in *Peter Squared* were good. They're nothing, Peter. High school at best. Now, I don't mean to offend you but you can't hold a candle to me when it comes to mathematics. And you know you could never write a novel. Besides that, Peter, you've got no friends and I do.

kengoldberg: I hope it doesn't bother you too much that I wrote a novel and you didn't. You're just not as smart as I am.

kengoldberg: So, what did you think about Sandy. Quite a looker, isn't she. Sorry you didn't get it on with her, but it's much too early in this story for you to get laid. Try being patient. LOL. Almost forgot. I'm talking to Mr. Patient Emeritus himself. ROFLMAO.

kengoldberg: Sorry, Peter. I have to sign off. My wife's waiting for me upstairs. I figure that at least one of us ought to get it tonight. LOL. And I don't think it's going to be you. ROFLMAO.

kengoldberg: Later.

***

Peter turned off his computer and got up from the desk to see Anna standing by the dining room table, stark naked, bent over, her exposed rear facing him. Peter stood frozen, not knowing whether he should just walk to his bedroom or try to help Anna find what she was looking for. As he vacillated back and forth, first starting toward his room, then stopping and turning back, then starting to his room again, to stop and turn back again, Anna periodically looked back, hoping Peter would approach her unsure what to do. Finally, she called out, "Can you come here?"

Peter started in her direction, noting the elliptical form of her behind. Her cheeks showed good symmetry. Peter detected no smells from her exposed rear, and there was only a small bit of discoloration due to two tiny pimples. Hesitantly, he walked up to Anna, bent over, and began scanning the floor hoping to help her out.

"There's nothing there," Peter said, unable to find the lost item on the floor. Anna looked at Peter puzzled, then threw her arms around him and hugged him.

"You're a real gentleman, Peter. I've never met anyone quite like you. Thanks for letting me stay."

Once Anna retired to Peter's deceased mother's room, he realized that Anna, just like Shirley, the girl who wanted to have sex with Peter, the one Tom Carroll once said, "I told you man, you should have fucked her then," was making an advance. For the rest of the evening, Peter lay in his bed, masturbating to images of Anna's behind, regretting his missed opportunity.

***

Peter worked at his desk Thursday morning, re-checking the calculation he had done everyday since Carl left the firm, along with the formula for tax returns completed during and after tax season: $0 + 0 = 0$. Anna continued to answer calls that were not coming in. Andrew arrived slightly late, greeted Anna first, then walked to Peter's desk and said,

"She's great! We have more leads now than we've had all year. Now, come to my office and we'll finalize our plans."

Peter and Andrew reviewed the plans. Andrew would fly out Saturday to meet friends in Indianapolis, then meet with Harold early Monday morning. Peter needed to book a different flight Monday morning so he could be there for the second meeting at 2:00 p.m.. Over the weekend, Peter should work on the proposal and put together a Power Point presentation.

Shaking his head, imagining his own erect penis powerfully pushing by his dual underwear, air conditioning filtration system, through his pants, he asked, "What's that?"

"Power Point? It's a program: State-of-the-art corporate presentations available to anyone," Andrew replied. "Have Anna help you if you're not sure how to do it. She'll know what to do."

Andrew smiled as he glanced Anna's way, watching her furiously record one message after the other.

***

At noon, Peter and Anna left the office and walked to the park. Before they reached Peter's bench, Herb, who was sitting in the middle, the seat Peter had hoped to take for himself, called out, "Hey folks. How you doing?"

Neither Peter nor Anna answered as Peter contemplated his choices – the right or left sections of the bench – while Anna walked cautiously, scanning the park to make sure her family wasn't there.

"Missed you in program," Herb went on. "Get up late folks?"

Anna dashed the twinkle in Herb's eye by saying, "I'm working for Peter."

"That's great. You've got a job. Hell, what I'd give to get one myself."

Peter and Anna sat down. Herb went on.

"Did I ever tell you kids I once was a lawyer? Made law review. Top of my class. Crazy times then: the war, civil rights. I worked down south with Martin Luther King himself. Yea, me and Marty were good friends. And Billy wanted me to help him defend the Chicago 7. I woulda done it, but the bitch just wasn't on the same page with me. For me, it was a passion. For her, just a stage. Her heart was into family, money, the suburbs, you know. Not for me, but I was a wimp, and she was a willing piece of tail, so there she wrote.

"Hell, I'd go back to corporate law now, but no one will take me back. Somehow. Somehow I'm gonna make it. One day at a time and wait for a chance.

"Peter. You work for a big firm. You guys must need lawyers. Your clients must need lawyers. Think you could give me a chance?"

Peter bit his sandwich, this time a hexagonal shape. Looking pensive, he chewed carefully making sure that each tooth bit into the morsel twice. After he swallowed, Peter looked at Herb and said, "I'm working on something now. If the chance comes up, I'll mention your name."

"GREAT!" Herb shouted. Here, take my card.

Herbert J. Whitmore
Attorney at Law

For appointment, call
212-637-1000 and ask for Herb in the Day Program

Motto: It's for you, that we sue.

Personal former friend of the Rev. Martin Luther King, Jr.

Peter looked at Herb's card and said, "Thanks."

***

After work, Peter and Anna walked home, Peter looking longingly as they passed *Private Booths, Sexy Girls*. In total silence, they took the uptown bus to Peter's apartment. After opening the door and leading Anna in, Peter reached in his pocket and fished out his notebook where he erased the number 1 by Anna's name and replaced it with 2. He also added an s at the end of the word *visit* on the line with her name:

Lifetime visitors:
1961 Sammy   23 visits

| 2002 Herb | 1 visit |
| 2002 Anna | 2 visits |

Peter prepared dinner: chicken and cereal. Anna took the cereal pouring the milk directly in the package, then tilting it toward her mouth so she could consume it without using utensils, her only Kosher alternative at Peter's place. Peter watched feeling pangs of passion, realizing that Anna, like he, would not use someone else's cutlery.

Peter ate his standard dinner, thinking about Anna the night before, standing naked by the table, bent over, exposing her rear, wondering if she was aware that her pants had fallen off. Of more concern, Peter wondered how he would masturbate tonight with Anna in the apartment. *Maybe, Howdy can keep her company.*

After dinner, Peter went into his bedroom and retrieved his Howdy Doody doll which he gave to Anna to take into his mother's bedroom with her. He then logged onto his computer and immediately received an Instant Message from kengoldberg.

kengoldberg: Guess what, Peter, I figured it out. The Base Peter system works. Peter Cubed equals 5. Now, you can jerk off 5 times to your heart's delight. In fact, you can now jerk off as many times as you'd like. Here's how it goes:

$2^0 = 1$
$2^1 = 2$
$Peter^2 = 3$
$2^2 = 4$
$Peter^3 = 5$
$Peter^4 = 6$
$Peter^5 = 7$
$2^3 = 8$
$Peter^6 = 9$
$Peter^7 = 10$

Then, we begin with
$John^2 = 11$ and so forth.

With this system, you can jerk off any number of times you'd like and be guilt-free.

Peter: Thanks. I'm not sure I understand how this system works.

While waiting for Ken's next message, Peter heard Anna open the door to his mother's room and walk back to the kitchen. She opened the drawer, removed a knife, and took it with her to the living room by Peter.

kengoldberg: Stop asking so many dumb questions, Peter. It works. You've got to trust me. If you don't, you'll be in bed with a chimpanzee instead of Anna.

After briefly picturing himself with a chimpanzee, Peter typed in,

Peter: I'm sorry. I just like to know the mathematics.

By now, Anna stood in front of him, completely naked, the kitchen knife in her hands.

kengoldberg: Well, stop worrying about the math. In fact, why don't you just get a life instead. Did you ever think there are other things to do besides math, cleaning all the time and beating off? Why don't you go to an art museum or play ping pong. Take up water polo. How about astronomy? You could study a foreign language.

kengoldberg: For God's sake, Peter, get a life for yourself. Find a nice girl, get laid, have a family, get your kids a cat and a dog, buy a house and a car.

Peter watched Anna insert the knife in her vagina. He cringed when he saw blood drip on his carpet.

kengoldberg: LOL. I was just kidding Peter. I know it's hard for you. I'm just playing with your head a bit. Now, don't go postal on me just because I teased you. By the way, don't worry about that relationship thing. It's all planned. You're going to have sex by the end of this story. I'm not going to tell you exactly when and how. That would spoil it for everyone else. Just keep beating the meat and trust me, things will work out soon enough.

Once she bled, Anna came out of her trance. Her face turning red, she dropped the knife on the floor and ran back to Peter's mother's room.

kengoldberg: Sorry Peter. I've gotta go. My wife is home. Did I tell you my other mathematical system. It's the Base Ken system. Ken^2 means I'm getting laid tonight and you're not. LOL. Bye.

Peter looked at Anna's blood stained knife on the floor, glad that the carpets were being changed next week, frightened by the knife that could so easily lop off his penis. He felt jealous that Anna could cut herself while he stayed tormented over the wish for self-castration, without the gumption to ever do it.

Peter found his plastic gloves so he could pick up the knife, wrap it in paper towels, and drop it into a plastic bag. He took it downstairs where the garbage cans were kept, and threw it away, knowing he could not castrate himself with this knife, tainted by Anna's blood, no longer safe for his personal use.

***

That night, Peter lay in bed, unable to sleep, having masturbated only five times. Determined to prove Ken right, Peter had struggled for hours to keep his hand off himself. As his organ throbbed, Peter tentatively grabbed it and began to rub. Before he could grow erect, he stopped, interrupted by an earth shattering scream from his mother's room. The next minute, Anna came charging in and jumped in his bed, tears in her eyes, wailing painfully, clutching Peter with all her might.

"Aaaaaaah!" she cried as her tears dribbled on Peter's night shirt. Suddenly, she sat up, looked at Buffalo Bob, and ragefully pointed her finger, "Him! It's him. Get him out of here."

Anna jumped off the bed and stormed the doll. She grabbed him by the head and threw him across the room. She stomped on him until his right arm was crushed and the left arm fell off. "You evil man. Get away from me. NEVER! NEVER AGAIN! I'm telling the rebbe. The whole congregation will know. I will never be silent again."

Then, she looked at Clarabelle Clown, certain it was her mother, and again pointed her finger accusingly, "You! You've been part of it all the time. You helped him fuck me. You won't get away with it. I swear. You're gonna pay."

Peter watched Anna attack Clarabelle Clown, tearing her head off her body just as she had assaulted Buffalo Bob a moment ago. Seeing his prized dolls, his childhood friends, torn to bits, Peter quickly left his room and ran to his mother's bedroom to lovingly hold the now frightened Howdy. Still intact, Peter stroked his painted, plastic head, rocked him, and hugged him, hoping to calm the doll down, "No one will hurt you, ever. I promise."

Howdy just looked at Peter, his expression sad, *Are Bob and Clarabelle OK?*

Peter tried to be strong but could not deceive the knowing Doody.

***

Peter put Howdy down on the bed and started out the room to check on Anna. Looking back seeing fear in Doody's eyes, Peter turned back, picked him up and held him behind as he peeked in his room. By now, the naked Anna was lying on his bed, exhausted. She looked up at Peter. Her eyes closing, she put her head back down and fell asleep. Peter looked at Howdy and said, "You're not safe here."

Peter put on his coat, and carrying Howdy, his blanket, and a tape deck, walked out the door the twelve blocks to Aunt Cindy's apartment. When he reached her door, he inserted his key, not sure it would work, having never used it on a Thursday before. The door opened and Peter went in.

Peter laid the blanket on the floor with Howdy on top. He carefully folded the ends over the doll before plugging in the tape deck. Peter reached in his pocket to retrieve a tape that he inserted in the machine.

Setting it for continuous play, Peter walked back to Doody to give him a kiss. He then left the apartment, double locking the doors, humming along with the music he played.

It's Howdy Doody Time.
It's Howdy Doody Time...

***

Back at his apartment, Peter looked into his bedroom and saw Anna sound asleep. He went to his tool chest and pulled out a tape measure. Calculating the distance between Anna's right elbow and the end of the bed, Peter figured that he would fit on his bed in the required position if he shifted his body 7½ inches to the right. Not wanting to seem forward, Peter walked to his closet to get his suit. Wearing combination 25162, Peter returned to bed assuming the required position. Watching Anna, he quietly masturbated through a hole in his pants pocket. Although he couldn't sleep, Peter still smiled peacefully knowing he had finished the night masturbating 6 times, $Peter^4 = 6$.

14 THE GREAT ESCAPE

Peter woke up Friday morning at 6:00 a.m. and followed his standard routine except for eating breakfast since it had been consumed by Anna the night before. He tried once to wake her before going to work himself, but she waved him off, yawning, "I'm staying home."

At work, Andrew met with Peter to teach him Power Point. "I know Anna's good, but maybe she hasn't done this. It's not hard. Let me explain it to you now."

After showing him the program, Andrew went back to his own office to return the messages Anna left him the day before. Peter sat at his desk, playing with Power Point, using its high powered graphics to present the calculation he did every day since Carl left the firm, along with:

Tax returns in tax season	0
Tax returns after tax season	+0
Total tax returns	0

At noon, Peter got up from his desk to leave for lunch. As he reached the door, Andrew called out from his office, "Peter, I've returned about half these calls. No takers. Next time, Anna's gotta patch the calls straight to one of us. You know what they say. The early bird gets the worm."

***

When Peter arrived at the bench, Anna was already there, fully clothed with a suitcase by her side. Herb arrived moments later, "How'd it go?"

Without responding to his question, Anna said, "I can't go back."

"You don't have to," Herb said. "I assume things have been okay with Peter. If he can't have you back, you can always stay with me."

"It's Friday, Herb. Sol will hurt me. I can't be with that man anymore.

73

I don't want to be hurt."

"Why don't you divorce him, Anna?" Herb asked.

"He won't give me a Ghet. He'll kill me before he does. I know him. I'm not safe. I went to the bank this morning. He thinks all the money is in his name, but that's not true. He forgot about our wedding account. We got a lot of money and it was all still there. I took it out this morning so I don't have to go back."

"You might need a lawyer," Herb said, handing Anna his card.

As Anna opened her purse to show Herb a very large sum of money, they heard a familiar voice, Dave, call out, "Anna. There you are. We were all worried about you."

Anna looked up, terror in her eyes, seeing Sol and her father by Dave's side.

"Aaaaaaah!" Anna screamed as she got up from the bench and started running away. Herb followed her as quickly as he could, his 60-year-old body worn from abuse. Peter was next, running at Herb's pace, younger and faster, but slowed by his efforts to avoid stepping on dirt. Dave, fit and spry, caught up quickly, the four pulling easily away from Sol and the Rabbi held back by their 19th century Hasidic garb. Anna reached the curb, opened the door of a taxi waiting for the light to turn green, and ushered Peter, Herb and Dave in. By now, her father and Sol were closing in. Anna cried out, "Port Authority. Step on it."

The light turned green.

As they rode, Anna checked her copy of the bus schedule: The 1:15 to LA was just about to leave. Inside the terminal, she pushed ahead of the line to buy four tickets. Before long, they were on their way, leaving the Hasids behind.

***

The group found seats in the 12th and 13th rows of the bus, Herb and Dave sitting right behind Peter and Anna. As the bus rolled out, Anna could see her father and husband wandering around, looking confused. Soon, the bus had crossed the George Washington Bridge and was traveling down the New Jersey Turnpike on its way to LA. Anna wistfully stared out the window, a position she maintained for the next two days.

For two hours, Peter wondered if he should deboard the bus in Philadelphia and look for Ken. Not sure what he'd tell Anna, he stayed in his seat as the bus left the station, up the Schuylkill Expressway, onto the Pennsylvania Turnpike, and out west. Then, a more painful concern crossed his mind: *Who will take care of Howdy?* At first, Peter cringed picturing Howdy all alone in the apartment, Then, he looked at his watch, saw it was Friday and thought, *He'll have dinner with Aunt Cindy Sunday.*

With a break in Pittsburgh, the group got off the bus to get something to eat. Anna gave Dave and Herb money so they could buy food at the bus stop. She opened her bag so she could consume the packaged Kosher items she had bought for the trip. Afraid of contamination, Peter ate nothing at all.

***

By Saturday, they were in the heartlands, traveling through rows and rows of corn and wheat. While Peter developed formulae for counting the number of plants in a row, ears on a plant, and the velocity of the wind by estimating the angle at which the wheat and corn stalks bent, Herb dreamed of life as a lawyer in LA while Dave thought of ways to get into Anna's pants.

Tired, Peter closed his eyes, soon picturing himself driving a tractor with Anna walking behind, vacuuming the dust. Together, they planted wheat in perfectly symmetrical rows. The wheat pushed through the ground. Anna beamed at Peter, her arms tight around his waist, saying, *Can we raise them Jewish?* Peter laughed, *You don't have to be Jewish to love Levi's.*

Anna dusted Peter's plate before giving him his sandwich, corned beef on rye. *Does it have mustard?* Peter asked. *No,* Anna replied. *I thought we'd try snot.*

Anna laughed and Peter wiped his sleeve to catch the mucous dripping from his nose. Herb put $40 on the table and told Anna: *Don't worry. It's his first time.*

Anna smiled, easing his erect penis in: *It won't be his last.*

Suddenly, Peter broke from his thoughts as he felt Anna jump out of her seat and vault herself over him, screaming "Traif, traif, traif."

Running up and down the aisles, she pulled at her hair and threw her hands back and forth. She grabbed the bus driver's arm almost sending them off the road. Struggling to stay in control, the driver left the highway and exited into a small Nebraska town. Anna took her hands off and let him steer the bus into town. Soon, they were met by two officers emerging from a police car with the words *Anderson Police*, written on its side.

The cops boarded the bus with their guns drawn. The driver pointed to Anna, "That lady's gone mad."

The policeman approached Anna who was now sitting calmly on a seat in the first row.

"What's the problem, Ma'am?" the officer asked.

"Nothing," she answered. "If you don't mind, I'd like to leave this bus."

The officer stared at Anna, sure he knew her from before,

"Take her the hell off," the driver cried. "That'll be great by me."

"Do you want to press charges, sir?" the officer asked.

"No way. We're going to California. Just get her the hell off this bus. I'll be fine."

Anna signaled Peter, Herb, and Dave to follow her off. The officer stopped Peter before he stepped off, "Who is she? I've seen her before."

Noticing the resemblance between the officer and Don Knotts and remembering one of the passages he had read on the bus, Peter flashed his copy of *Peter Squared* and said, "It's here."

The policeman grabbed the book and said, "You Easterners are sure weird."

Remembering Ken's response when he last lent his book to Herb, Peter just said, "Check it out. It's online and at fine book stores everywhere."

Peter walked off the bus, reached in his pocket and retrieved his notebook, writing, *Tell Ken, the next time we talk, a policeman's going to buy your book.*

NEBRASKA

15 THE BOWLING ALLEY

On Sunday morning, Peter woke up in a hotel room bed, fully clothed, his tie dangling to the left approximately 65% of its mass on the half of his body defined by the central meridian formed with an imaginary line starting at the topmost point of his head, through his penis and landing squarely between his toes. Although his penis hung slightly to the left, his belly button was 5% off center and there were no other identifiable body parts which would do in constructing this line. Peter took his tie in his left hand and shifted it slightly to the right to accurately bisect his body.

Peter looked around. Lacking the posh elegance of his Washington, D.C. hotel room two years ago and the quality and comfort of the room he stayed in on business in Indianapolis, but considerably cleaner than the one he had in the Catskills years ago, Peter reached for the end table and found his notepad and writing supplies, recording,

June 7, 2002. Anderson Nebraska. Third best hotel/motel I ever visited.

Peter returned the pad where he found it and looked around now sensing the same presence in his bed that he experienced the night before he took this trip. There, sprawled on the right side of the bed except for one leg crossing over onto his side was Anna, her right breast 63% exposed above the sheet. Peter checked his zipper to make sure it was closed, then looked at his watch: 6:00 a.m. Peter remembered riding through Ohio two nights before, watching the exits intently, waiting for the exact moment he crossed into Indiana to adjust his watch, pleased that he made the change in under two seconds, far better than his performance two years ago when he crossed the time zone in the air on a plane.

Peter thought back to the night before and recalled how Anna landed in his bed.

***

"I'm with Peter," Anna boldly declared draping her arms around him while Herb signed for the rooms and Dave stood in the lobby playing with a leaf on a nearby plant. Peter stood still, his body rigid, his eyes fixed ahead, focused on the colorful, flowered wallpaper all around the lobby. He counted twelve flowers per square yard. With nine square feet in a square yard, he predicted one flower in two-thirds of all randomly selected square foot sections of the wallpaper, two flowers in the other one-third of his selections.

"Can we trust you alone?" Herb chuckled as he winked at Peter. "She's married you know."

Anna stroked Peter's hair, glaring at Herb. "Stop that Herb. Don't scare the poor boy off."

Peter smiled having just finished checking out his 12th randomly selected square foot section, finding two flowers in exactly four of them.

When they got to the room, it was quite late at night. Exhausted from the ride, Peter looked to see where he could sleep. There were two double beds which, unlike his own apartment, were both in the same room. Peter sat in one of the two chairs also in the room, hoping that Anna would quickly pick her bed so he could lie down to sleep in his. While he waited, Anna began dancing erotically, slowly removing her clothes, grinding her hips, causing Peter to feel aroused. Hoping she would not get angry at him as his erection grew, Peter quietly placed his right hand in his pocket and, skilled at the art, reached through a hole and taped his assembly of tissue paper and plastic bag around his penis, masturbating to her undulating moves. When Anna lay on the bed farthest from the door, her clothes off, her right leg bent to expose her crotch, Peter glanced away and, fully clothed, climbed into the other bed.

At first, Peter placed himself squarely in the middle. To his shock and dismay, Peter watched Anna get up from her bed and walk to his, climb in and wrap her bare leg tightly around his pants. Cringing as he thought of her vaginal fluids staining Suit No. 3, Peter looked away while Anna rubbed herself up and down his leg, screaming as she came.

Realizing that Anna was straddled in an asymmetrical position, Peter shuffled his behind toward the front of the room, hoping that the combined mass of their bodies would distribute evenly between the left and right halves of the bed. Following a final climactic contraction, Anna rolled on her back toward the right side of the bed. Peter shifted quickly to the left hoping to re-establish even distribution of their combined weights over the surface of the bed.

"That was wonderful," Anna said. "Sorry you couldn't get into it. We'll try again."

She then winked at Peter and added, "I'll give you time to take your clothes off tomorrow."

Anna fell asleep.

Peter looked across the room and saw that Anna had thrown the covers off the other bed onto the floor. Peter decided it was better for him to stay in bed with her rather than risk getting contaminated using sheets that had been on the floor. Not wanting to seem forward, Peter slept in his suit and masturbated once more ($2^1 = 2$) through the hole in his pocket before falling asleep.

***

Peter was jarred back to the present when he heard someone knock on the door. At first, Peter thought he heard a seven knock 3-4 pattern, three evenly spaced soft knocks, a pause, then four consecutive knocks (two loud, two soft). Reconsidering his first assessment, Peter thought, *Maybe that's only five knocks: three soft knocks, a loud short knock, and a loud rolling knock, like a drum roll, with two trailing sounds.*

Herb called out, "Peter, you up?"

Peter glanced toward his penis before realizing what Herb meant. "Yes. I'm awake."

"Good. How about breakfast?"

Peter realized that he did not buy anything to eat in the frenzy out west. It was Sunday, the day he would normally stay home and pretend to pray before visiting Aunt Cindy.

Far from her apartment and having missed work Friday afternoon, he decided to adjust his schedule and continue his calculations this morning. When it was lunchtime, he would find a place to buy food and a local park where he could eat it.

"No," Peter started to call out when Anna stretched and said, "Who's that, Peter?"

"Herb."

"Where?" she asked looking around the room.

"He's on the other side of the door."

"Well, let him in," Anna chuckled. Peter put his work down and got up to answer the door.

"Geez, I thought I'd be out there all day," Herb said, before noticing Anna half-clad with just the sheet covering her breasts, and Peter standing there in his now wrinkled suit.

"Oh!" Herb said with a devilish smile. "You could have told me to come back later."

Anna shook her head and looked at Herb, "It wouldn't have made a difference, Herb. Believe me."

Herb noticed the suit for the first time, nodded his head glancing back at Anna and again asked, "You sure you don't want breakfast?"

"Of course I want breakfast," Anna said. "Give us a few minutes and Peter and I will be right there."

"Great," Herb said. "In the coffee shop in ten."

Herb closed the door and Anna got dressed. Peter returned to the desk and started working on his calculations again. So engrossed in his work, he was surprised when Anna tugged at his shoulder and said, "You ready?"

Not knowing what to say, he sheepishly followed her out the door.

***

In the coffee shop, Peter and Anna approached Herb who was sitting with Dave. The waitress brought coffee; Peter pretended to drink his while the others talked.

"OK, Anna," Herb said. "You brought us here. What did you have in mind?"

"What I had in mind didn't actually happen," Anna answered.

"What do you mean?" Dave asked.

Herb tapped Dave on the arm and gestured toward Peter.

"Oh!" Dave said.

"Now that we're here. What are we going to do?" Herb asked.

"I don't know," Anna said.

"I want to go back home," Dave chimed in.

"OK. Anna doesn't know what she wants to do. I say we stay. Dave wants to go home. I guess you're the tie-breaking vote, Peter. What do you say?"

Deep in thought, Peter failed to answer Herb's question as he remembered that he needed to be in Indianapolis tomorrow – *thank God I won't have to adjust my watch* – and replayed in his mind the conversation he had earlier in the week with Andrew when he left: *particularly proud of his idea that there could be a comprehensive family entertainment center where men could masturbate to girls and dancing horses while their wives and children bowled nearby.*

"He's thinking," Herb said to his friends. "No shoot-from-the-hip decision from Peter. OK, Petey, what'll it be?"

"Let's go bowling," Peter said.

"Bowling?" Herb laughed. "We're 1500 miles from home and you want to bowl."

When the waitress returned with everyone's orders, Herb asked. "Is there a bowling alley in town?"

"There sure is; the only decent thing to do here. It's old and run down. The owners have been here for ages and ought to retire. But they don't charge much. And if you don't mind waiting every couple of three shots for them to fix the machines, you'll have fun. The beer's pretty good and it draws a nice crowd."

"Then it's settled," Herb said. "After breakfast, we bowl."

"Where ya folks from by the way?" the waitress asked.

"New York," Herb responded. "Didn't recognize our accents?"

"No, but I noticed your plan to bowl after breakfast on Sunday morning. This is church country, you know."

***

At Herb's suggestion, Peter picked up the tab. The foursome got up from their seats and walked out the restaurant. Noticing a much younger and prettier waitress serving the other side of the shop, Dave walked over and asked her, "Excuse me. Where's the bowling alley?" She smiled coyly seeming to sense Dave's interest, then explained how to get there.

Following her directions, the four friends turned right upon leaving the hotel and walked four blocks down Main Street, to the edge of town, where they saw a sign announcing:

Lincoln 63

Camp Outward Bound   15

On the left across the street, fifty yards back from the road, there stood a rectangular building sporting the sign: Anderson Lanes.

The group crossed the street and walked to the front door. Inside, an older woman was dusting the seats where the bowlers would sit. A younger man with a limp pushed a broom up and down each alley. A third man, wearing a cowboy hat and string tie, stood by the main desk, counting money by a cash register. Herb pushed the door, and it easily opened letting them in.

No one noticed the group until they practically reached the desk. Startled, the man looked up and said, "How'd you folks get in?"

"Through the door," Herb laughed.

"You're easterners, ain't you?" the man asked recognizing Herb's New York accent.

"Yea, just got in. Thought we'd bowl a game or two."

"We ain't open yet," the man said. "Start at twelve on Sunday, 5 PM during the week, all day Saturday."

As Herb and the man got into small talk, Herb explaining his role in the civil rights movement, the man introducing himself as Fred Sommers, long-time Anderson resident, *Peter winked at Anna and said, "Let's do it now." Anna smiled broadly and led him to the women's bathroom. She opened a stall and sat down, spreading her legs to invite him in. Peter dipped his head partway into the toilet to let his tongue touch her inviting clitoris. As he passionately licked her, Anna groaned*

82

with pleasure pulling his head tightly to her crotch. When they finished, Peter smiled and drank the water straight from the bowl.

STOP HIM, Aunt Cindy screamed. HE'S DRINKING RIGHT OUT OF THE BOWL.

"So what do you say?" Herb asked Peter, jarring him out of his thoughts. "They don't open for another hour and a half. Want to come back later?"

Peter reached in his pocket, pulled out his handkerchief and wiped his mouth, relieved there was no liquid on his lips. He looked at Herb and realized Herb wanted something from him. With no clue what it was, Peter stood and stared blankly until Herb said, "Peter. It's OK. If you don't like this place, we don't have to bowl."

"I like it," Peter said. "Is it for sale?"

"For sale?" Fred exclaimed. "I think of selling it every day. But who's gonna buy it? Sue and I have wanted to get out for a long time. Our son lives in Oklahoma. He's asked us to come. But there ain't no one in town that wants it, 'cept Jud over there."

Fred pointed to the limping boy sweeping the lanes. "He got nothing to buy it with, so we'd have to sell it for a piece of the profits. And he ain't too smart so a piece of nothing ain't much."

"Nothing," Peter said.

"What?" Fred asked.

Peter again looked blankly, ashamed for correcting Fred, while completing the calculation in his head. *Zero times anything is zero. A piece of nothing is nothing.*

Nothing $\leq$ ain't much.

Fred shrugged his shoulders and sighed, "I guess Sue and me is here to stay."

"What if you got a cash offer?" Peter asked as he thought:

X $\geq$ ain't much $\geq$ nothing

Defining X as any cash offer in excess of what Jud can produce over the course of his lifetime. Jud looks like he's ...

"Take it in a heartbeat," the man replied.

"OK," Peter replied, "How much?"

Herb laughed, Fred went on to say. "Now, there's a city wheeler dealer for you. OK. How much? The property's gotta be worth $8,000. The building could be turned into a warehouse. Maybe $100,000. The equipment's old but it still works: $50,000. There a bunch of unsold merchandise – shirts, shoes, bags, undrilled bowling balls – say $25,000 at auction. The fixtures could bring in $10,000. And goodwill, a buck and a half. Put it together, I'd say the place could go for ..."

Fred reached for a piece of paper when Peter blurted out.

"$193,001.50."

"OK, one hundred ninety what the hell did you say?"

Before Peter could repeat his number, Fred said. "Tell you what. $200,000 and the place is yours."

"I'll buy it," Peter said.

"You'll what?" Herb gasped, a stunned look across his face.

"I'll buy it," Peter said, drawing his checkbook out of his pocket. "Who should I write this to."

"Wait a minute," Herb said. "You can't be serious."

"Why is that?" Peter naively asked.

"Because you just don't do business like that. You've gotta look things over, haggle and daggle, hire appraisers, bring in engineers, talk to your accountant, bring in your lawyer."

"I'm an accountant," Peter said. "Aren't you a lawyer, Herb?"

"Well, yes," Herb stuttered.

"And Dave and Anna could be the appraiser and the engineer."

"Can I be the engineer?" Anna blurted out. "I've always loved trains."

"I don't want to be no appraiser," Dave protested, kicking his foot yet knowing there were no other jobs left.

"Hold on, everyone," Herb said. "Anna, you ain't no engineer and Dave's not an appraiser. But I am an attorney so if you really want to do it, I can guide you through."

"Hold on a minute," Fred said. "I've gotta talk to my lawyer, too. Give me a minute and I'll get him on the phone."

Fred left and quickly called his son, asking what he thought he should do. In the meantime, Dave picked up a bowling ball and rolled it down an alley. Herb reviewed some details for the sale with Peter. Anna took Peter by the hand and walked him down Alley #6.

Can we have children, Anna asked, as she watched Peter's penis grow large. Together, they walked into the study where he stood before her father and asked for his daughter's hand. Have you studied Torah, father asked. I jerk off a lot, Peter replied. Will you keep a Kosher house? I only eat food purchased that day, Peter replied. Will you make my daughter happy? The rabbi questioned. I'll fuck her in the ass whenever she wants me to. Peter replied. Sol always let me have her, too. Anna's father explained. Of course, Dad, Peter said, as her father shook Peter's hand firmly, agreeing to let them wed.

"It's a done deal," Herb replied, beaming with pride. As Herb shook Fred's hand, too, Peter pulled a disinfectant swab from a package in his pocket and, trying not to be seen, wiped his hand clean.

16 THE DANCER

After dinner, Herb and Dave went to their room, Anna followed Peter to theirs. Feeling sad, thinking about Howdy alone in Aunt Cindy's apartment, Peter walked to the desk and opened the box with the laptop computer he just bought. He completed the registration and rebate forms, and neatly disposed of the packing materials. Then, he went on line to look at his mail.

Wow, cuminme really missed me, Peter thought counting thirteen messages since he last checked Friday morning. *A prime number, too.*

Peter opened the first message and followed the link to cumine's pornographic website when he heard a chime and saw on the screen:

The Internet user kengoldberg has sent you an Instant Message. Would you like to Accept?

Ken! Thought Peter, his penis now fully erect.

He clicked yes and read:

kengoldberg: Hi Peter, what's up?

Peter hesitated hoping his erection would subside.

kengoldberg: We know what's always up, Peter. What's new?

Peter: I'm here with Anna and Herb. Dave came, too.

kengoldberg: Great! You made it. I was a bit worried. My wife and I have been screwing like bunnies all weekend. I lost track. Did she do you on the bus?

Unsure what to say, Peter glanced over to Anna who was now sitting on the bed, completely naked, seeming in a trance, looking Peter's way with her finger in her nose.

Peter: I don't think so.

kengoldberg: LOL. You wouldn't even recognize a blow job if you had one. What a jerk. ROFLMAO.

kengoldberg: Don't worry. You didn't miss anything. She didn't do you at all. I hope you don't mind all these teases but we're coming along just fine. I still can't believe I didn't get the Pulitzer for *Peter Squared,* but with this action, *Peter Cubed* is sure to win it now. Anyway, you still can't touch but I don't mind you looking if you want. Really, try beating off now before she takes her finger out of her nose.

His penis already erect, Peter slipped a plastic bag over his penis and climaxed while looking at Anna. As he came, Anna removed her finger and placed it in her mouth, consuming the object she had just removed.

kengoldberg: With your hangups, that should keep you off her bones for a while. LOL. Don't worry, you'll get it soon.

kengoldberg: By the way, good luck tomorrow. I heard you're buying the bowling alley. Maybe, the wife and I will come down in a few days to check it out.

kengoldberg: I've never been to Nebraska. I bet there are some hot farm girls out there, itching to get it from a famous author. LOL. In fact, scratch the wife thing. I'll tell her I'm meeting my publisher. She'll never know. HAHAHA. Worse comes to worst, I'll write myself into the script with Anna. ROFLMAO. Ain't gonna let a little snot get between me and friends. HAHAHA.

kengoldberg: Bye now. Beat off once for me. LOL.

***

After Ken signed off, Peter smiled broadly thinking, *Wow. Ken's coming to Anderson.* Seeing him smile, Anna walked over to Peter and said, "Whatcha thinking, Peter?"

Peter stiffened imagining the naked Anna, tainted by snot, approaching, touching him. He looked up to see her fully clothed and smiling sweetly.

"You look happy, Peter," Anna said, kissing him lightly on the forehead. "I'm glad."

Looking at her face hoping to keep his eyes away from her breasts for fear that he'd offend her, Peter tried to think of something to say but nothing came out.

"I like seeing you smile. You seem serious so much of the time."

Again, Anna waited for Peter's reply but he still said nothing.

"You shocked me, buying the bowling alley. Are you planning to settle here?"

Another pause, still no response.

"I sometimes think that you and I could get together. I bet I seemed spacy before while you were at your computer. I was trying to imagine what life would be like if you and I got together. I could really dig running a small business together."

Anna's face turned mournful. "I don't know what I'm going to do about Sol. I am married. I know I've been a bit forward with you. Maybe, you're not ready. Maybe, you don't even want me at all. It's OK. I've gotta figure out for myself what I'm gonna do, with or without you. Anyway, I hope you know I really love you. Think about it."

***

On Monday morning, Herb knocked on Peter's and Anna's door at 8 AM, inviting the couple to join Dave and him for breakfast. The four friends walked to the coffee shop while Peter pictured himself inside Anna, scoring a hundred per cent before Miss Weintraub changed his grade to 72%.

Once seated and served, Peter moved his food around his plate while the others ate.

"It's all set, Peter," Herb said. "We close at eleven. Here are the papers. What do you think?"

Peter took the documents from Herb's hand. The first page of the contract had four paragraphs, the first one quite short. The second and fourth paragraphs were long while the third paragraph was so short, it seemed more like an indented comment than a paragraph.

There are four people at the table, four paragraphs (or sections – three paragraphs and one indentation) on the first page. Dave hasn't been that involved so let's call him the indentation/brief paragraph. Herb and I are really handling this deal so we should be the big paragraphs and Anna can be the small paragraph.

Of course, Anna and I shared a room the other day. If we had sex, we could've been the big paragraphs and let Herb be the little paragraph. I wonder if Anna wants to have sex with Herb, too. Then, they can be the big paragraphs and I'll be the little paragraph.

"Does it meet your approval?" Herb asked, breaking into Peter's thoughts.

"Yes."

"Then it's a done deal. Congratulations, Peter," Herb said reaching across the table to shake his hand.

As Peter took Herb's hand, he pictured Anna on her knees, sucking his penis, saying, *Thank you Peter for letting me be the big paragraph.* Herb took another bite of his breakfast as Dave asked, "Why did you buy it, Peter?"

Peter said nothing. Herb chimed in, "Yea, why *did* you buy it?"

Even Anna, who was now sitting at the table next to Peter, asked, "What do you have in mind?"

Peter started perspiring. Everyone leaned forward to hear his response.

"I've always wanted ..."

Choking on his words, Peter paused, the group still glaring intensely, listening to his words.

"To run ..."

Anna leaned forward, Herb remained where he sat, his posture unchanged, Dave began to purse his lips to form the letter B. At the same moment that Peter began vocalizing the sound "pee," Dave had already let out a "bow" sound, their verbalizations blending to form:

Pboewlping Shalley

"A what?" Herb asked.

"A bowling alley," Peter replied.

"Well, that's what you got," Herb said.

Anna stuck her right finger in her ear and shook it around. "I must be hearing things."

"You often do," Herb quipped.

"I thought you said peep show."

"I wish he had," Dave added. "I walked all over this fucking place last night. Can't find a damn thing to .. you know what I mean."

"I do," Anna said, placing her hand on Dave's.

***

At 11:00 a.m., Peter and Herb were sitting with Fred Sommers and his lawyer, Bert Anderson, while Anna and Dave tossed balls down the alley. Dave kept trying different methods of throwing the balls – spinning in pirouettes, using his left hand, lying on his back tossing the ball over his head, and kicking it like a soccer ball – all things he thought might arouse Anna after her suggestive response. Anna meanwhile could see Sol's hateful face in the ball and began poking the holes imagining she was poking his eyes out. Herb haggled vehemently over meaningless points, pretending to be a world class lawyer. He insisted that the contract specify that Peter owned the parking lot and the gravel, and that Fred explicitly warranty the bottle of Windex left in the supply closet. Peter, meanwhile, pictured naked women dancing at the end of the lanes while the men sent bowling balls in their directions. Children played kickball and the best looking girls fed Peter grapes.

Halfway through the negotiations, at noon, Peter stood up and started to walk out.

"Where are you going?" Herb asked.

"To the park. It's time for lunch."

"Lunch!" Herb shouted. "We haven't finished the deal."

"Oh," Peter said. He looked at his watch again. "It's lunchtime."

"You can't go," Bert protested. "You haven't even signed the contract."

88

"Where do you want me to sign?" Peter asked.

"Here," he replied.

"OK," Peter took out his pen.

Herb stood up. "We're not done. I've got one more demand."

"OK," Bert said rolling his eyes. "What is it now?"

"Uh, uh," Herb muttered, "Uh. The bathrooms need to be clean before you leave."

Fred replied, "Clean the bathrooms? They're clean already."

"My final offer. Clean them again or the deal's off," Herb answered, his tone confident.

"OK," Fred said "But nothing more."

Herb quickly penciled in a provision that the bathrooms would be cleaned. Peter signed the document and walked out the door. Anna, freed herself from Dave's groping hands and rushed out to follow Peter.

Herb turned to Dave. "I hope he has something in mind. If I'm not mistaken, we're open for business tonight. You know how to work these machines?"

"No," Dave replied. "But I am handy."

"I saw," Herb said.

Dave made a face before saying, "My Dad was a builder. He taught me a lot. I've worked on cars, done drywall, know plumbing. I'll figure it out."

As Herb and Dave walked around to prepare for this evening's crowd, Peter found a seat in the local park. Anna approached him and asked, "Mind if I sit next to you?"

"No," Peter replied after looking at the bench. The seats were all unoccupied. Peter felt pangs of guilt realizing he had taken the cleanest part of the bench for himself.

"Do you like me?" Anna asked.

Embarrassed, Peter didn't respond.

"I like you," Anna went on to say.

Peter looked down.

"I don't think you like me. You turn away when I talk to you. You won't look at me when I take my clothes off. Why don't you like me?"

Still, Peter said nothing, continuing to eat his sandwich. The two sat in silence for several minutes more.

"Peter. I want to make love to you."

Still unable to respond, Peter took a final bite from his sandwich which he chewed methodically.

"Peter. Answer me. Will you make love to me?"

Peter held his head down and said, "I can't."

"Why not?"

"I'm not ready," Peter answered, Ken's face from the book jacket prominently in his mind.

"When will you be ready?"

Peter thought about Ken's promise that he'd get laid in the second book. "Soon. I think very soon."

"I'll wait," Anna said with resignation. "Of course, I'm not sure how long I can hold out. You saw Dave fawning all over me."

The two sat in silence for a few moments more. Trying to break the tension, Anna asked, "So, why *did* you buy a bowling alley."

"It's hard to explain," Peter said.

"You like to bowl?"

"No," Peter said. "I hate bowling."

"So why did you buy it?"

Again, Peter clammed up.

"No," Anna replied. "I'm not going to accept that. If you're not ready to sleep with me, that's OK. But don't close me off like that. Why did you buy the alley?"

"I don't know," Peter said, surprised by his own willingness to open up. "When I was a kid, everyone hated me. They all made fun of me, and I came to hate them. The worst was a time I got invited to a party. It was at a bowling alley. I thought they had finally accepted me. I didn't know what to do. I put the balls in the gutter. I thought I was doing well. I didn't realize that the idea was to knock the pins down. Everyone laughed."

"So, why would you buy the alley?"

"I want to turn it into a peep show."

"A peep show!" Anna laughed. "That's great! I love it. How are you going to do it?"

"You don't want to know, do you?" Peter asked, suddenly aware of Anna's interest in what he thought and did.

"Yes, I do," Anna said. "I really do. I think it's a great idea. And from what I can see, they don't have any peep shows here anyway. Tell me your plans."

Fighting off the desire to calculate the number of days since April 2, 1970 when Max Lerner offered him a job with Lerner and Schwartz, Public Accountants (the last time someone took interest in him), Peter went on, "I don't really have plans. I just thought that a peep show/bowling alley would be a great place for the whole family. I always see these men hiding their faces at the peep shows. Many wear wedding rings. They never talk to me. They don't talk with each other. I bet they miss their families. If the peep show was in a bowling alley, their wives and children could be having fun nearby while they're getting off."

"Wow!" Anna said. "I've never heard of that before. You are really smart."

Anna wrapped her arms around Peter's neck and without giving him the chance to push her away, kissed him on the cheek. "Tell me more."

With Anna's encouragement, Peter began explaining his ideas. He described to Anna in detail, the standard peep show layout: it's X-rated magazines, video tapes for sale, cabinets of sex toys, private video booths, private dancers, and the carousel.

"I thought I'd start with a carousel. One girl can dance for a number of men peeping from private rooms all around the outside. Then, I would build the video rooms, purchase my inventory of magazines, videos for sale, and sex toys. Finally, I'd build the private booths, once I hired the girls. I think that's the hardest part, getting the girls."

Anna looked around, noticing a church across from the park, and the few people walking by, none with the varied and off-beat styles of a New York crowd.

"I know what you mean," she said.

"In fact, looking around I may have to even hold off on the carousel. I don't know how to find that first girl."

"I'll do it," Anna said.

"You will?" Peter asked.

"I love you, Peter," Anna said as she touched this gentle man, so different from Sol. "I'll do anything I can to help. As long as I'm off my medicine, I don't mind taking my clothes off. I'd be happy to do that."

Peter moved slightly toward Anna, wanting to give her a hug. When he froze up, Anna gently patted him on the arm and said, "It's time to go back. We've got a lot of work to do."

17 THE BETTER BUSINESS

At 1:10 pm, Peter and Anna returned to the alley to find Herb and Dave busy sending bowling balls down lane 8. After each turn, the automatic pinsetter prepared the lane for their next shot. Herb called out, "Dave's figured it out, Peter. He's a mechanical whiz. It looks like we're ready for business. I tell you, this guy can do anything.

"I see from that sign on the wall," Herb said as he pointed his finger, "the place opens at 5, the leagues start at 6. We'd better get ready for the crowd. You're the boss. Tell us what you want us to do."

"Can you build a carousel?" Peter asked.

"A carousel? What do you mean?"

Picturing the twelve viewing stations around the carousel at *Private Booths, Sexy Girls,* Peter realized that his had to be in powers of two. He multiplied 16 booths by 4 foot frontage which he then divided by π. Peter pointed to the lobby and said, "We need a carousel here 20 feet in diameter, with 16 private rooms circling around. There should be a chair in the room, a pole in the middle, and some way to play music, too."

"Why do you want to do that?" Herb asked.

"Anna's going to dance inside. The men can watch while their wives and children bowl."

"Watch! Watch what."

"Watch Anna dance. Nude. They can masturbate while the rest of the family bowls."

"You've gotta be kidding," Herb laughed. "You mean you want to turn this bowling alley into a peep show?"

"Yes."

Herb looked at Anna who nodded her head yes. He crunched his face letting his bottom lip protrude out, shrugging his shoulders, shaking his head playfully back and forth. "I'm game. Dave, what about you?"

"Sounds great to me. I'll be the first customer."

"OK. Peter. You and Dave better figure out how you're going to build this carousel before five. Anna, you should practice your routine."

"What about you, Herb? Can you help?" Peter asked.

"You're damned right I'm going to help," he said as he started out the door.

"Where are you going?" Peter called out.

"I'm on my way to court. I'm spending the afternoon at the law library. Hell, this is what I've been waiting for for years. And believe you me. You are sure going to need a lawyer now."

***

Once Herb left, Peter walked to the main desk where he saw two stools, the cash register, a complicated control center to operate the alleys, and rows of cubby holes containing white and red shoes, all with numbers on the back. Peter recalled the day he had gone bowling and the lady behind the counter insisted that he trade in one of his shoes for two of theirs. Although impressed by the orderly way in which the shoes were lined up, Peter cringed at the thought of different people wearing the same shoes. He opened his pocket notebook and wrote down:

Purchase foot sized plastic bags.

He looked in the corner and saw an empty, cardboard box. Placing latex surgical gloves on his hands, Peter picked up the box and began placing the shoes in the box, careful that their numbers formed accurate equations:

$3 + 7 = 10$

Peter placed three shoes, sizes 3, 7 and 10 in the box together.

$5 \times 7.5 = 37.5$

Peter found four shoes: size 5, children's 3, and a pair of men's $7\frac{1}{2}$, giving him the necessary elements for the equation he sought.

As Peter completed his project, Dave came up to grab his attention.

"I think I've got your carousel worked out. I can build you one but that'll take time. I've seen them at the peep show. You may be better off looking around on the internet to see if you can order one from a supplier before you have me build one. For now, we need to go to an office supply store. They sell standing dividers that separate work spaces. We can set sixteen of them up in a circle and cut 4X4 holes near the top to look through. I'll cut another small slit about four feet from the bottom for the people to put their money in. We'll need some more dividers to create enclosures around each booth for private viewing. We also need a cheap stereo system and a chair for Anna inside. Finally, we should pick up a batting tee at the sporting goods store. She can use that as a pole. It won't be great, but it's the best I can do now. Here's a drawing. If you like it, I'll go downtown and get what we need."

Peter looked at the plan and agreed. He gave Dave a credit card to purchase the items, then wrote him a list.

1. Buy five gross, two quart plastic bags.
2. Dispose of bowling shoes.

At first, Dave looked aghast. "You're not getting rid of these shoes are you? How's anyone gonna bowl without them?"

Peter responded with his usual vacant stare.

"Oh, I get it. If they can't bowl, they've gotta peep. Great thinking, Peter."

Dave left the alley. Peter sat on the stool, removed his calculator and completed the calculation he had done over and over again, many times, since Carl left the firm.

***

While music was blasting in the background and Anna did traditional Jewish dances, fully clothed, not yet ready for an undress rehearsal, a group of men, two in dapper business suits, the third wearing a work shirt and Western string tie entered the building and walked right up to Peter.

"Welcome, friend," the casually dressed man said.

"We're from the Anderson Better Business Association," a second man said as he gently placed his hand in front of his colleague to remind him who was representing the group. "We want to welcome you to town."

Peter stared blankly, noticing that one of the men had a mustache, two did not. Two had black hair, one was bald. Peter continued to look for an attribute that was common to all three men when they ended his search by introducing themselves.

"I'm William Anderson, President of the Anderson National Bank," the leader said offering his hand. "This is my brother (pointing to the other man wearing a tie), Steve Anderson, President of Anderson Community Farm and Loan Association. Finally, we have Jeb Anderson. He's a grocer. So what brought you to town? And why did you decide to buy a business here?"

Peter stood speechless, not knowing what to say.

"Are you a professional bowler?" Steve asked.

Peter looked awestruck.

"Maybe a professional trouble maker," Jeb added.

"Come on, Jeb," Will scolded. "Don't scare him away."

"He don't mean nothing," Steve added. "It's just that the bowling alley's always been in the family. Kinda hard to think some Easterner's gonna own it now."

Peter glanced down to his copy of the contract. Seller: Fred Sommers

Will noticed Peter's glance and chimed in, "Cousin Fred. Remember the day he married Sue. Still can't believe they didn't give their kid the Anderson name.

"So, Mr. Branstill," Will said, his eyes now piercing, no longer trying to seem friendly like he had before. "You really want to set up business here in Anderson, don't you?"

Peter stayed silent.

As the men walked away, Dave returned wheeling boxes from Anderson's Office Supplies. Without saying another word, he went straight to work putting together the carousel. By now, Anna had completed her dress rehearsal and was starting to dance without any clothes.

***

Peter turned on his laptop and, before long, he was on the internet, ready to read his email. For the first time in months, he found more messages from

andrew@lernerandbranstill.com than cuminme. Peter also saw an email from Ken.

Peter opened Ken's message first.

To: peter@lernerandbranstill.com

From: kengoldberg@greatauthor.com

Peter, give me a tingle. 215-BIG-DICK.

Ken

Not completely sure what Ken meant by a tingle, he wrote in his notebook.

Look up the word TINGLE.

Peter then opened Andrew's messages in the order they had arrived. Tracking the progressively deteriorating tone of his remarks, Peter figured that Andrew was getting 7% angrier with each successive effort to contact Peter.

The first message read:

Hi Peter. I'm here with Harold. Didn't see you at the hotel. Did you check in somewhere else? Maybe, you've got a honey here in town.

The last message read:

Where the hell are you? I'll break your balls.

Somewhere in the middle, Andrew had implored Peter to contact him by IM if he used Instant Messenger, sign up if he didn't. Andrew gave Peter his IM screen name:

Andylookingforguys

Peter opened his IM screen to type in a message to:

Andylookingforguys

95

Peter: Andrew. I'm on line now. Peter.

Within seconds, a response appeared:

Andylookingforguys: Where the hell are you?

Peter: In Nebraska.

Andylookingforguys: Nebraska! You were supposed to be here with me today.

Peter: I know. I'm sorry.

Andylookingforguys: Sorry! That's not enough. We haven't had a damn bit of work for months. We have a chance to get Harold back and you're in Nebraska. What the hell happened?

Peter: I don't know. Anna brought me here.

Andylookingforguys: Anna. You mean the cute secretary we hired last week?

Peter: Yes. She wanted me to go with her and Herb.

Andylookingforguys: You and Herb? A fucking threesome. That's great. I never ask you a damn thing about your sex life. I never intrude on you one bit. I support you no matter what the cost. And now, after 20 years of work, you take your first vacation ever when I fucking need you.

Peter: It's not actually a vacation. I don't know what you would call it except that I bought a bowling alley today.

Andylookingforguys: So you bought a bowling ball. You could've bought one in New York, or Indiana, or fucking anywhere.

Peter: No, I bought the alley.

Andylookingforguys: LOL. Gotta give it to you Peter. You've still got that same deadpan sense of humor, even if we are going down the tubes.

Peter: I'm serious.

Andylookingforguys: I guess that's good for you. Congratulations. Maybe it's a better move than staying with a dying firm. Anyway, I'm still here in Indy. I'm going to meet with Harold again tomorrow. He was pretty pissed off when you weren't here today. I told him that he is not the only account in the world and that you were very busy, helping another client. I don't know if he bought it but he said he'd give you until tomorrow to come up with your recommendations. It's my last shot to make something happen. Any ideas? You know, if I don't get him back, I'm gonna have to close the business and you're gonna have to give me a job as pinsetter.

Peter: You can have a job if you want. In fact, you can run the alley if you want. If Harold wants, he can own the alley with me.

Peter pictured himself standing with Harold, their pictures being taken, proud owners of the alley, welcomed into the Anderson Better Business Association by Will, Steve, and Jeb Anderson, Harold in charge of the bowling alley, Peter running the peep show.

Andylookingforguys: Now, there's an interesting idea. I read this wrong. Here I am trying to talk Harold into coming back to us. You're out there doing something. It's brilliant.

Andylookingforguys: You already suggested entertainment. And there you are in the Heartlands. I'll tell Harold tomorrow. Maybe we can fly out on Wednesday and see your operation. Great work, Peter. Talk to you soon.

Peter: Thanks.

Peter: By the way, if you find those guys, ask them if they'd like to work here, too.

18 OPENING DAY

At 5:00 p.m., a family of four, a man, his wife, and their two boys, walked in. Timmy, nine years old and the younger of the two, immediately spotted the carousel and asked, "What's that!" His father, Deacon Anderson, responded, "Don't know, son. Let's see."

Timmy and his Dad walked into one of the private viewing booths where they saw a hand-written sign by the money slot,
$1 five minits.

"Can we, daddy," Timmy asked, his voice filled with excitement.

"No, son. It's one of them new virtual reality video games. The devil's work. Let's just bowl."

Disappointed, Timmy held his head down and proceeded with his family. When the pouting failed to work, he gave in, smiled, and skipped ahead to get his shoes.

Deacon Anderson took the lead and approached the desk, ready to get their lane. He waited a few minutes while the man behind the counter seemed engrossed in calculations. Tommy, Timmy's older brother turned to his father and asked, "What's he doing?"

"Be patient," the Deacon replied. "He'll be with us in a moment."

"Uncle Jeb told me the guy's an idiot," Tommy added.

"Now don't talk that way, son," Deacon Anderson responded, checking his own anger knowing that teens will be teens. "He just bought the business. It takes some time to learn."

The Anderson's waited five minutes more before the Deacon, himself getting impatient, tapped on the counter and asked, "Sir. Can you help us?" Peter looked up stopping his calculations, still not saying a word.

"He doesn't talk, Daddy," Timmy said tugging on his father's shirt.

"Hush," the father said holding his finger to his lip. "He's

98

handicapped."

"But, I want to bowl," Timmy said, now almost ready to cry.

The impasse ended when Herb, who had been standing by the door, welcoming the customers, handing out business cards for his law practice, looked to the front desk and saw the crowd queuing up to the speechless Peter Branstill. Herb rushed to his rescue.

"What are you doing?" Herb demanded.

"I don't know," Peter answered.

Aware of the restless crowd, Herb quickly took charge asking the Deacon, "How many?"

"Four," he replied before inquiring. "Is there something wrong with that man?"

"Just a bit nervous," Herb replied. "Nothing to worry about. You said four. OK. Go to alley 1."

Herb got ready to call out *next* when the Deacon said, "We need shoes."

"OK. How many?

"You mean what size, don't you. There's four of us."

"Of course," Herb responded. "Sorry but I'm a bit nervous myself. I haven't worked since I was a promising lawyer at Cromwell, Douglas, McDougall, Halperin, Dooley, and Smith. My wife Teri pushed me to work there. My heart was really into civil rights. You know I worked side by side with Marty in Alabama. Marty had a dream, well more of a thought until I told him it should be a dream. I mean I've had dreams, too, not wet dreams but regular dreams. The other night I was dreaming that my law practice really grew. I was a famous civil rights lawyer, well respected by my colleagues, honored by the president, standing in court arguing a very complicated human rights case. But that's another story. Getting back to Dr. King, did you know that he wanted to give his speech in a small park in Biloxi. I said, think big. Let's go to DC. Could you imagine what would have ..."

"The shoes?" the Deacon asked again.

"Oh yes, the shoes. How many? I mean, what size?"

As his father began giving his family's shoe sizes, Timmy called out, "Daddy, they don't have any shoes."

Herb looked back to see the empty cubby holes.

"Peter," Herb asked. "Where are the shoes?"

"I got rid of them," Peter replied. "Give them these."

Peter handed Herb a box of plastic bags.

By now, the crowd had grown quite long, their complaints vocal and loud.

"We want to bowl," an older woman called out from the back.

"They don't have any shoes," a scrawny fellow in wired-rimmed glasses cried out.

"You've fucked this place up," Chester, a quite brawny bowler said.

"If you don't like it, take your fuckin' business somewhere else you piece of hillbilly shit," Herb said his face red with rage.

"Hillbilly what?" Chester said stepping forward rolling up his shirt sleeves when a much louder noise emerged from the front of the place.

Realizing that her husband, Mo, was standing in the carousel gawking at the naked Anna spinning gaily, stark naked, to the sounds of Hava Nagila, Emma Ford let out an ear shattering, "EEEEEEEK!"

She jumped into the viewing booth swinging her purse at Mo's head. A large woman, Emma lost her balance and, trying to steady herself, grabbed her husband bringing him and the partition down. Like dominoes, the entire set-up came tumbling down leaving Anna in the open, standing bare.

A mixture of applause from the Bob Anderson Tool and Die Plant bowling team, laughter from the children, gasps from the clergy, and catcalls from the members of the Women's Decency League, Anna went scurrying from her spot to the women's bathroom only to be greeted by shrieks from the women already there. She quickly darted out and ran to the men's room where a peeing man looked at her, shocked but happy that she was there.

By then, Officer Barney and his deputy, Tex, charged into the place. As the townspeople scurried in different directions, the officers handcuffed Peter and Anna (Barney taking the naked Anna while letting Tex handle Peter), and led them to jail.

Herb rushed from the building to bail the couple out. Dave climbed on top of the counter and announced today's New Management Special: Free Bowling

A crowd-pleasing masterstroke, Dave's move was spoiled by a few grumbling patrons unhappy to wear plastic bags over their feet.

***

At 10:30 p.m., Sol knocked on the Pearlman apartment door.

"I know where Anna went," Sol announced to his father-in-law, his expression somber.

"Where?!" the Rabbi questioned, anxious to learn of his daughter's whereabouts.

"It's hard to explain," Sol said. "But she's in Nebraska."

The Rabbi held his head and cried out in pain. "Every year. The same thing."

He reached out to his son-in-law, "I'm so sorry Sol. This must be very hard on you. I'm afraid to ask. What did she do?"

"Oy," Sol said. "Worse than ever."

"How's that?" the Rabbi inquired.

"Come with me. I'll show you."

Sol led his father-in-law up one flight to the apartment of Max and Gertie Berman. Neither the Klingers nor the Pearlmans owned a television, a decadent sign of the Americanized world, but the Bermans did and this was the only way they could see the 11:00 p.m. news.

"I called Sol as soon as I saw it, Moishe," Max said. "Fox has the news at 10. The other networks should have it at 11."

Turning on Channel 2, CBS, Anna's family stayed glued to the TV on the edges of their seats as they saw the newscaster introduce the headline story.

"Today in the unlikely hamlet of Anderson, Nebraska, a major Civil Liberties story unfolds. We now turn to our Lincoln, Nebraska affiliate, KOLN, for the report."

"At 11 o'clock this morning the citizens of this quiet, sleepy, conservative mid-western town in the heart of our nation's breadbasket were buzzing with excitement anticipating a modern, state-of-the-art bowling alley and entertainment facility under the management of Peter Branstill, its new owner. But dreams of carefree bowling after Sunday church were quickly dashed, mired in scandal. Branstill gave a new twist to the old hook ball, with the hooker ball. I guess the new owner thought the game needed more spice than just spares and strikes."

The scene switched to show Anna screaming and running through the crowd to the rest rooms, the picture altered to poorly hide her private parts. Sol and the others sat wide-mouthed as they saw what was there. The announcer interviewed Mayor Anderson who promised to tar and feather the Yankees out of town. Herb appeared next on the screen with an ACLU lawyer by his side, promising he'd take the case to the Supreme Court and beyond.

"We will be heard in court. We will be heard in Appeals Courts, and we will be heard in the Supreme Court. And if we don't get justice, we will be heard in heaven by the Reverend Martin Luther King himself who is a personal friend of mine, until we get justice."

The ACLU lawyer quickly took the microphone from Herb and explained in more objective detail his organization's stand on the rights of people to have access to pornography.

Max turned his TV set off. Sophie cried. Sol anguished with pain, "G-d. What should I do?"

Rabbi Pearlman calmly replied, "I'll tell you what we are going to do. We're going out there to get her. We'll apologize to those people."

"We can't do that," Sol said. "They're anti-semites. They'll kill us before they have a chance to hear what we have to say."

"No they won't," the rabbi continued. "We'll leave tomorrow morning. We'll get there Wednesday night. We'll take the Yeshiva boys and go in a caravan. G-d will protect us."

***

Finally bailed out of jail, Peter and Anna returned to their room just past midnight. Anna plopped on the bed while Peter went to the desk to boot up his computer.

"I'm pooped," Anna declared. "Hope you don't mind if I pass tonight."

Anna peered at Peter looking for a response. Peter clicked on his internet service provider to get on line.

Anna continued, "It's really been exhausting, Peter. I can't do anything else. OK with you?"

Peter typed in his password and was now on the internet, the screen indicating there were several unread messages.

"I can't do anything, Peter, unless you just wanna do it simple and quick. But, we can't stay up all night and fool around."

Anna began walking to Peter who by now was reading cuminme's message. Close enough to see three women and a horse on the screen, she noticed Peter lurch slightly forward and give out a sigh.

"Jerk," she said just loud enough for Peter to hear.

PETER BRANSTILL IS A JERK. PETER BRANSTILL JERKS OFF.

Anna returned to bed, stretched out, and was soon asleep.

Peter saw that the next two messages were from andrew@lernerandbranstill.com. He opened the first. It read:

Peter,

Talked with Harold. He loves your idea. Wants in. He suggests setting up a corporation, Branstill Entertainment and making it a subsidiary of Sterling and Warner Industries. He'll purchase 49% of the company and leave you the controlling share: 51%. Eventually, you'll go public and trade on the New York Stock Exchange. He suggests that you be the president and CEO, he'll be the Chairman of the Board. Harold is planning to come out later this week to finalize the deal. I know it's premature, but I think it would be classy for him to get credit as soon as possible. Unless you object to those terms, why don't you put up a sign on the building:

Branstill Entertainment
A division of Sterling and Warner Industries, Indianapolis, Indiana

Great work, Peter. You've really nailed it this time.
Andrew.

Peter opened his notebook and wrote: Ask Dave to paint a sign.

Peter pointed the cursor to Andrew's next message, the subject:

DON'T DO A DAMN THING

Before he could open it, another message popped on the screen:

The Internet user kengoldberg has sent you an Instant Message. Would you like to Accept?

Peter clicked YES failing to open Andrew's message.

kengoldberg: Hi Peter. What's happening?

Peter: I bought the bowling alley today.

kengoldberg: Mazel Tov. Anything else?

Peter: It didn't go too well. I kind of wanted to make the alley different. Anna sort of danced and, well, we got taken to jail.

kengoldberg: You're kidding. Why'd they arrest you?

Peter: Anna was dancing without her clothes on.

kengoldberg: Wait. You got a webcam there? Let me see.

Peter: She's asleep. I still don't know why she's in my room. No. I didn't get a webcam with this computer.

kengoldberg: Selfish sonofabitch. If she's dancing nude for the whole world, why can't I see? My wife's not feeling well so I'm all alone and you know what that means. Gotta do something to get through the night. Could've used those pictures.

Feeling bad for Ken, Peter typed in,

Peter: Have you seen cuminme? She's got nice pictures. Do you want me to send you some of hers?

kengoldberg: You're such a jerk, Peter. I don't need those pictures. I was just kidding. My wife isn't sick. She's up and well and raring to go. Here, I'll put her on.

kengoldberg: Peter, this isn't Ken but Ken's wife. Forget those pictures. Use them yourself. Believe me, the big guy doesn't need them. Take your goddamn pictures and beat off to them yourself, you fucking jerk.

kengoldberg: Be with you in a minute, honey.

kengoldberg: So how'd you like talking with Mrs. Goldberg. Pretty hot, wouldn't you say. Anyway, I'm on my way upstairs so I can't stay on any more. If you don't have a webcam, why should I talk with you? Not that I need the pictures. I just want to check out Anna. Make sure she's good enough for you. I told you I have her penciled in as your first lay.

kengoldberg: (from Mrs. Goldberg not Ken Goldberg) Get the hell off the computer, Peter.

kengoldberg: Sorry Peter. That was Mrs. Goldberg. She's just a little impatient. You understand, don't you?

kengoldberg: (again from Mrs. Goldberg, not me) I hate you Peter. You won't amount to anything. You'll never have a girl. You don't have a life. No one likes you.

kengoldberg: OK, honey. I'm coming. Let me just sign off.

kengoldberg: (Mrs. Goldberg once more) You're a piece of shit Peter. You'll never get it.

kengoldberg: Gotta go, Peter. Talk with you tomorrow. I'm coming honey. No, I don't mean I'm cumming. LOL. But coming. But, I'll be cumming later. ROFLMAO.

Peter scrolled back through the transcript of their conversation and reread Mrs. Goldberg's words: *Get the hell off the computer*, so he turned off his machine without reading the message Andrew sent after he saw the TV evening news:

DON'T DO A DAMN THING

19 GROUP THERAPY

Peter arrived at the bowling alley Tuesday morning to find a group of middle-aged women, on their knees, holding candles, in prayer. Several men stood with signs:

BAN PORNOGRAPHY
CHRISTIANS FOR DECENCY
CLOSE THE ALLEY

Nearby, there were three other men wearing bowling shirts and bowling shoes with signs of their own:

BOWLING YES: OBSCENITY NO.
KEEP THE ALLEY CLEAN
VISIT AL'S VIDEO

By the corner of the building, there were trailers and vans, marked as belonging to the major news networks, reporters and photographers all around.

Herb and Dave were already in the building when Peter and Anna walked in. Looking worn with bags under his eyes, Herb called out:

"We're OK, buddy. I've been working all night. Got a court order to restrain the town from interfering with your business. The only thing is that we can't serve kids. It looks like there are children's leagues on Saturday morning, so we'll have to get rid of all signs of peeping then. Otherwise, Dave's painted a sign. No children allowed. 18 and over only."

"No children?" Peter asked. "But that's the idea. I don't want these men pulled away from their families while they're beating off. If the wives and kids can't be here, it'll be like any other peep show."

"I know," Herb said. "I tried to push the point. I almost had the judge eating out of my hand. I told him you were the true champion for family values. I think he got scared, and wanted to wait for a full hearing Thursday before doing any more. He kept saying over and over again that he would have to come here and see the place, in operation, before he could rule. And of course, this thing is gonna go to the Supreme Court before it is settled once and for all. In the meantime, we'll have to stay with the temporary carousel so we can put it up and take it down depending on whether kids are here. Sorry, but it was the best I could do."

Peter thanked Herb, then asked Dave to paint the sign Harold asked him to put up. He then returned to the counter and resumed the calculation he had been doing at work every day since Carl left the firm.

***

At 10 a.m. while Peter continued to calculate, Dave flirted with Anna, and Herb kept drafting his legal briefs, the door opened with an unexpected group of bowlers. Surprised by their entrance, Herb quickly glanced at the sign which announced business hours: Monday through Friday, 5:00 p.m. to 10:00 p.m.. He looked at Peter who had not budged from his seat, then turned to the woman who appeared in charge of the group and said:

"Sorry, Ma'am. We're not open."

"I know," the tastefully dressed and quietly attractive, professional appearing woman in her mid-30s replied, "that it's closed to the general public. But this is bowling day for the mental health center."

Slightly ashamed at himself for having failed to recognize the telltale signs of his former comrades, Herb looked beyond and saw a cadre of followers in the poorly coordinated clothes of mental illness and poverty. The group tagged behind the woman as she reached out her hand and said, "I'm Penny Smith. You must be Peter Branstill. Welcome to town."

Herb returned the handshake while correcting her assumption. "I'm Herbert J. Whitmore, Esquire, Chief Counsel for Branstill Entertainment, a sub-division of Sterling and Warner Industries, and a former personal friend of the Reverend Martin Luther King, Jr. Mr. Branstill is over there."

Penny looked at Peter, and remembering what John had told her when he came to Anderson after traveling with Anna in *Peter Squared,* said, "I heard of him before. I was told he's a very successful businessman who has been very kind to the mentally ill. If he's not too busy, I'd love to meet him."

"We'd better wait," Herb said as Peter was intent re-doing his standard calculation the twenty-sixth time today. "Can you tell me about bowling day?"

"Sure. We've been coming here Tuesday mornings at 10:00 for years. We stay two hours. From 10 to 11, I run group therapy. From 11 to 12, Chip does a music group. Anyone who needs to can talk with either Chip or me while the other does group. Or, they can bowl. I hope I wasn't being rude. That's Chip," Penny said pointing to a younger man in his mid-twenties holding a guitar. Chip nodded and waved to Herb.

"Well, it sounds like you're here to bowl, so let's bowl," Herb handed out plastic bags for the patients to wrap over their feet after assigning them the lanes they would use.

***

Andrew paced around Harold's Indianapolis office trying to think of a way to convince Harold to give him another chance.

"We don't really know what happened, Harold. I know the news sounded bad but you've got to admit that Peter was onto something. Who knows why that woman took her clothes off in the alley? But I can't imagine Peter being involved!" Andrew protested, knowing that he'd have to omit the fact that he recognized Anna and that he first met her with Peter in front of his own favorite whore house.

"I'm sure Peter had nothing to do with this," Harold tried to assure Andrew. "But it's still not good for business. Can you imagine if we had locked down the deal, and Sterling and Warner were involved? The board would have me for lunch."

"I know. But Peter isn't involved and there are lots of small towns where we can float the idea. Let it lie. We'll talk to Peter soon and straighten this whole thing out. You're not involved so it can't hurt you in any way."

"I guess you're right, Andrew. But I still can't announce a change in accounting firms right now with this going on as much as I truly hate Carl. Maybe in a few weeks."

"Thanks," Andrew said finally able to sit down.

"Did you notice by the way," Harold added with a twinkle. "That gal was quite a looker."

The men laughed until the phone buzzed with a call from Harold's secretary Marianne, "Mr. Sterling. There are some gentlemen out here to see you."

"Tell them to wait," Harold replied with a start, turning off the intercom. "Marianne's good. She protects me from the vultures."

Harold noticed the light blinking on his phone indicating that she was trying to reach him again. He ignored the calls hoping to share an off-color joke he heard with Andrew. His efforts proved unsuccessful when

Marianne opened the door and called out, "I'm sorry Mr. Sterling, but this is really important."

Harold cupped his hand and whispered to Andrew, just loud enough to make sure Marianne could hear, "Not nearly as important as the man who fell in love with a sheep."

Harold's devilish smile quietly vanished as Marianne informed him there were members of the press outside. Before she could finish prepping Harold, two men, a reporter and a photographer, barged in. While one flashed pictures, the other demanded that Harold answer his questions.

"Is it true that Sterling and Warner is behind the debacle in Nebraska? What is the relationship between Branstill Entertainment and Sterling and Warner Industries? What is an Indianapolis concern doing pushing smut on the good, god-fearing people of Nebraska?"

"We're not involved at all!" Harold insisted.

"Then why are you meeting now with Andrew Lerner, Branstill's long-time partner and associate."

"Well, uh, uh, well, uh yes we know Peter Branstill, but we have no connection to what he is doing now. Mr. Lerner and I both vehemently dissociate ourselves from Mr. Branstill's perverse activities."

"We have on reliable sources," the reporter went on as the photographer took Andrew's pictures, "that Branstill's pornographic ring goes far deeper than just this venture in Nebraska, placing him at such illicit boutiques nation-wide as *Private Booths, Sexy Girls* in New York, and the *Capital Girls* in DC. Further, we have an affidavit from one John Mintz of Rapid Falls, Michigan who goes by the screen name DirtyDavid, that Mr. Lerner peruses the internet, seeking contacts with children using the IM screen name: andylookingforguys."

Andrew and Harold shooed the reporters out.

"What the hell is going on!" Harold screamed.

"I don't know," Andrew replied practically in tears.

Harold turned on the television to CNN where they saw pictures of Peter and Herb in front of Anderson Lanes, a hand-made sign on the door.

Branstill Entertainment
A division of Warner and Sterling Industries, Indianapolis, Indiana

***

From her carousel, Anna watched the patients, somewhat longingly, remembering the times she spent at Midtown Mental Health Center Day Treatment Program. Penny seemed confident and helpful, sitting in a circle talking with her group. Anna decided she should talk to Penny about her problems with Peter.

At 11:00 a.m., the group broke up. Several patients walked to the unattended snack bar while others stepped outside to smoke cigarettes. Anna put on her robe and walked out of the booth, approaching Penny.

"Can I talk with you a minute?" Anna asked.

"Uh, well," Penny stuttered, hesitating because Anna was not enrolled in the program and could not be billed for their talk. Quickly, she felt ashamed that she thought that way and said, "Sure. Can you wait a minute?"

"OK," Anna replied and walked back to the booth.

Anna waited for twenty minutes while Penny took care of two telephone calls and listened to one of the patients tell her about a gift she got from her mother. In the meantime, Dave entered the carousel to look at Anna.

As Anna stood fully clothed, Dave implored, "Come on Anna. Dance for me."

"Some money, this time?"

Dave, disgruntled, reached in his pocket and found thirty-seven cents. He dropped twelve cents in the slot, putting the quarter back in his pocket. Anna stood there eyes wide open in disbelief.

"Come on, Anna. I'm horny."

Anna removed her robe and wiggled her leg while Dave jerked off. Meanwhile, Chip rounded up the patients and formed a circle to begin music group.

Penny approached Anna's carousel where, instead of knocking on the door, she entered one of the private viewing booths that circled the structure. Intrigued by her visit to a peep show, she put a dollar in the slot. Anna started to spin around the room, dancing the hora to the sounds of Hava Nagila. So excited to have a paying customer, Anna failed to notice that Penny was the one watching her. When she finally realized who was there, she reflexively covered her breasts with her arms. Penny laughed and called out, "Don't be ashamed. Hold on. I'll come inside."

Penny left her private booth and walked around to the entrance to Anna's carousel. Inside, they shook hands. Penny asked, "What were you doing?"

"The hora," Anna replied. "It's a traditional Jewish dance. We always do it at weddings and Bar Mitzvahs."

"Really," Penny inquired. "Can you show me how?"

"Sure," Anna answered, taking Penny's hand. Shortly, the two women were dancing gaily around the room. Penny laughed, "This is weird. You're naked and I'm fully dressed."

Anna let go of Penny's hand. "I'll put my clothes on."

"No," Penny said stopping her. "This is your place, and I'm your guest. I'll take mine off. Anyway, it seems like a lot of fun."

Meanwhile, Pat, a particularly unstable man who had been recently released from the hospital, became angry when Chip wouldn't let him play the guitar. He spewed out a string of invectives, then stood up from his seat and walked close to Chip, his pose threatening. While Chip wasn't scared, he still thought it best to get Penny's help so he could go on with the group while she talked with Pat. Chip asked Joe, a fairly stable member of the group, to find Penny. Hearing her laugh from inside the carousel, Joe knocked on the door. When Penny didn't answer, Joe walked into one of the booths and called out, "Is Penny in there?"

Anna cried back, "It'll cost you a dollar,"

"I don't have one," Joe replied.

"Can you wait?" Penny asked again.

"I think Chip needs you."

At Penny's encouragement, Anna pulled up the screen exposing both of the women unclothed. Shocked by the display, Joe forgot why he was there and immediately ran back to the group.

"She's naked," he screamed.

"Of course," Chip said. "This is a peep show. Did you find Penny?"

"In there! Come quick. She's standing in there."

Chip rushed to the carousel as several patients followed behind. By now, Pat had stopped his tirade, much more interested in seeing Penny than playing the guitar. Chip entered the carousel while several patients stood outside, some putting change in the slots. Anna lifted the screens. Excited to have a large crowd, she began dancing the hora while Chip and Penny talked, Penny completely exposed. Suddenly, Penny realized that everyone was watching her, quickly put her clothes back on and rushed out the carousel.

Joe called out, "Hey everyone. Let's have group in here." The patients picked up their chairs and moved them inside the carousel, many still unaware of what had gone on. Chip asked Anna if she could put her clothes back on and leave the room. Once settled in their new circle, Chip turned the music back on and used the group to discuss ethnic musical forms, starting first with traditional Jewish tunes. For the rest of the hour, Chip and his group sat in the carousel while Anna and Penny talked in an adjoining party room. One local man who was quite drunk had walked through the unlocked door of the building and entered a booth. Irate to see group therapy instead of Anna dancing nude, he approached Peter to demand his money back.

***

Once alone, Anna started to talk and unexpectedly bawled out of control.

"Penny. I'm so unhappy. Please help me."

"Sure, Anna," Penny calmly replied, glad to be back at her trade, fully clothed. "What's bothering you?"

"Look at me. I'm an Orthodox Jew, dancing nude in the middle of nowhere. Ten months of the year, as much as I hate my husband, I follow the laws. I go everyday to our program and sit there quiet as a mouse, always dreaming that I'm in love. I hear voices. I cut myself. My family thinks I'm crazy."

"And what do *you* want to do?" Penny asked.

Anna started bawling again as she cried, "I want to be with Peter."

"You want to be with Peter?" Penny responded, her tone sympathetic, her technique reflective, the type of response that earned her As in school.

"Yes. I really want him."

"Have you told him?"

"In a way I have and in a way I haven't. It's strange Penny. I'm kind of afraid to tell you. You're going to think I'm crazy."

"Well, Anna. I don't usually think in terms of people being crazy, so I doubt that's a term that will come to mind for me. But suppose I did think that or something that was like that. So what?"

"I don't know," Anna replied. "I guess you would think I was sick, that I had an illness, that I was mentally ill."

"And what if I did? Haven't you spent your whole life with people thinking you were mentally ill?"

"That's true. They always make fun of me and treat me bad, and hit me, and ..." Anna suddenly held back when she pictured her father raping her.

"So being mentally ill is a way of saying you are bad, or that you are in danger. I don't know if you are mentally ill. I wouldn't care or treat you any differently if I thought you were. But what you just said to me is very human, that you met a man, Peter, and that you really want to be with him. Even if you are mentally ill, that sure sounds like an awfully normal thing to feel. So, why don't you tell me more about you and Peter."

"It's so complicated. Peter's a goy, my husband's a Jew. The law says I can't be with Peter. Even if I got a Ghet, we still couldn't marry. Sometimes, I think I'm someone else, just so I can imagine making love to him without feeling guilty. Then, it gets near summer and I figure I can do what I want since Yom Kippur will come soon. It's June and I've been trying so hard to get Peter to sleep with me. Even if he does, it won't help me have what I really want."

Penny looked at her watch and realized it was coming close to twelve and that she'd have to go back to the clinic with the patients. She opened her appointment book and looked for an opening.

"This is something that's going to take more than a few minutes,

Anna. Why don't you come back to the mental health center tomorrow at 4:00, and we'll really have a chance to talk."

20 THE MITZVAH MOBILE

At 5:00 p.m., Anderson Lanes reopened for business. Dave had painted a new sign, *18 and over only*, unnecessary since no one brought their children. Several league bowlers came with their own shoes and balls, and lettered shirts identifying their teams on their backs. Many stopped at the door, but left when they saw they'd have to pass through the catcalls of the Women's Decency League, the admonitions of the clergy, and the cameras of the media. The few that entered found their teams in shambles, not enough players on either side, plus no service at all. Peter sat transfixed at his table completing calculations while Herb was consumed preparing legal briefs. Dave was glued to his booth around the carousel where he could watch Anna dance nude. The bowlers had to operate the pinsetting machines themselves, and go to the next alley whenever they broke. Soon, it became clear that there was nothing to do but watch Anna dance. Even that failed to work with the protesters quite well organized, quickly calling mothers and wives to catch errant bowlers peeping.

By the end of the day, there was little business done at all. Peter completed his ledger for the second day's receipts:

Bowling fees	$0
Plastic bags	$0
Concessions	$0
Arcade games	$0
Exotic dancing	$40.25

A skilled accountant, Peter quickly divided the final line item into three subcategories:

Exotic dancing

Peter	$40.00 (4 visits @ $10, $2^2 = 4$)
Dave	$0.25
Other peepers	$0

***

At 11:00 p.m., the bowling alley closed and just as Peter and his friends began to leave, a black limousine with Harold and Andrew in the back pulled up.

"Peter," Andrew called out, his voice stern, a glare in his eyes. "What's going on?"

"Andrew," Peter replied, overlooking the stare, smiling slightly glad to see his old friend. "How are things in New York? Are we getting any more business?"

"I'll give you the business," Andrew said. "I don't know what the hell you had in mind, but we're partners and I can sure as hell tell you, we're getting sued."

Herb perked up when he heard Andrew's words. He quickly pulled out a business card from his jeans, rubbed it to smooth out the wrinkles, and handed it to him.

Herbert J. Whitmore
Attorney at Law

For appointment, call
212-637-1000 and ask for Herb in the Day Program

Motto: It's for you, that we sue.

Personal former friend of the Rev. Martin Luther King, Jr.

Herb stopped short when suddenly a bright light shined in his eyes.

"Turn that damned thing off," he called.

"Mr. Whitmore, I understand that you are chief counsel for Branstill Entertainment."

Recognizing that he was being interviewed, an opportunity for publicity to fuel his fledging practice, Herb broke into a broad smile and responded, "Yes, and former best friend of the Reverend Martin Luther

King, Jr."

"Dr. King?" the reporter questioned, thrown off by Herb's comment. "Is this a civil rights case? We didn't notice any African-Americans here."

"Civil rights? Of course this is a civil rights case," Herb responded shocked that anyone would think otherwise. "We have a long history of black people jerking off to white people and white people jerking off to black people, so we're gonna take this all the way to the Supreme Court even if Medgar Evers, a dear friend of mine too, has to come out of his grave and kick some butt."

"I'm a bit confused," the reporter went on. "We understand there are several actions here. The town of Anderson has filed suit to close the bowling alley. The prosecutor is calling a grand jury for possible criminal charges against you and your associates. Mr. Sterling tells us that you have misrepresented his relationship with you by advertising that Branstill Enterprises is a subdivision of Sterling and Warner Industries. How do you account for that?"

"I say, don't fuck with us," Herb replied. "There's gonna be interrogatories, and discovery, and writs, and pleadings, and motions, and judgments. Hell, I wouldn't be surprised if old man habeas corpus don't get involved in this damn thing. This is big man, real big."

***

Wednesday morning, Peter got out of bed at his usual time, 7:00 a.m. He walked to the bathroom and urinated bending his knees at the required angle, and showered according to his standard procedure, having reminded himself of his morning routines by re-reading how they were described in *Peter Squared*. Without looking once at Anna, he walked out the door and went to the bowling alley. Shortly afterwards, Herb and Dave stopped by to pick up Anna and join him there.

By the time they arrived, the protests were in full swing. CNN was interviewing Emma Ford, the first woman to see the naked Anna. Behind her, the women of the Decency League prayed to an 8-foot plastic statue of Jesus with a cardboard sign draped around his neck,

Let he who peeps be the first one stoned.

The bowlers had set up a vigil of their own: two kegs of beer standing side by side with a bowling pin on top. Until the peep show closed, they promised to add one pin each day. Harold erected an information booth with pamphlets and brochures describing the activities of Sterling and Warner Industries. Hoping to improve PR, he announced his firm's plan to donate funds for the needy youth of Anderson. Meanwhile, several needy youth slipped around the back, hoping to sneak in and look at Anna.

Anna had already entered the building as Peter completed his 10th

calculation. Dave called to Herb and said, "Don't turn around. You ain't gonna believe this."

At that moment, a caravan of vehicles with New York license plates careened around the corner heading straight for the front of the alley. When Herb saw the highly Orthodox men and women begin to come out of the cars, he opened the door as he and Dave walked in and called to Anna, "Sweetheart, I hate to tell you. They're here."

An older woman wearing a mink stole looked around after leaving the car. She held her hand to her brow to protect her eyes from the sun, and demanded, in a loud voice, "Is there a bathroom here? We need a bathroom. We've been in the car too long."

The Reverend walked up to the woman and offered his hand.

"Get your paws off me, mister," the woman responded. "I need a bathroom. Is there one in there?"

"Yes, my dear woman," the Reverend replied, his voice soft trying to atone for the gaffe he did not understand. "But, it's a din of iniquity in there. Please, let us find a more suitable place for a woman of your high moral values to use."

"Look, mister," the woman said, "When you gotta pee, you gotta pee. We've been in this car for hours and Moishe won't stop. No. The big man has to drive the whole way. Just cause he's got a bladder like an elephant doesn't mean we all do. I can't tell you how hard it is to sit for hours, hearing nature call, and your husband won't stop. 'Just another mile or two,' he says. One mile, then another mile. I have to pee!"

The woman pushed past the minister and walked into the bowling alley. Before she got to the bathroom, her attention shifted hearing the sounds of Klezmer music. She walked to the carousel where she saw the sign asking for a dollar to lift the screen. Undeterred by this makeshift structure, she pushed her hand through the opening and she saw her daughter wrapped around the batting tee, completely nude.

"Schmendrick!" she screamed as she shoved the partition aside and rushed up to Anna pointing her finger, "You meshugina slut. Get your clothes back on right now and we're out of here, young lady. What will I tell your father?"

"Tell my father?" Anna called back, her face red with rage. "Daddy's been fucking me for years, seven to be exact, while you stand by. How the hell do you have the nerve to tell me what I have to do?"

While the women yelled back and forth, Dave zipped his pants and ran out of the carousel. He saw the mob begin to form, the mood turning bad. Quickly, he ran to the front and locked the door.

Meanwhile, Rabbi Pearlman had gotten out of the car and was looking around, "Where's my wife?"

The Reverend approached him, "In there."

The rabbi began walking to the building when the Reverend added, "You can't get in. They've locked her inside."

By now, the occupants of the other cars were on the street. Besides Anna's family, there were twenty Lubovitch Yeshiva boys riding in the lead car, the Rabbi Itzhak Rubowski Memorial Mitzvah Mobile. Mr. Feldman, his wife, and seven children were next, driving a 1987 Chrysler Imperial. Manny, the caterer, and his wife, followed in a Chevy station wagon, the back stuffed with pots and pans, and other kitchen supplies. A family of Russian Jews, recent immigrants to the United States, emerged from the fifth car, an old Ford Fairlane. Finally, there was a Dodge Grand Caravan, overstuffed with more, bearded young men in traditional Hasidic attire, just like the ones who rode in the Mitzvah Mobile.

As hoards of Lubovitch Jews poured out on the street, many walking behind the bowling alley to urinate either North or South as allowed in the *Jewish Code of Laws*, Sol walked to the front of the alley, his father-in-law Rabbi Pearlman by his side, and called out hoping Anna would hear,

"You're ferblandzhet! Let your mother out. You're going to get it now."

Fueled by the Jew's passion, Reverend Anderson walked to his side and said, "We're with you, brother. In the name of the father, the son, and the holy spirit, we're with you."

Soon, the ladies of the Decency League broke out in song: *Onward Christian Soldiers*. Rabbi Pearlman tugged at the door. When it failed to open, he cried out, "They've got her. My wife's a hostage."

Harold picked up his cell phone and dialed 911 to summon the police. While waiting, Chester came to the front and asked, "What's happening?"

Andrew informed him, "They're locked in. They've got the rabbi's wife."

"Let's storm 'em," the bowler said.

"The door won't budge," The rabbi replied.

Jimmying the door himself and seeing it was firmly locked, the bowler tapped his knuckles on the plate glass door then said, "Stand back."

He walked back to the edge of the sidewalk holding his 16 pound, Brunswick Fuze Detonator bowling ball. He took four steps forward and let it roll. At first, the ball headed for Sol. Five feet before the door, less than a foot before hitting Sol, it hooked left and rolled directly to the door, breaking the glass squarely in the middle.

With glass still intact on each side of the hole, Chester's friend shook his head and said, "It's a split. Gonna be a tough spare."

Forgetting his original goal, Chester stopped to ponder the situation, wondering how he could knock down the rest of the door with a single ball.

While he thought, Officer Barney drove up to the alley, blew his whistle and demanded that the crowd calm down.

***

Officer Barney stood by the front of the alley imploring everyone to back off. "Someone. Tell me what's going on?"

"My wife," the rabbi said. "They've got her in there. I'm afraid she's not safe."

"And my wife, too. I want her back," Sol added.

"OK," Barney replied. "Let me get this straight. We've got a damn peep show in there, and a bunch of horny men out here. And you fellows are telling me your wives are in there watching. I'd beat my wife sideways if I found her fooling 'round with no woman."

Barney then looked carefully at the men, noticing their Hasidic garb. "You know. It could be your duds. No offense, but I think my wife would go for women too if I dressed like that."

"Officer, please," the Rabbi protested. "There's got to be something you can do. My wife is being held captive and my daughter's broken every religious and moral law."

"Your daughter ain't Sue Perkins, is she?" Barney asked.

"No," the Rabbi answered, somewhat annoyed by the officer's cavalier attitude.

"Whew," he said. "I was helping Sue break a few moral laws myself last night."

Barney and the deputy cackled with laughter proceeding to give each other high fives.

"This is no joke," the Rabbi said. "This is a violation of civil, moral, and rabbinical law."

"You mean like the Bible. Well correct me if I'm wrong. Hey Rev. Come here and back me up on this one. Wasn't there a whole lot of begatting in the Bible? This one begat that one who begat that one. It was one helluva a begatting party, right Rev."

"Barney," the Reverend implored. "These folks are serious. This one is Anna's father. This is her husband. They have a right to see her. She must be committable. You know she is mentally ill."

"Well, before we go and commit no one, we've gotta make sure it's legal. If you ask me, this is no way to solve the problem. What you should've done you can't do cause there's too many witnesses to get away with it now. Hell, if she were my wife, I'd knock her off. I'd get some farmboy to visit her, maybe deliver a package for me. Then, I'd wait in the bushes. Once she opens the door, Bam! Bam! Bam! I shoot her fucking head off, throw the gun on the porch and call the cops. She's dead and they fry the goddamn farmboy.

"You can't do that now. Everyone here knows you want to kill her.

You're just gonna have to leave her alone until court on Thursday. You know Judge Anderson's gonna close the place up. She'll be outta work. She'll beg you to take her back. Once she's home, knock her fucking teeth out if you want to.

"In the meantime, take a tip from me. Go to Mel Anderson's Men's Shop and get yourself some cool clothes. You dress like that and the judge might just rule for the bitch."

21 GOING BACK IN TIME

Inside the alley, Herb began to pace, frightened ever since the bowling ball crashed through the door. "You've gotta do something, Peter. It's just a matter of time before they break down the door. We won't be able to hold out too long, and they're gonna fuckin' lynch us. Whatcha gonna do?"

"I'll ask Ken," Peter said, going back on line.

kengoldberg: Hey Peter. Good to see you. What's up?

Peter: It's not good, Ken. We're locked in and Anna's mother is here, too. She's screaming at Anna while the crowd outside is trying to break the door down. Herb thinks they're going to lynch us.

kengoldberg: You know Peter, I've got a very busy practice with a lot of things to do. Why can't you deal with these problems yourself?

Peter: I don't know, Ken. I'm sorry. What should I do?

kengoldberg: Maybe what you should do is stand up on your own two feet and start managing your life. God, Peter. You think you'll ever get laid if you keep acting like this. No girl wants a wimp like you.

kengoldberg: Imagine if I were like you. Hi honey. Let's go to bed. I'm Peter Branstill and I want to have sex now. Can we do it?

kengoldberg: Sorry Peter. I've got a headache. Maybe tomorrow. And tomorrow she says tomorrow and then tomorrow again. And you never get it because you're a loser.

kengoldberg: You know what I say, Peter. Tomorrow? You've gotta be kidding. I could've had anyone I wanted. We're gonna do it now, and we're gonna do it whenever I want to. And you let her know she'll be out on the street if she thinks otherwise. That's what you tell women. You don't wimp out. You don't mince words. You let them know who's in charge and that they're damn lucky you even give them the time of day. Keep that in mind, Peter. I didn't make you the stud you are so you wouldn't get laid.

Peter: Thanks for the advice, Ken. I'm still not sure what to do about the things that are happening outside.

kengoldberg: It's not that hard and I'd really like to help you. But I can't. Did I tell you? I'm giving a speech about mental illness next week. It's about nut cases like you. It's a big psychological conference and I need a lot of time to prepare for it. I can't do any writing this week so you're kind of on your own. I know this is bad timing for you and you really need me, but too bad. You'll just have to figure it out. Now, don't do anything I wouldn't do, and keep the faith, power to the people, this little light of mine, Tippecanoe and Tyler too, you can bring the man to the mountain but you can't bring the mountain to the man. If they haven't lynched you by next week, I'll be able to work on the story again.

kengoldberg: Anyway, I think you got the idea. Figure it out for yourself and don't mess things up too much and I'll be back next week to salvage the story.

kengoldberg: Signing off. Toot-a-loo.

***

Peter rested his head on the desk after signing off. Herb came up and asked, "What did he say? Any good ideas?"

"Not really," Peter replied, feeling pressure in his groin. He got up and walked to the one standing viewing booth on the otherwise demolished carousel and watched Anna, hoping to relieve himself. When Anna saw Peter, she stopped arguing with her mother and began to dance. Surprisingly, Peter was unable to have an erection. After half-heartedly rubbing himself, he left the booth, quite defeated, and returned to his desk.

"Hey, Peter. Why the long face?" Herb asked.

"I don't know," he said. "Something changed. I can't put my finger on it."

"Like what?"

"Ever since Ken signed off, I just don't feel the same."

"Hm, anything in particular?"

"He's got to work on some speech he's giving next week. He told me we were on our own since he doesn't have time to write this week. All of a sudden, he's not writing and I don't really feel like jerking off anymore."

"That's interesting," Herb said. "Do you know what Ken means to you?"

As Peter pondered the question, Anna approached from the other side, no longer undressed but wearing an ordinary sweater and skirt.

"Hey, Peter. What happened? That was a first in there."

"I don't know. Ken told me he's going to be away for a week. I got so nervous I thought I'd feel better after going to your booth. It usually works for me. I don't know why it doesn't now."

Anna gently patted Peter's arm saying, "I get it. Something feels different for me, too."

Peter looked at Anna. He liked her touch and could feel himself slightly aroused. He placed his hand on hers and said, "This is what I mean. Before, I would have just ..." Peter paused blocking the term *jerked off* before continuing. "you know what I mean. And that would be that. This time, I can't do it. Yet, I look at you and I kind of feel like, you know, like you and me here. Like really doing it, not that I'd put that on you now, but ..." As Peter stumbled over his words, Anna smiled and replied, "Funny, it's the same thing with me. If you said that to me before, I would have ..." Anna thought to herself, *I really mean Connie would have*, a thought she knew she needed to keep private, "... just done it, no feelings, no real contact, just something right here and now. But, I'm not in that place either. There is something strange happening."

Herb laughed and said, "I don't know, but it sounds like you kids need to go out on a date."

Peter and Anna smiled at each other, Peter saying, "A date. I've never been on a date in my life."

"Me neither," Anna added. "A matchmaker hooks me up with one horrible guy, and that's my life."

Peter added, "But at least you've, you know, done it. I'm 45 years old and still a virgin. The closest I've ever gotten to a girl is from behind the peep show partition. A date. I wouldn't even know what to do."

"Me, neither," Anna laughed.

"OK, kids. It looks like I've gotta teach you guys a thing or two. I may be a drunk, but I did have a life before. I dated, got married. Hell, it didn't work out but at least I know something about what it's like. OK, the date. What do you kids like to do?" When neither responded, Herb realized that neither had any experience doing anything normal that might be fun, so he asked the next question.

"What do you want to do? Use your imagination. Tell me one thing you want to do that you've never done before, barring sex, which you'll get to later. What do you want to do?"

Peter shrugged his shoulders and said, "I've always wanted to do the mambo."

The three laughed heartily before Herb walked away from the table leaving the two lovebirds to talk with each other. Anna told Peter, "I've never done the mambo, but I know the hora. When we have parties -- weddings, bar mitzvahs -- the women dance with the women, the men with the men."

A few minutes later Herb returned with some notes written on a scrap of paper.

"Listen guys. I just called the Arthur Murray Dance Studio in town. The lady says they got a last minute cancellation. It's a crock if you ask me. I bet she don't have no business at all. But, in 45 minutes, you guys are having a dance lesson and she's going to teach you the mambo.

***

Herb led Peter and Anna out the back door to a car waiting there. Taking a circuitous route until they lost the two cars that followed them out of the bowling alley parking lot, Herb doubled back to town and dropped Peter and Anna off at the Arthur Murray Dance Studio. Once inside, they were greeted by Mrs. Anderson, an older woman in casual attire, with some makeup that could not mask her otherwise dowdy appearance. On the walls of the studio, there was a picture of Arthur Murray and posters of several other well-known dancers like Fred Astaire, Gene Kelly, and Judy Garland.

Mrs. Anderson frowned when she recognized Peter and Anna from the paper, but welcomed them anyway, needing the work. She started the lesson with dance basics. Along with the mambo, Mrs. Anderson covered the basic two step, tango and waltz. When Peter stepped on Anna's feet, Mrs. Anderson took Peter aside and danced with him herself.

After the lesson ended, Mrs. Anderson sold Peter and Anna a discount package of ten lessons, two a week, promising that they would be proficient dancers by the end. If they needed more lessons after that: half-price.

Herb was waiting in the car as they left the building and were out on the street. Sitting in the back seat, Peter placed his arm around Anna, ready to kiss her, when Herb turned toward them and said,

"I hope I'm not getting ahead of myself, but I figured you lovebirds would want to go out for dinner. I made a reservation at the Anderson Room at the Holiday Inn, best restaurant in town, far better than the coffee shop. I also figured if this was going to be your first real night, you should have the best. I booked the honeymoon suite and had them move your things there. You should start things anew."

Anna giggled. Peter said nothing.

***

The hostess led Peter and Anna to their table. Engaged in small talk, holding hands, they kept putting the waitress off ordering their food. Finally, on her fourth trip to their table, already on their second bottle of wine, Peter apologized for the delay and quickly looked at his menu. He ordered the veal parmesan, feeling unexpectedly peaceful eating food that someone else prepared. Anna asked for ham, commenting to Peter after she ordered, "I'm just not into Kosher tonight."

Dinner went on, endlessly, far past closing time, Peter and Anna in no hurry to leave. Anna giggled pointing to the waitress, "She's pissed. We'd better let her go home." Peter paid the bill leaving a very large tip to atone for their romantic delay. They embraced as they rode the elevator up to their new room.

***

The next morning, Peter awoke to the sound of the telephone.

"Hello," he answered as Anna still asleep rolled over and placed her arm across his naked chest.

"Peter, it's me," Herb said.

"Uh, um, well," Peter stuttered trying to think of what to say.

Understanding the situation, Herb quickly said, "Listen buddy, I know this is bad timing. I really didn't want to call you, but it's pretty important. Can we get together now?"

Peter cupped the phone and turned to Anna, "Herb wants me back at the alley."

Anna frowned protesting, "No."

"What should I do? He's says its important."

"Ask him what it is."

"What is it, Herb?" Peter asked.

Cupping the phone again, Peter said to Anna, "He won't say. Just that it's real important."

"Can he come here?" Anna asked. "Maybe, he doesn't have to spoil the whole day."

"Herb," Peter said returning to the phone. "Can you come here?"

Herb paused before answering, "That'll work. I just don't want to intrude."

"Hate to tell you, buddy," Peter chuckled, "but you've already done that."

They both laughed, then Peter said, "Really, you know Anna. She doesn't mind. Just come over here, we'll talk about whatever, and maybe keep the meeting short."

"Great, I'll be there in 20 minutes."

Peter hung up the phone telling Anna that Herb would be there shortly. He tried to get up to put his clothes back on but Anna grabbed him by the arm, pulled him to the bed, and kissed him passionately while she mounted herself on top.

Peter and Anna had both climaxed and were still giggling when they heard Herb knock on the door. Peter called out, "Wait a minute."

Peter scurried quickly to get his clothes back on before answering the door. Anna wrapped herself in the sheet, then sat on the edge of the bed. Peter opened the door to let Herb in.

Herb greeted Peter while Anna picked up the phone to order coffee service for three. Peter invited Herb to sit at a table in the room. He pulled the table close to the bed where Anna sat.

Herb opened by saying, "I'm sorry to bother you, but I just spoke with Ken. He really wants to talk and says it can't wait."

"I'm surprised," Peter said. "I thought he was working on his presentation. He told me he'd be out of contact for a week."

"And he was. He must have been on line while working on his project. I saw he was there and sent him an IM. I didn't think he'd have time to talk. I just wanted to say hello. He asked how you were doing and I told him what happened with you and Anna. I thought he'd be proud. He said he needed to talk with you and asked me to get you back on line. I don't know what it is, but he seemed to feel it was urgent."

Peter booted up his computer and was shortly on line. Immediately, a message showed up on the screen indicating:

The Internet user kengoldberg has sent you an Instant Message. Would you like to Accept?

Peter clicked yes and Ken was on line.

kengoldberg: Peter. What are you doing?

Startled, Peter tried to think about what he should type when a stream of IM messages came flooding in from Ken.

kengoldberg: Why did you fuck Anna?

kengoldberg: I told you you'd get her in the end. Why are you fucking her now?

kengoldberg: You couldn't wait. I can't go away for a week without you doing whatever the hell you want to do.

kengoldberg: Is this what I get for caring about you? I brought you into this world. I raised you.

kengoldberg: I gave you a friend: John. You were all alone before. Don't you care that I did that for you? I introduced you to Anna and Herb. Before that, you were jerking off to any stoned dancer in town. Now, you're masturbating to just one girl. You can see her any time you want. Doesn't that mean anything to you.

kengoldberg: You're selfish, Peter. You're goddamn selfish. This is what I get for all I've done. I'm gone for an hour and this is what you do to me. You betray me for a piece of ass.

kengoldberg: Tell me, Peter. What do you really want? Put it out in the open. You want to get laid? Say it if that's all that matters to you. Well, you just might want to know that you were going to get laid soon. I had it planned. It would've happened by the end of the book. Not intercourse, but your first blow job. I figured you could have intercourse by my third or fourth novel at worst. But you couldn't wait. That's what's fucking wrong with young people today. No one waits.

kengoldberg: So, I hope you enjoyed what you did. Did you have a good time at my expense? What are you going to do if Anna gets pregnant? I suppose you figured I'd just write in an abortion if that happened. No way, mister. I have values you know. Well, I'm not going to bail you out this time. Maybe, the kid'll have Down's syndrome, or a cleft palate, or chronic skin infections. Just don't expect me to bail you out every time you decide to do what you want.

kengoldberg: Really Peter. I knew you were messed up but I never thought you were this selfish. I'm very disappointed.

Peter, Herb, and Anna looked at each other in total shock. No one knew what to do. Finally, Peter typed on his screen.

Peter: I'm sorry.

kengoldberg: SORRY!!!! You're sorry. So you think this can all be made right by saying you're sorry. It's not going to happen. You say you're sorry if you step on someone's foot or burp at dinner. You don't say sorry for this. This is just plain wrong.

Herb looked at Peter. "Why don't you ask him what you can do to make things right?"

Peter: Really, Ken. I'm sorry. Is there anything I can do to make this right?

kengoldberg: Well, maybe. How much to you want to right this thing.

Peter: I really do. I appreciate everything you've done for me. What can I do?

kengoldberg: You don't appreciate anything. You think this is the fucking Donna Reed Show, and that you can go out and meet a girl, have a family, and not give a damn about me.

Peter: But I do care about you Ken. I know you've done a lot for me. I see how far I've come. But this thing with Anna seems good. It's new and I'm scared, and I do need your support.

kengoldberg: Damn you, Peter. You don't need me for anything. You just want to get laid. You're fucking selfish. You'll go off with Anna, have a family, and never turn back. That's what happens. Tell you what. You want a normal life so much? I'll give you one.

Peter turned to Herb. "I don't get it."

"It is weird," Herb replied, as Anna threw her arms around Peter, forgetting for a moment that Herb was there as the sheet covering her breasts dropped exposing her slightly.

After a moment's pause without another IM from Ken, Peter mused out loud, "I wonder what he's doing."

"I don't know for sure," Herb replied. "He said he was going to give you a normal life. Maybe, he's writing some new text."

Suddenly, the three of them heard laughter emanating from behind the door to another room in the honeymoon suite. Two children, Joey and Lucy, burst into the room still wearing their pajamas.

"Mommy, Daddy," the children screamed as Lucy jumped into Peter's arms, and Joey ran toward Anna. Peter held the girl, feeling warm yet puzzled by her presence. A golden retriever, Rex, came charging from behind, jumping on Peter and Lucy, knocking them over. As the dog licked Peter's face, Lucy giggled, "She loves you, Daddy."

Confused, Peter could not even remember his formula for calculating contamination from a licking dog.

The computer screen beeped signaling another incoming IM.

kengoldberg: I hope you're happy now. I guess you won't be needing me anymore so I'll be on my way. Have a good life.

Peter: No. Please stay.

kengoldberg: Why should I? You don't need me now. You can write your own story. Maybe I'll just visit a peep show while you fuck the hussy.

"Damn him," Anna said as Peter typed in his next message.

Peter: Ken. Don't leave. Just tell me what you want me to do.

After another long pause, the IMs continued.

kengoldberg: Well, I guess I should apologize a bit to you. It is part my fault, leaving you alone to work on my presentation at such a critical stage in the story. I still have to make the presentation but maybe I can cancel a few appointments this week. Then, I'll use some old material I had from a presentation I did last year. It's a new audience, they haven't heard me yet, and probably won't notice the difference. This will give me time to continue to work on the book.

Peter: Thanks, Ken. Is there anything I can do now to make it up?

kengoldberg: Nothing much except to hold onto your seatbelts. We're going to wipe out this entire day and go back to where we started. Hold on.

kengoldberg: OK. I just blocked out the text starting at *kengoldberg: It's not that hard and I'd really like to help you. But I can't. Did I tell you? I'm giving a speech about mental illness next week* up to the present time. I'm going to press the delete button. OK here goes.

Anna instinctively reached for Joey as he started to cry. Lucy clung onto Peter tighter than ever. Herb looked awestruck and Rex whimpered quietly. Nothing happened.

Peter: What happened?

kengoldberg: I pressed delete but got a message, Are you Sure with two boxes, Yes and No. I just stopped for a moment to read the text. You know, it really is a good story. You and Anna did well, romancing each other, considering it's your first time. I actually feel a bit proud of you.

Peter: So we can keep the story?

kengoldberg: No. Sorry. As much as I'd like to let it stay, it's not my story. Hell, authors have written lots of good love stories. And people have nice experiences like you and Anna did all the time. But, it's not my story. I've got to be true to myself as a writer.

Peter quickly tried to think what he could do to keep the experience he had with Anna. He started to type.

Peter: Please Ken, keep the text. It's really good. You're going to sell more copies of this book than you sold the first one. It'll make people feel good, and ...

But before Peter could finish his message and send it into cyberspace, Ken pressed the *Yes, I am sure* button, sending Peter back to his bowling alley, peep show.

kengoldberg: It's not that hard and I'd really like to help you. But I can't. Did I tell you? I'm giving a speech about mental illness next week.

kengoldberg: On the other hand, this is really an important place in the story. I guess I can cancel a few patients so I can work on my speech and still write your story. It won't matter much for them anyway. They're just a bunch of losers.

22 TWO TO THE FIFTH

While Peter continued his calculations and Herb prepared his arguments for tomorrow's hearing, Anna quietly put her clothes back on and walked out the back door. She looked at her watch, 2:00 p.m., two hours until her appointment with Penny.

Damn that Ken, Anna thought to herself, angry that he took her wonderful night with Peter away. Remembering the soft feel of his tongue darting in and out of her mouth while his huge penis filled her inside, Anna knew that she would never dance nude again. Neither Peter nor Herb noticed Anna's departure when Harold and Andrew entered the building.

"Hi Peter," Harold said, hoping he might calm things down by using a light and friendly approach to address the issue. "We sure missed you this time. We've all come to count on your visits. Can't wait till you come to Indy. I think I've found the place where you'll eat. They serve anything you want: Sushi and Grits R Us. My treat. All I ask is that you take that sign off, close the peep show, and tell the press this was just a bad mistake. I'd sure like to keep this out of court if I can. Too much press will just hurt business."

Before Peter could answer, Herb jumped in front and began arguing civil liberties, civil rights, human rights, immigration rights, transcendental rights, and right to life laws.

"We'll never back down," Herb insisted. "With God on our side, we'll fight until we see your eyes turn white."

Harold tried to get past Herb and resume his conversation with Peter when Andrew called out from the carousel.

"Harold. Look here. Anna's gone."

Harold turned and looked toward Andrew to hear Dave shout at him, "No, I'm not going to take her place. Now, get out of here before I punch your lights out. And I'm not meeting you in the men's room either."

"Cool it guys," Harold called back. "Let me finish with Peter, then I'll get to you."

Harold turned back but Peter was no longer there. Herb continued to pontificate on the vast legal, moral, scientific, anthropological, and culinary aspects of the case.

***

Peter left the bowling alley and walked down Main Street to Mel Anderson's Men's Wear hoping they carried his favorite suit. Ken had brought him back to his senses and, feeling dirty wearing and sleeping in the same suit all week, he needed something else. The salesman expressed regret that they did not have the exact suit Peter wanted, but showed him one that was comparably drab. Peter bought it and ordered four more which the salesman promised would be here by next week.

Peter next stopped at a small grocery store to buy enough food to last him twenty-four hours. Finally, he reached the Holiday Inn and went to his room. When his magnetic key did not work, he returned to the front desk.

"Hi, Mr. Branstill," the clerk cheerfully said, "How can I help you?"

"My key doesn't work."

"Let me see."

The clerk looked at the card carefully. "This is for your old room. We changed the code when you moved to the Honeymoon Suite. Let me get you another card for your room."

"I want to go back to my old room," Peter said.

"Oh," the clerk inquired. "Anything wrong with that suite. It is the best in the house."

"I just want my old room back."

"OK," the clerk replied. "Let me check to see if it's still available for you and Mrs. Branstill."

"Mrs. Branstill?" Peter puzzled. "You mean Anna. Mrs. Klinger. She'll be staying in the Honeymoon Suite."

The clerk lifted his eyes and paused before composing himself and saying, "OK, Mr. Branstill. Let me check on the availability."

Before going to the register, the clerk handed Peter a brochure from the First Baptist Church, "This is where the Mrs. and me go. Great bunch of folks there."

Peter had just started counting the number of three letter words in the brochure when the clerk returned to say, "Sorry Mr. Branstill. That room is no longer available. Strangest thing cause it's empty. But someone called in and reserved it for the whole week, even though they're not here, and may not get here for a day or so. Anyway, can I give you another room."

"That's fine," Peter said trying not to lose his place having counted seventeen three-letter words so far.

"OK. I'm sorry but it'll take a few minutes more. Darnedest thing happened this morning. Our computers went down. They act like it's yesterday, Wednesday morning.

***

Refusing the clerk's offer to help, Peter brought his belongings down from the Honeymoon Suite to his new room in four trips ($2^2 = 4$), and placed them on the dresser in symmetrical fashion. He set his laptop on the table and soon was on line, talking with Ken.

Peter: I'm here, Ken, in a new room, without Anna.

kengoldberg: What do you want, Peter, a medal?

Peter felt sad as he hung his head down.

kengoldberg: Come on, Peter. Get over it. That shouldn't have hurt you so much. OK. You do deserve some credit giving up that hussy. It's my fault anyway. I thought she was the right one for you, but she's no good. She'll open her legs (or spread her ass) for anyone. You need a good wholesome girl.

kengoldberg: Anyway, how's your new room? Does it suit you well?

Peter: It's nice. Not as fancy as the Honeymoon Suite but it'll be fine.

kengoldberg: Hey. That's not my old Peter. Maybe nice to the ordinary eye, but you're Peter Branstill. Have you checked it for dirt yet.

Peter: This chair is clean.

kengoldberg: Peter. One clean seat works in the park. You're gonna sleep there. Maybe you forgot shacking up with that hussy all these nights, her pussy juice on your clothes, but you've gotta be cleaner than that. I'm surprised, and a bit disappointed. I would have thought you'd check it out more thoroughly.

Peter: You're right Ken. I'll get to it soon.

kengoldberg: Do it now, Peter. **NOW!**

Peter: OK, Ken. I'll sign off right now and check it out.

kengoldberg: **WHAT!** Don't you dare sign off. You're going to stay on line and report to me step by step everything you do to make sure that room is clean. Listen up and listen carefully. This is what you're going to do.

Through a succession of IM messages, Ken directed Peter to go downstairs and ask for four rolls of paper towels with which he would cover the entire floor, the beds, and all the surfaces. Then, step-by-step, Peter was to look under each tear-off section of the towel and rate its cleanliness according to the Graduated Dirt Rating Scale. Further, Peter had to clean every place with dirt rated 35 or higher. Finally, Ken added a masturbatory requirement.

kengoldberg: While you're cleaning and before you go to sleep, you need to jerk off $2^5 = 32$ times.

Thirty-two times! gasped Peter. *I've never done that.*

Peter: Why?

kengoldberg: It's the fluids, Peter. You contaminated yourself with immoral fluids staying with Anna. It's not just the semen emitted, but the semen that has built up inside. It's different from the semen you get when you stand in front of a dancer or beat your meat to a horse. This semen is bad. It comes from impure thoughts and lustful feelings. You get it when you touch a woman instead of looking at her safely through a glass partition. Your body is tainted, your prostate overworked, and you've created poisonous fluids lying in the arms of that wanton woman. You have to bleed those fluids out of your system before you can be strong again.

kengoldberg: Someday, you'll have a woman. You'll consummate your relationship with her through a hole in a sheet to protect you from contamination by her bodily fluids. You'll be safe from contact with perspiration, saliva, oily hair and traces of urine. You'll wear a condom with a tiny hole in the end to let you impregnate your partner while minimizing the risk of contact with her pussy juice.

Confused, his orders were clear. Peter jerked off once, and began to rate the dirt in his room.

***

Anna arrived at the clinic for her first therapy session with Penny. In tears, she blurted her whole story out including her frustrating relationship with Peter, annual sexual habits, and how much her father and husband abused her. A half hour later, she stopped talking and hung her head in shame.

Penny waited to make sure she was done, then softly spoke.

"Anna, I'm so sorry you hurt that much. But there is hope. I think I understand your problem, and if I'm right, it can be easily treated. First, let me ask you a few questions. When did your father start molesting you: as a child or were you already an adult?"

Anna thought. "I don't remember him doing it when I was young. Would that be a repressed memory?"

"Possibly. It's also possible he never hurt you until you grew up. When is your first memory of him raping you?"

"Hanukah, 5756. He told me he had a very special Hanukah gift for me. I followed him into the bedroom. Mom was there. She told me I had to do it."

As Anna's eyes welled with tears, Penny calmly went on. "5756?

132

That's 1995 in the Christian calendar. And when did Sol start beating you?"

"About the same time?" Anna answered, puzzled by Penny's questions.

"Did you ever have a better relationship with Sol?" Penny asked.

"Oh, yes. We had lots of fun. We kept a Kosher house and believed in the same things. We were disappointed I didn't have children. I never got pregnant until after my father ..."

Anna's voice tailed off as she welled up in tears and could faintly hear the voices chanting:

You're no lady, killed the baby.

"It's OK," Penny soothingly replied. "Do you want to talk more about what happened with your Dad?"

"No," Anna answered. "I want to tell you about Sol."

Anna took a deep breath before continuing. "We were disappointed. We wanted a family. Besides that, things were good. I liked to be naughty and tease him. He would blush whenever I sucked his penis. You know, that's not really allowed in Orthodox law."

"And the mental illness, the hospitals, the trips out west: When did they start?"

"About the same time," Anna answered.

Penny rose from her seat and walked to the bookshelf. She removed her copy of *Peter Squared* and brought it to Anna. "Here, Anna. I want you to read the Acknowledgment."

Anna began:

"I want to thank my brother-in-law, Seymour, a man of humor and wisdom, who encouraged me to write Peter Squared over dinner conversation, November 23, 1995."

"Thanksgiving, 1995," Penny emphasized. "Just one month before the abuse began."

"I'm confused," Anna revealed. "What does this mean?"

Leaning forward imagining herself a great therapist, Penny said, "What you have, Anna, is author induced, group psychosis. You, your family, Peter, Herb and everyone else involved in *Peter Squared* are caught up in Ken Goldberg's delusional system. Each of you were abducted against your will and forced to be characters in his book. When people are molested in dysfunctional families, the problem always starts in childhood. When a normal, healthy, moral father starts molesting his daughter after she becomes an adult, it is always indicative of an author-induced clinical state."

"Wow," Anna responded. "I can't believe this. Does it happen often?"

"Quite a bit lately. There's always been some author-induced psychopathologies, but not like now. We know Lenny was once a used car salesmen who sold John Steinbeck a lemon. Steinbeck took revenge by making him a character in one of his books. There's a wonderful article about it called, *Who's the Mouse? Who's the Man?*

"The earliest known case of author-induced psychopathology involved a credit counselor named Silas Marner. George Eliot was broke and sought Marner's help negotiating with creditors to consolidate her debt and establish a repayment plan. Marner did his best, but things had gone way too far for Eliot. She ended up in debtor's prison. Enraged, she took revenge by making Marner a pathetic miser.

"These situations were quite rare in the past, but this keeps changing as technology substitutes for imagination. More and more authors cannot conjure up their own interesting characters and seek ordinary people to take parts in their books. I've seen an enormous rise in author-induced psychopathologies with the advent of modern video games, projection TV, and the Rush Limbaugh Show."

"And this only happens with authors?" Anna asked.

"We're not sure. There are some researchers who believe there are artist and composer induced psychopathologies, too. Recently, a historian uncovered an invoice from Madame Augustine Roulin's personal physician dated just before Van Gogh came to live with her family. The document diagnoses her with anorexia nervosa and orders her to take leave from her job as a show girl. Except for the influence of Vincent's art, we have no way to explain how she became so fat and dumpy like her husband, the postman.

"Then, there's Beethoven. For years, historians thought Beethoven soured on Napoleon after he composed Eroica. He wrote a letter to a friend just before he began writing the symphony. The translation is not clear but he seems to say something like, *Bonaparte should squeeze the world by its balls*. What do you think? Could Beethoven have been the one to make Napoleon the madman he was?

"The good news is that the condition is easily treated. Insight alone is the cure. The bad news is that you can't change Peter unless he wants to change himself. Because he's the main character, he'll have the hardest time freeing himself from Ken."

"What should I do, Penny?" Anna pleaded. "I love him."

"First, you need to confront your husband and the rest of your family. We'll do that tomorrow morning, here in my office, at 9:00. Once they've made amends, which they surely will do once they understand what happened, you have to talk with Peter. You'll have to be strong. Either he gives up Ken or you have to give up Peter."

23 ORDER IN THE COURT

At 4:45 pm, Herb paced frantically, wondering where Peter and Anna were. He walked up to Dave who had just put the carousel back up.

"Something's wrong," Herb told Dave. "They should be here. We open in 15 minutes. What will we do?"

"No shit," Dave exclaimed. "Anna's not here?"

"I don't know where Peter is either."

"Damn him," Dave said, picturing Peter humping Anna. "That girl's got awful taste."

"Good taste or bad, we need to do something. I'm prepared for the hearing and I'm sure we'll win in court. But we've gotta be open for business. I don't want them thinking they've got the upper hand."

Just then, there was a knock on the front door. The men looked over and saw Harold and Andrew standing there.

"It's early!" Herb called out.

"We want to talk," Harold said. "Before you open for business."

"What's there to lose?" Dave said. "There ain't gonna be no business tonight anyway, not with the machines all broken down and Anna not here."

Herb half-heartedly agreed and went to the door to let Harold and Andrew in. Dave kept his foot pressed against the bottom of the door to prevent the crowd from rushing in as the two men squeezed by.

After Herb locked the door, Harold started to talk. "Is Peter here?"

"Not right now," Herb said trying to think of what else to say. "Uh, he's out recruiting girls. By tomorrow night, we'll have a full stable."

"Let's not horse around and come to the point," Harold replied. "I've got a proposition for you. Things are awfully hot. This crowd's not gonna let anyone in. The media's still on my tail about being part of this, which you know I'm not. So, here's what I think we should do. The hearing is tomorrow. We know this is going to the Supreme Court ..."

"And Martin Luther King if need be," Herb interjected.

"That's right. I forgot Reverend King," Harold responded rolling his eyes. "Anyway, it's not going to end soon but at least there'll be a temporary decision tomorrow. Why don't you just keep the place closed tonight, see what happens, and then we'll decide. It'll be real helpful for me and the firm to seem like we talked some sense into you. Frankly, I kind of like the peep show idea, and might go into it with you and Peter sometime down the pike. With my money, you'll do ten times better. For now, I'm concerned about image. Sterling and Warner fell badly in the market today. If it rebounds this week, I'll sell out, then go with you. A deal?"

Herb did not like the deal and felt like arguing the point. But neither Peter nor Anna were there and he knew there were no other dancers coming. Reluctantly, Herb agreed to stay closed.

"Thanks, man," Harold said. "I'll let you star in our first film."

"At my age?" Herb laughed.

Earnestly, Harold replied, "Our market research shows that older, gay men are our most under-served population. Think about it."

Harold called out to Andrew as he was walking to the men's room with Dave, "Andrew, let's go."

"Now?" Andrew asked.

"Yes. It's important that we not be associated with this group too long. We'd better go."

As Andrew put his wallet back in his pocket and returned with Harold, Dave called out, "At least give me half."

***

The crowd began to disperse after Harold informed them of his successful negotiations to keep the alley closed tonight. He willingly gave interviews to all the networks, sure that his efforts would help cleanse the corporation's name.

Herb and Dave locked the building and walked back to the Holiday Inn, Dave stopping at Al's Video Shop, Herb going straight to Anna and Peter's room.

"Who's there?" Anna called out hearing Herb knock on the door.

It's me," Herb replied. "Are you guys decent?"

"More decent than you'd know," Anna answered.

Anna opened the door and let Herb in.

"Where's Peter?"

"He took another room," Anna replied. "Two floors down."

"Why'd he do that?"

"Not sure," Anna said. "He didn't tell me. He just did it. I think it has something to do with Ken."

"I'm not surprised. That was pretty wild what happened the other day. Anyway, I closed the lanes. You weren't there and it was just a matter of time before Dave took his clothes off and started dancing himself. In fact, I think he negotiated something with Andrew before I made him leave."

"Dave," Anna laughed. "Now that's one man I never want to be with."

"Hm," said Herb. "Any interest in me?"

"Herb!" Anna answered with shock and surprise. "Stop that."

"Sorry," Herb said.

Anna put her hand on Herb's. "You shouldn't be. You're a nice man and who knows, in my old days I might have done it just for the hell of it. But not anymore."

"Really?" Herb asked.

"Really. I'm changing. I'm not gonna fuck around anymore. I'm not gonna strip. I want a life, something real."

"Are you going back to Sol?" Herb asked.

"No. That's over. I'm gonna tell him tomorrow. If Peter's willing, I want to start seeing him. If he's not, I'll get a job and a place of my own, and try to live a normal life."

"Sounds good, Anna. I'm happy for you. But what about Peter? You just said he got his own room. Is this a step back in time, or does it mean something else? Are you and Peter cooling off? Do you think you'll get back together again?"

Looking sad, Anna answered, "Something else. I want to be normal, not a prude. I'd love to have him stay with me. But, I don't think it's going to work. You see, I'm out of this story. Peter's not. He's too enamored with Ken. I think he's always going to be a character."

"He is a character," Herb said, hoping to inject some levity into the conversation.

"Thanks, Herb. You're a sweet guy," Anna said, giving him a kiss on the cheek.

Herb smiled, "Sure, you couldn't use one last fling before leaving the book?"

***

At 9:00 the next morning, Anna, Sol, Rabbi Pearlman and his wife were all assembled in Penny's office. Penny began by asking who would like to speak first. The rabbi chimed in offering the first words, a Barucha he devised thanking the Lord for the fruit of the session.

Anna went next, "Daddy, let's get this out in the open. You've been fucking me for years and I'm really upset. How can you do that?"

"Anna," her mother jumped in. "He's your father. Talk to him with respect."

"And why did you allow it?" she added, tears starting to form in her eyes.

Anna's mother stood up and started to yell at her using curses in both English and Yiddish, her points unintelligible beyond the fact that Anna never liked her chicken.

Penny stepped in, "Mrs. Pearlman, please sit down. Perhaps it's my fault for not setting the rules before we began. In family therapy, we sit in our seats. We don't get up. We discuss feelings and thoughts and refrain from taunts and invectives. We expect to be heard and are expected to listen to each other. Your daughter just asked you why you allowed your husband to molest her. That's a question. Surely, there's an answer."

Anna's mother sat back in her chair and took a deep breath, thought and then answered, "Her father needs it. He's a man."

"And you, Rabbi Pearlman? What's your thought to your daughter's question about why you molested her?"

"Sophie is right. I'm a man. What could I do?"

"What did you used to do?" Penny asked.

The rabbi looked at his wife. They smiled at each other. Sheepishly, he looked at Penny.

"So let's ask another question. What happened between you and Sophie that you stopped looking to her to meet those needs?" Penny asked already picturing herself the keynote speaker at the annual conference of the American Association for the Study of Author-Induced Psychopathologies.

"I don't know," the rabbi said. "What happened?" he asked looking at his wife.

"I don't know either," Sophie said.

"Do you remember the last time you had relations?" Penny went on.

Anna's parents both smiled, Rabbi Pearlman responding, "How could I forget?"

"So what happened the next time you wanted to be with your wife?"

"I don't know. I don't think there was a next time. It was great one day. The next day it seemed the thing to do to be with Anna."

"That's how I felt too," Sophie answered.

"Is that what it says in the Talmud?" Penny asked, knowing she was pressing hard.

"No," the Rabbi answered, lowering his head. "Never."

"So what do you think happened?" Penny went on.

"I just don't know. All I know is that I'm so ashamed of myself."

Sol then chimed in. "That was 5756 wasn't it?"

"Yes," Sophie said.

"That's when things changed with us, too, Anna," Sol added now looking at his wife.

Anna cried, "You hurt me so much, Sol."

"Oh Anna," Sol said, reaching over to touch her with no concern if she was clean. "I don't know what happened."

"I'll tell you what happened," Penny said. "It's called author-induced psychosis.

Penny went on to explain, much as she did the day before, the syndrome. The foursome listened in awe until she was done.

"Any thoughts?" Penny said. "Where does this leave you?"

Rabbi Pearlman was the first to respond. "Very puzzled. Very ashamed. And quite horny. Let's go back to our room, Sophie, when this session is done."

Penny chuckled then turned to Anna and Sol. "And what about you two?"

Sol seemed to stumble on his words, afraid to speak. "I don't know." he finally said.

"Sol, it's all right. I've always loved you, but it isn't going to work for us anymore. I love another man. I want a Ghet."

Sol seemed hurt and relieved at the same time. "Actually, there's a girl here in town, Vicky. She's a descendent of Anderson Jews who had to convert to save their lives. Anderson was once a thriving Jewish community, devastated by the United States Calvary in the battle of Little Shetl, led by General Adolph Custer and his Lieutenant, Ulysses S. Anderson. There are many ethnic Jews still living here. Vicky and I want to marry and lead the revitalization of this one-time vibrant Jewish community."

"I wish you well, Sol," Anna said. "I hope she turns out to be right for you."

***

The Bailiff instructed all to rise as Judge Tyrus Anderson entered the court. He opened the session with the cases of Anderson, Nebraska vs. Branstill Entertainment, and Sterling and Warner Industries vs. Branstill Entertainment. Christians for Decency, Bowl America, and the Republican National Committee were all present with lawyers offering friends-of-the-court briefs. Herb represented Peter and was still grumbling because he failed to garner further support from the ACLU, or to bring in the American Psychological Association, Playboy Magazine, Al's Video or the NAACP.

"Why the hell do you think we'd be interested in this case?" the Executive Director of the local NAACP chapter replied, slamming the phone down before Herb could describe his former association with the Reverend Martin Luther King, Jr.

The judge asked the attorneys to state their appearances, then called a brief recess to let Herb, who was suddenly beset with diarrhea, take a quick bathroom break.

"Where's your client?" Judge Anderson barked upon Herb's return.

"I don't know, your honor," Herb said, hiding the fact that Peter wouldn't come to court until he finished cleaning his room. Unbeknownst to Herb, having only talked to him through the door, Peter had seven masturbations left before reaching the required number: 32. Finding it progressively harder to jerk off, emitting no semen at all in the last two attempts, Peter nevertheless stayed to the task after Ken squashed his hopes for dispensation.

kengoldberg: Stop! Of course not. It's like drilling a tooth. The dentist goes a bit beyond the decay to make sure the tooth's totally clean. You'll be pure once you reach 32.

James Anderson, Anderson's city solicitor, opened the case seeking a permanent injunction against the peep show.

"It violates zoning laws," the lawyer said.

"It violates child welfare laws," he added his voice a bit louder.

"It's obscene," his face now red.

"It's an eyesore and a fire hazard," now shaking with rage.

"The dancer's a Jew," he screamed to the gasps of the crowd.

"And, it violates God's law, too."

Judge Anderson took his time picking up the gavel and pounding it to quiet the now agitated crowd. "Nicely put Jimbo. By the way, Mom wants to know if you and Alice can come over for dinner tonight."

"Let me see," Jim replied looking at his calendar. "Sorry, bowling night."

"Is your client here, Mr. Whitmore?" the judge asked.

Herb replied, "No, your honor. He'll be here soon."

"Well, that's not good enough, sir. I think we've got a default judgment brewing up here."

"Wait a second, your honor. Mr. Branstill isn't used to central time. He comes from the East. I'm sure his watch is on Eastern Daylight time. That's why he's late."

"Eastern daylight time?" the judge scoffed. "Then, he would've been here an hour ago. What are you talking about?"

"I mean, I changed his watch to Central Time last night just to make sure he got here on time. I forgot to tell him I did that, so he probably thinks it's an hour earlier than it is. He'll be here soon, I guarantee it."

"Adjusted his watch?" Judge Anderson responded more incredulous than ever. "How could you do that if he was wearing his watch?"

"He was bowling, and took it off because he can bowl better without it on so I changed it thinking I would help him. I didn't want to interfere with his bowling and waited to tell him. He got strike after strike all the way to the tenth frame. You can't talk to a bowler without jinxing him if he's heading for a perfect game. So, I had to wait. By the time he missed the final strike, I forgot to tell him what I did."

The Judge scrunched his brow. "Tell you what, Mr. Whitmore. It's 10:20 now. If you're telling me the truth, Mr. Branstill should be here by 11:00. We'll take a brief recess. If he isn't here by then, I'm issuing a default judgment and throwing you in jail for contempt of court."

The judge banged his gavel and said, "Court adjourned until 11:00."

Herb quickly got out of his seat, ready to dash out when the judge called out, "Bailiff, hold that man. Don't let him go. Mr. Branstill's got a watch. He'll have to remember to get here on his own."

***

The hotel clerk joined Anna at the door outside Peter's room.

"I can't just let you in ma'am. Mr. Branstill is entitled to his privacy and he already told us you're not married."

"He's in trouble," Anna insisted. "You've got to let me in."

"I need more to go on than that," the clerk answered, still refusing to open the door when suddenly he and Anna heard, emanating from the room, a painful moan.

"Quick," Anna demanded, grabbing the master key from the clerk, opening the door quickly. They both started in, the clerk covering his eyes and backing off when he saw Peter lying on his back, his eyes glazed over, holding his very red penis, half-heartedly rubbing it up and down. Anna rushed in as the clerk walked away.

"Peter," she cried, shaking his arm forcing him to release his grip on his organ. "What are you doing?"

When Peter just moaned, Anna ran to the bathroom where she found a washcloth, wetted it, and placed it on his head. Anna grabbed Peter and held him in her arms saying, "Darling, I was so worried about you."

"I've got four more to go," Peter replied, trying to get his hand back to his organ, tears in his eyes.

"Why?" Anna asked. "You don't seem to feel like it."

"Ken," Peter groaned. "I have to."

Peter pointed to the computer across the room. There, Anna read the transcript of his IM conversation with Ken, revealing line by line Peter's efforts to get dispensation, Ken's adamant demands that he keep jerking off.

"Peter," Anna said, returning to the bed, no longer sympathetic at all, her voice harsh. "I love you, and I want you. And I'm going to have you, or someone else I can love, like you. I'm leaving Sol. I'm going to have a life. I'm out of this book. It's up to you what you want to do."

Peter looked quizzically at Anna, then pulled his pants back on and asked her what she meant. The explanation clear in her mind, Anna quickly and succinctly told Peter what she knew. "What do you want to do?" she ended.

"I know you're right. I don't know if I can do it."

"All you have to do is decide that you're giving up Ken," Anna said. "You may hurt. You may mourn. It'll be hard. Just make that decision and I'll be by your side."

With that, Peter and Anna hugged. Overjoyed, Anna began to passionately kiss Peter. He smiled and said, "Hold it, Anna. We'll have to wait. I'm not avoiding you now. I just need some time."

Peter pointed to his crotch to explain his dilemma.

***

Anna released Peter from her embrace and asked, "By the way. Where's Herb?"

"Oh my God!" Peter exclaimed. "He's at the courthouse. The trial started an hour ago."

Quickly, Peter and Anna left the room and rushed downtown. Arriving five minutes later, they could see, through the glass windows of the courtroom door, Herb standing in front of the judge, waving his hands. They opened the door and heard the judge furiously pounding his gavel demanding that Herb sit down to let him make his ruling. The argument stopped when Dave saw Peter and Anna arrive and called out, "They're here! Peter's here!"

Peter walked down the aisle to the front of the courtroom while Judge Anderson sternly looked on. Peter went up to Herb and whispered in his ear.

"No, Peter. We can win," Herb replied, loud enough for many to hear. "We'll fight to the end."

"I don't want to fight," Peter said. "Something's changed. I need to heal."

"Mr. Whitmore," the judge demanded. "Are you ready to proceed."

"Uh ... uh ... well your honor. I'm not sure. Let me confer with my client, please."

"We've waited long enough, Mr. Whitmore. Let's get on with the case or I'm making summary judgment."

"Your honor," Peter spoke up. "May I speak for myself?"

"Hell," Judge Anderson replied. "You couldn't do any worse than this clown."

"Objection," Herb cried out. "I'm declaring this a mistrial and holding you in contempt of court."

The judge shook his head, "Go on, Mr. Branstill. Open your case."

"Thank you, your honor."

24 THE SPEECH

Peter confidently walked to the middle of the courtroom and said, "Your Honor Judge Anderson, Town Solicitor Anderson, Mayor Anderson, citizens of Anderson, the media, visiting Jews, Harold and Andrew.

"I came to Anderson to open a peep show, my lifelong dream. For years, I've wanted a place of my own where good people, ordinary people, family men, their wives, children, friends and neighbors, could come together, live as comrades, congregate as a community, socialize in peace, fraternize with their neighbors, bask in harmony, peep and bowl together. *I was wrong.*"

Peter paused, his timing perfect, expecting the gasp that came. He went on.

"Yes, I have sinned. I was wrong. Sure, it's a noble cause, but the means far too radical. People are people and men are men. But for God's sake, if you're going to jerk off in a bowling alley, do it in the bathroom."

Peter let the few cheers subside. Then, he said, "Tomorrow morning, I am ordering my staff to tear down the carousel and install five new, state-of-the art, high tech, Brunswick bowling lanes. Tomorrow morning, I am ordering my staff to open our doors, and as penance, give the good citizens of Anderson, Nebraska a day of free bowling. Tomorrow morning, I am ordering my staff to keep the lanes open 24 hours a day for round the clock play. Let's bring the *owl* back in bowl.

"Over the next several months, we will expand our operation. We will tear down the back wall and build out, into the former rear parking lot, a full service health club. Our snack bar will offer a wide selection of health foods and Glatt Kosher cuisine along with our standard menu of hot dogs, pizza, and beer.

"Later this year, I will purchase land outside of town and build the Anderson Adult Book Store. With tastefully appointed signage, we will not

144

only serve the peeping public but provide jobs for deserving young women. I intend to work closely with the Department of Public Assistance to insure that Branstill Entertainment does its part in your welfare to workfare program. Dancers will receive living wages, vacations, and full health benefits. Men who bring their wives and children will masturbate comfortably knowing we'll have a wide variety of social and recreational services for their families in a distinct section of the building.

"Next year, I plan to erect an adjourning building near the peep show to house the new Anderson Center for Marriage Counseling and Sex Therapy. I'm offering the position of Director for that facility to your own Penny Smith.

"I hope to later create a non-denominational center for religious studies open to people of all cultures and faiths. Orthodox Jew, Fundamentalist Christian, Muslim, Hindu, and Atheist alike can come together to communicate and learn, attacking the roots of hatred and bigotry. I will offer two fellowships for studies in human relations to be administered through the College of International Studies at Nebraska State University. We will encourage peoples of all faiths and nationalities to settle in Anderson which will someday become a model of diversity and tolerance, a demonstration project for rational living in the 21st Century.

"I want to apologize for any pain I may have caused you good people. But after all, pain is part of growth."

When Peter finished, the crowd sat stunned, no one knowing what to say. Finally, Bufford Benson, Democratic Candidate for mayor, an assured loser in the election running against the Anderson clan, a man who never bothered to campaign, stood up, clapped his hands, and announced,

"I hereby withdraw from the Mayoral election to throw my support to Peter Branstill, Anderson's next mayor."

Mayor Anderson, who had been in office 20 years following the equally lengthy terms his father and grandfather had served, grabbed his brother's gavel and started banging it, crying out, "This is out of order."

Herb immediately began rifling through his law books.

Herb, Judge Anderson, and Town Solicitor Anderson met to discuss the issue while Mayor Anderson argued furiously with Former Candidate Benson. Quickly, it was determined that not only was Benson free to relinquish his place on the ballot in favor of Peter, but that everyone staying in Anderson today, five days before the election, was eligible to vote. Crying foul, Mayor Anderson argued fruitlessly to force Rabbi Pearlman's group out of town.

***

That afternoon, Herb sat in his room reflecting on the day. He was glad that Peter and Anna were finally together, and that Dave had joined a Bible study group instead of thinking about sex all the time. He laughed trying to picture old Rabbi Pearlman in bed with Sophie. Sol seemed really happy with Vicky. And Herb was glad that he could finally get Dr. King off his mind. Sure, he admired the man but they were never personal friends.

Herb thought about Teri. *I wonder how she's doing. It's been seven years since I've seen the kids.*

Herb thought he could call but he realized he didn't know her number. *Dr. Parker, the dentist. Gerald Parker.*

Knowing they lived in or near New Rochelle, Herb picked up the phone to call information. He started to dial when he remembered he could find the number himself through the internet. He put the phone down and went on line.

As soon as Herb logged in, he received a message from kengoldberg.

kengoldberg: Herb. You there?

Herb: Yep. How's your workshop coming?

kengoldberg: Not good. I can't concentrate. This whole plot is driving me crazy.

Herb: How's that?

kengoldberg: It's just not going the way I hoped it would. It's so out of control. When I wrote *Peter Squared* I was in charge. Peter was just as bizarre as I wanted him to be. He got a little better after he met John, cared for him and broke down. Eventually, he went back to his old life. I got some criticism because the book lacked a happy ending. I got some good reviews too, applauding me for resisting that old feel good thing. Whether people liked it or not, I had control.

Herb: I thought it was a good story, too. I always appreciated that you put me in at the end.

kengoldberg: You're welcome, Herb. You've always been a good friend.

Herb: You, too.

kengoldberg: But this second volume is all wrong. I started with the idea that we'd take off where we ended, you, Dave and Anna meeting Peter. I figured Peter would be Anna's next conquest. They're both pretty whacked. I'd have them travel together to Anderson, make Peter completely unable to respond to Anna in any way until the end. Yom Kippur would pass and Anna would become morbidly depressed. I figured Peter would hear her wailing, naked, in the peep booth, and touched by her pain, actually enter the booth. She sobs, leans her head on his shoulder, the way John did it in *Peter Squared*. Peter has an erection; Anna unzips his fly. The book ends with Peter getting his first blow job while Anna tolerates doing it without worrying that she's violating Kosher dietary laws, consuming his semen. The story stops there.

Herb: Wow, Ken. That is a great story. So what's the problem?

kengoldberg: Everything, Herb. It all went wrong. It started when Anna led Peter from the bench right to the Waldorf and made love. For all his inexperience, Peter proved a helluva lover, way out of context for the way I created him.

Herb: But that was a fantasy, not a reality.

kengoldberg: Not when it first happened. You can't imagine how dumbstruck I felt, sitting here at my computer, watching them do it with such pizzazz. Hell, I made love that night, and it wasn't half as good. I didn't know what to do. I figured I could give Anna a split personality, call the other person Connie, and turn the whole thing into a fantasy.

Herb: And it was a great idea.

kengoldberg: I know. But it's crazy. I kept fighting cats and dogs trying to keep Peter the way he was, while he's proving to be this great studmuffin. I don't know how he learned to do it, but you've gotta realize, it's been very hard on me trying to keep him in character.

Herb: Well, you've been doing a great job.

kengoldberg: Thanks, Herb. I've tried. But this now takes the cake. I take one week off writing and here he goes, having the romantic moment of his life. I know I could delete the text, but I'm beginning to wonder if that's the right thing to do.

Herb: Are you thinking about making some major change?

kengoldberg: Yea, Herb. I hate to do this. You know my heart is into writing a literary novel, not some crappy, feel good jive. But, I've got to accept reality. Peter just isn't the strange Kafkaesque character I thought he'd be. I should really think of him more like the Gene Kelly type: upbeat, energetic. I may have to change the plot and end it something like this.

Herb waited for Ken's next IM to come, but his computer froze. By the time he rebooted and got back on line, Ken was gone.

***

Later that evening, Herb was lying in bed watching *I Love Lucy* reruns when the phone rang.

"Herb, Pick me up. I'm at the airport."

"Ken?" Herb asked. "Is that you?"

"Who the fuck did you think it was? Now, pick me up at the fucking airport."

"That's Lincoln, Nebraska. It's an hour away. Why don't you take a limo?"

"God damn you!" Ken shouted. "Now get in your fucking rental car and pick me up at the fucking airport."

Herb shivered as he heard Ken slam the phone down. He sat there trying to decide what to do when the phone rang again.

"Herb. Where are you?" Ken demanded.

"I'm here. In my room," Herb replied.

"Did you tell Peter anything?"

"No," Herb answered. "He's not even here. He's with Anna in ..."

"Shut up!" Ken screamed. "Just get the hell out here. You should've been on the road already. I'm sick and tired of waiting all day long. Don't say a damn thing to Peter and get your fucking ass here."

Herb pondered the situation knowing that yesterday, Ken was in total control. He wouldn't dare defy Ken lest he'd be back on the street drinking again. Ken was powerless now. Yet, Herb longed to know what Ken was about. He even felt sorry for the pathetic author.

"OK, Ken. I'm leaving now."

"Good. I'm at Terminal B. I shaved my mustache and dyed my hair black. I'm wearing a green tie and there's a small stain on my pants: must have spilled something on them in the bathroom on the flight."

"OK," Herb said. "I'll get you a room and be right out."

"NO!" Ken shouted. "Just get here. I've already taken care of the room."

***

Herb saw Ken pacing outside when he arrived at the Lincoln International Airport. He pulled the car up to the curb and said, "Hey Ken. How you doing? You look good with the mustache off and no grey hair. Looks like you lost some weight, too."

"I can't eat a fucking thing with all this shit going on with Peter."

"I don't know, Ken," Herb replied. "I'd think you'd be happy for Peter. He's sure the happiest I've seen him since I got into this book. And I'm not sure why it bothers you. Peter still needs your help figuring out what to do, and learning how to be in a relationship. Remember, Anna's still married, and Peter's not Jewish. They've got a lot of issues to work out, either in therapy or in literature, as they move along."

"Herb, my books aren't about happiness," Ken scoffed. "They're not feel good comedies. Even when my characters do well, they're never really joyful. Sure, I use humor, but that's just to help the reader tolerate the awful things I say. My books tell of misery and human suffering, pathos and the struggle to find meaning and purpose out of hopelessness and despair. My characters don't just run around, get laid, and learn to do the mambo whenever the hell they want to."

Herb looked at Ken deeply. Not wanting to believe what he was hearing, he tried to lighten things up.

"Really, you should try the mambo. It's a good dance."

Herb began to move his feet while vocalizing a mambo beat. "Da da da da da da. Da da da da da da."

"Stop it!" Ken screamed. "Let's just go before I re-write you into a drag queen."

***

When they got to the Holiday Inn, Ken cautiously looked around before getting out of the car. Sure that Peter was not around, he scurried to the lobby and approached the clerk at the front desk. Holding his hat to cover his face, Ken asked for his room.

"Is that for one, sir?" the clerk asked.

"Yes," Ken replied. "Now give me my damn room."

The clerk looked surprised but contained his reaction and asked Ken, "Will that be smoking or non-smoking."

"Idiot!" Ken responded. "I've already paid for my room. I called you two days ago and asked for Room 427. You idiots told me it would be ready whenever I got here."

"Oh, yes," the clerk said, now remembering the strange request to keep Room 427 free. "It's all ready sir."

Ken took the key and picked up his bags, walking to the room. Herb followed. When they got there, he commented, "Hey. This is the room Peter and Anna had when they got here before moving to the Honeymoon Suite."

"Fuck you!" Ken shouted. "They're not on a honeymoon. They're pathetic, tragic, literary characters who need to learn a lesson about listening to their author. I don't want to hear this honeymoon shit anymore."

Herb shrugged his shoulders and said, "That's fine, Ken. I won't say anything more. But you're gonna have a hard time teaching them anything. Those kids are really in love."

Ken looked at Herb with hate in his eyes. He then raised his hands, put them squarely on Herb's chest, and pushed him back hard, making him stumble and fall just outside the door. Ken slammed the door shut leaving Herb on the hallway floor.

Ken then turned on his laptop and opened his file, *Peter Squared Sequel*. He thought to himself, *Idiots. They're all idiots. But I think this will work. As long as I'm here, I can keep my eye on Peter while I finish writing the book.*

Ken quickly recorded the story of his arrival at the airport and his trip to the hotel with Herb. He saved the text, loosened his tie and laid down on the bed.

Comfy bed. Ken looked to his right and saw a second, double bed.

I wonder which bed Peter slept in, Ken thought.

Let's think: Peter is so number obsessed, he probably had a formula. Ken played with the numbers deciding that Peter would call the first bed he encountered entering the room Bed No. 1, the second bed, Bed No. 2. Since Peter was sure to think it odd for him to be sharing a room with a woman, he'd want to sleep in the odd numbered bed.

Ken lay down in Bed No. 1 imagining Peter and Anna making love. Before long, Ken pictured Anna riding busses, making out, giving blow jobs, stopping at bars, having anal sex, getting beaten by Sol and raped by her father. Ken imagined Anna, dark and thin, a poignant lost look in her eyes, lying in the bed while the voices screamed. He laughed imagining impotent Peter trying to screw her. She must have hated him, closing her eyes, wishing it would be over. *I want a real man like you,* Ken could imagine her saying as his organ got hard. Ken pictured her lying beneath him while his large, throbbing penis penetrated her hole. Anna cried and shivered, melted and screamed. Beads of sweat formed on her brow, and mucus ran from her nose. Her vagina bled and her body quaked. Anna climaxed over and over again to Ken's magnificent thrusts, finally digging her nails deeply into his skin while the couple climaxed together. Ken looked down to see a large semen stain on the bedspread beneath him.

THE ELECTION

Editor's Note: Because of Ken Goldberg's deteriorating mental state, the publisher has cancelled his contract. Rabbi Moishe Pearlman has graciously agreed to author this final section. Rabbi Pearlman's impressive religious and secular literary credentials include eighteen highly regarded commentaries on Talmudic law and his delightful Dad-Daughter Haggadah. He writes the weekly gossip column, *Matchmaker, Matchmaker*, for the Hasidic Daily World and is the chief screenwriter for the popular television series, *The Little Schul on the Prairie*. On a disconcerting note, we have been unsuccessful in our efforts to enjoin Ken Goldberg from staying in Anderson, Nebraska and entering this book. Any appearances by him in this last section are without the publisher's permission. The publisher will vigorously pursue civil and criminal remedies to protect this book from his further influence.

25 BORN AGAIN

On Friday morning, Peter woke to hear his hotel telephone ring. Struggling to free himself from Anna's sleepy embrace, he reached for the phone and said, "Hello?"

"Who's that?" Anna scowled. "Make 'em go away."

"It's Herb."

"Shit! What does Ken want now?"

Peter held his hand up motioning to Anna to stop talking, "What's up, Herb?" Peter asked.

"Uh-huh, uh-huh, uh-huh," Anna heard Peter say as she sat up in bed, her expression cross.

"Is that necessary? This is our first night really alone."

Following a pause, Peter reluctantly said, "OK. We'll be there."

Anna frowned, pursed her lip and sulked, "No. We're not going."

"We have to. Remember what happened yesterday?"

"How could I forget?" she said, a smile starting to break through as she tried to hold onto her sour expression.

"Not that, silly. In court. Remember, I'm running for mayor."

"And you should," Anna said. "You'll be great. But why are we getting up so early this morning."

"The election's Tuesday. We really gotta move."

"Tuesday. This is June. Elections are held in November."

"Not in Anderson. Elections here are always on Flag Day. I'll explain later. Now get some clothes on that cute ass and let's go. We'll pick up where we left off tonight, and tomorrow night, and every night after that."

"I love you," Anna said hugging him one more time before getting out of bed.

***

152

Herb and the committee were already there when Peter and Anna entered the banquet hall at the Holiday Inn. Shocked to see a large *Branstill for Mayor* banner, telephones, copiers, fax machines, boxes of campaign buttons and literature, Peter said, "Wow. You've been working, haven't you?"

"All night," Herb replied, "while you two were getting your beauty rest. Get lotsa sleep?" he added winking his eye.

Peter and Anna took seats at the table with Herb and the rest of the Branstill for Mayor campaign committee: Dave, Harold, Penny, Rabbi Pearlman, Andrew, and Former Mayoral Candidate Benson.

"Now, we've got four days," Herb opened. "The election's on Tuesday. I hope no one minds but I've appointed myself campaign manager. OK?"

No one dissented. Several members of the committee nodded their heads yes.

"OK. Dave, you're our detail man. I want you to handle press releases, set-ups, transportation, wardrobes, PA systems, anything and everything to make the campaign run smoothly. Can you do it?"

"Hell, yes," Dave replied. "You know, I majored in administration in college before my first psychotic breakdown."

"Great," Herb answered. "It'll look good on your application if you decide to go back.

"Andrew. You're the finance guy. People! If you need money. Here's your man." Andrew flashed the thumbs up sign in return.

"By the way. Let's not forget where these funds are coming from, Harold, take a bow."

Harold made a fake bowing gesture still sitting in his seat followed by a salute with his right hand.

"Hate to tell you, but I'm not as noble as you think. Once the campaign is over, I'm setting up WS Entertainment, Inc., a subsidiary of Warner and Sterling Industries. Our first location will be here in Anderson. Right, Mayor Branstill?"

"Zoning?" Peter quipped. "Did I hear someone say the word variance?"

"Now, Rabbi Pearlman. You're our liaison to the religious community. Do you want to tell us ... Oh, shit! I forgot the opening prayer. Did you want to say something, Rabbi?"

"Sure," Rabbi Pearlman replied.

Keeping with the levity of the meeting so far, he said, "Baruch Atau Adonoy, Elohanu Melach, now, let's win this damn thing!"

"Dad," Anna said affectionately, touching her father's hand realizing that she knew, for the first time in years, that he wasn't going to shove it up her ass.

"Penny. You have a lot of contacts with the civic leaders of the town, particularly people outside the Anderson family. Any thoughts?"

"Yes, but I'd rather hear what Benson says first. He knows the community better than I do. What do you think, Bufford?"

"I reckon you fellas are like the tortoise trying to ketch that dang hare. The Andersons have this town wrapped up tighter'n a stallion on a mare in heat. I jist ran cause it was somethin' to do. Hell, I didn't even want the dang job. And frankly, Rufus ain't doing so bad. I figures you got a helluva job if ya wanna win this dang thing."

"Well, we want to win it and we are gonna win it," Herb responded. "What do you think would happen if the election were today."

"Why you'd get crushed flatter'n a tire that jist ran over some dang nails."

"I don't think it's that bad," Harold added. "CNN has Peter with 42% of the vote, and he just came into town."

"That's 9 points short of 51%," Peter said.

"What does that mean in actual votes?" Andrew asked.

"I don't know," Benson said, "Only 2000 people voted the last dang time."

"Forty-two percent of 2000 is 840 votes," Peter said. "We'd need to convince 161 people who would've voted for Anderson to vote for me. On the other hand, if Anderson would've gotten 1160 votes to my 840 votes today, I could also win be convincing 321 people who weren't going to vote to vote for me. So, if x is the number of voters previously committed to Anderson who switch to me and y is the number of voters who didn't plan to vote but now vote for me, I win with any solution (x,y) where $2x+y$ is greater than or equal to 321."

Herb laughed, "He may have gotten laid but he's still the same old Peter."

Anna who was seated next to Herb slapped him saying, "Herb!"

"Sorry Anna. I didn't mean it that way," Herb said, his face now red. "So, how are we going to get these votes."

Rabbi Pearlman spoke next. "Peter'll win the Jewish vote. That's 38 Type Y votes from our group. The Jews who are already here are pure Type X votes."

"There ain't no dang Jews here!" Benson shouted out.

"Sure are," the Rabbi replied. "You just don't know it cause everyone here is so damn prejudiced; they hide their heritage. But, that's going to change. Once we build the synagogue, the Jewish Community Center, and set up a Yeshiva, they'll come here in droves. In twenty, thirty years, Anderson will be a predominately Jewish town."

"Hmmph," Benson grunted, when Andrew interrupted the interchange. "Rabbi, are you sure they'll all vote for Peter? He isn't Jewish you know."

"True. What's your position on Israel, Peter?"

"It seems like a nice place. There's a website with hot girls from Tel Aviv. It's very good."

"Tel Aviv," the Rabbi said. "That's a good start. Why not start a student exchange program and announce it at the first Annual Hasidic-Christian Pitch-In Picnic today?"

"Great idea," Herb chimed in hoping to stop this discussion and move on to the next order of business.

"Benson. Any ideas where we can get some votes?"

"Kiwanis. It's the only dang place in town you don't find Andersons. They're all Rotarians. Farmer Brown was gonna talk 'bout cross-fertilization of wheat but he fell off his dang ladder th'other day. They need a speaker more'n a pig needs slop. I can get Peter on today. And the lunch is great. It's better'n a dang thunderstorm in the middle of a drought."

"Can't do that. Peter's got to be at the picnic."

"Can't pass on Kiwanis no more'n a hungry farm boy can pass on a piece of Flo Anderson's homemade apple pie. Ya need the votes, and I already promised."

"What can we do?" Herb asked.

"I'll do it," Anna said.

"What do you think?" Herb asked, looking at Benson.

"Hell yes! A pretty thang like her. They'll love her more'n a coyote wants to get into a chicken coop."

"OK. Peter does the picnic, Anna Kiwanis," Herb said jotting it down.

"Now, the media. Where do we stand there?"

Andrew fielded this question. "We've got it covered. Harold's got some of his best advertising men putting together the ad campaign right now. Watch."

Andrew picked up the remote control starting a video on a large, projection TV screen. To everyone's surprise, the commercial showed Peter describing his vision of a better Anderson. He even attacked Mayor Anderson for allowing a peep show/bowling alley into town. The ad ended with the campaign theme song:

> Happy Days are here again,
> Peter Branstill's here and you know when,
> He cleans up this town it will be swell,
> And the Andersons can go to [pause]
> Happy Days are here again.

"Catchy," said Anna.

"Pretty gutsy," added Peter. "You sure we want to hang the peep show on him. After all, I brought it here."

"Doesn't matter," Harold said. "We air this Monday night. It'll be too late for him to make that point."

"By the way, where did you get those clips. I don't remember making those speeches. This isn't something Ken wrote, is it?" Peter asked.

"No," laughed Harold. "The boys in advertising say it's state of the art, virtual reality. They had some graduate students at the University of North Carolina whip it up from a few pictures we sent them of Peter. Hard to believe they can do that."

"What about the press. Is the local paper covering the campaign?" Herb asked.

"We're way ahead of local coverage," Andrew said. "This campaign is making national news."

"I know," said the Rabbi, "That's how we knew Anna was here. Even before you decided to run for mayor, all the networks were covering the bowling alley, peep show story."

"But, how's that gonna help Peter's campaign?" Herb asked. "Don't we need local coverage?"

"No," Penny jumped in. "Everyone watches CNN. The psychological effect of bringing Anderson national attention will help Peter much more than it helps Anderson."

"And it can't hurt Peter's chances at a run for the governor's mansion next year," Andrew said.

"Let's challenge Anderson to a debate," Harold suggested. "They're sure to cover it."

"Great idea!" Herb replied.

"Hm," thought Peter out loud. "I don't know if I'm quite ready for that."

"Sure you are," Herb responded. "You'll do great. I'll prepare you personally Sunday morning."

"Can't do that," Benson said. "Rabbi Pearlman's plan or not, we got more Christians here than bees on a dang honeycomb. He's gotta go to church Sunday morning."

"Don't forget Saturday morning either," Rabbi Pearlman protested. "You won't get the Jewish vote if you're not in schul."

"OK," Herb said. "We've got the picnic and Kiwanis at noon. Schul Saturday morning, church on Sunday. We need to fill the rest of the weekend. Penny, Bufford. Get some ideas to Dave right away. What else?"

"I think we still have a problem because of *Peter Squared*. Peg Anderson just brought in a big shipment. She owns Anderson's Book Nook. They could sell out. Everyone'll know about your sexual habits by

Election Day," Dave commented.

"And not just Peter," Harold chimed in. "I'm up to the chapter that describes Anna's shenanigans. I like the bit about you taking it up the ass, but it'll still hurt us."

"This is a big problem, Herb," Penny said. "We're really between a rock and hard place. We've gotta debate Anderson but you know he'll bring it up."

The group sat silently for a moment until Peter spoke out. "I'm not going to be ashamed of my past. I'll just tell my story openly and honestly."

"That'll work!" Benson proclaimed. "Folks here love born again better'n potato salad at a picnic."

"Tell them you'll fast on Yom Kippur," the rabbi added. "It'll all be forgiven."

As Benson and the Rabbi scowled at each other, Herb suddenly perked up and said, "Barbara Walters. Can we get an interview with her?"

"I think so," Harold said. "She went to college with my wife's cousin. I'm sure she'll do it."

"Great!" Herb exclaimed. "This'll be better than Bill and Hillary."

26 THE CRYPTOGRAMS

After the group dispersed, Herb went up to Ken's room at the Holiday Inn where he found Ken angrily pacing around.

"Calm down, Ken. It's not so bad. Peter's happy, and Anna doesn't hallucinate anymore. With a happy ending, you'll sell ten times more copies of this book than *Peter Squared*. People'll love it. I've even been thinking that we can adapt it into a musical. Watch."

Herb started shuffling across the room singing, to the tune of *Officer Krupke* from *West Side Story*,

Gee, Officer Barney, you don't understand.

Peter's got to peep because he's that kind of man.

It ain't that he's crazy. It's not what he ate.

It's just that he wants to masturbate.

"Damnit," Ken shouted as he threw a lamp across the room, knocking his Howdy Doody doll to the floor. "I don't write crap. I'm an intellectual and an artist. I don't care about sales. Someday, *Peter Squared* will be a classic. This book could have been a classic too if that goddamn Peter Branstill didn't fuck things up!"

"Be honest, Ken. How many copies of *Peter Squared* did you sell?"

"What's your point, Herb?" Ken said drawing dangerously close to his friend, his finger pointing. "What's your fucking point!."

"Look," Herb replied, backing away as far as he could. "The first book was great, but it never sold well. What makes you think this second book will do any better the way you want to write it?"

"Come on, Herb," Ken said derisively. "It'll catch on. Even if I have to wait until I'm dead, it'll be a great best-seller."

"What do you mean by that?" Herb demanded.

"Don't worry," Ken replied, going to the dresser where he picked up a picture of his wife and children.

Ken's calmness scared Herb. "I'm calling Penny."

Herb started to pick up the phone, but Ken grabbed it and slammed it back down. "I don't need Penny, I don't need no two-bit social worker. Did you forget, Herb? I'm a psychologist."

Taking a deep breath, Herb replied. "I know you are. And you're a good one, too. But this can happen to anyone. You don't have to feel ashamed. And remember how you developed Penny in *Peter Squared*. She's very insightful. I'm sure she can help."

Ken stumbled looking for words in reply but he couldn't think of them. He sat on the bed next to Herb, his head in his hands. "I used to be like her."

"I know you were, Ken. And you can be that way again. But now, you need help."

"I don't know who the hell I am, Herb. You're right, I was just like Penny once. That's how I got all my ideas for the book. But it sapped every damn thing out of me. I was exhausted and tired and wanted to call it quits. But everyone told me I was a writer and that I should keep writing. I'm not up to this, Herb. This second volume is too damn much for me to do. I can't focus on my patients and all I want to do is write plot, control people, have them masturbate and make them as crazy as I can. I was never like that before."

"Come with me, Ken. We're going to see Penny."

Ken cried and hugged Herb before agreeing to see Penny.

***

The Kiwanians welcomed Anna warmly to their group. Knowing that she was Jewish, they prepared a special lunch of Empire Kosher chicken in a casserole made with Campbell's Cream of Mushroom soup.

After lunch, the president of Kiwanis introduced Anna. She walked to the lectern and said, "I want to thank you for inviting me to speak today. In less than a week, I've learned that the finest people in the world live right here in Anderson, Nebraska."

Anna waited for the applause to die down before she could go on. "You all know that my fiancé, Peter Branstill, is running for mayor. The record is clear. He is the candidate for decency, tolerance, prosperity, freedom, family values, individual enterprise, education, civic services, parks, recreation, community development, law and order, rugged individualism, social programs, and a dynamic student exchange program with Tel Aviv. That's my fiancé, that's your candidate, and that's the next mayor of Anderson, Nebraska." With her voice at a feverish pitch, Anna concluded. "Peter Branstill."

The Kiwanians rose to their feet in hearty applause. After the applause again died down, Anna continued.

"You don't need me to point out the many gifts Peter has to offer. I will not presume that I can tell you, the educated and urbane citizens of Anderson, how to vote. Only you, the people of Anderson, the heart and soul of this community, its leaders in commerce, service, and faith, its movers and shakers, only you can decide who you think is best to be this fine town's mayor."

Anna took another breath while the crowd once more applauded her.

"Instead of giving you another tired and worn, hackneyed campaign speech, today I'm going to do something different." Anna reached out and took the hands of the Kiwanians on each side of her. As they all took their neighbors' hands, the group formed a large circle outside the tables in the middle of the room.

"You've seen me dance nude to Klezmer music. Now, everybody, with your clothes on, let's do the hora."

On cue, a Kiwanian stationed by the sound system pushed a button causing the sounds of Hava Nagila to fill the air. Spontaneously, the men began to dance, around the room, holding hands, following Anna's lead as she taught them the hora.

***

Peter walked around the park, shaking hands with Christians and Jews alike, careful to avoid direct contact with the Hasidic women, not wanting to offend them in case they were unclean. Peter kissed a baby, shared a laugh with the Reverend Smith, and argued a small legal point with Rabbi Pearlman, using his best Talmudic insights. So engrossed in the camaraderie of the event, he didn't notice Andrew walk to the speaker's platform and announce. "Ladies and Gentlemen. I give you an honored resident of Anderson, Nebraska, a man who can dance circles around his opponent with quadratic equations, no longer a nerd, from peep show to politico, a man who doesn't mind getting his hands dirty fighting for the people, a fiction come true, the next Mayor of Anderson, Nebraska, Peter Branstill."

The crowd applauded as Peter hopped onto the platform. His tie half undone and his shirttails coming out, he called out, "You folks know how to throw a helluva party."

There was laughter and clapping. A Yeshiva boy raised his fist in the air. "Shalom Brother!"

When the crowd quieted down, Peter took a deep breath and said, "This election is not about me. This election is not about Mayor Anderson. This election is about the people of Anderson."

After more applause, Peter went on.

"We're not talking about individuals. I don't question Rufus Anderson's ability to run the city services. Hell, he can pick up my garbage anytime. I'm talking about values. I'm talking about people. And I'm talking about a vision for Anderson, Nebraska that will propel us into the 21st century."

With his voice raised, Peter went on, "I see an Anderson, Nebraska that is a model of life, liberty, and the pursuit of happiness. I see a Mecca of wealth and prosperity, where family and community, black and white, Jew and gentile, gay and straight, husband and wife, worker and boss, doctor and patient, bowler and pinsetter, and dancer and peeper, can all live together with love and respect, while having a damn good time."

Peter ended his speech saying, "Anderson, I love you," throwing kisses out to the crowd.

***

Herb and Ken arrived at the mental health center which was two blocks from the hotel, on East Main Street. At first, Penny was awed to meet Ken Goldberg and almost asked him to autograph her copy of *Peter Squared*. Quickly, she recognized the signs of a man in the midst of a nervous breakdown, her expression turning somber. "What happened?" she said, looking more at Herb than Ken.

"He's in bad shape, Penny. He needs to go in."

"Why do you say that, Herb?"

"I've been there before. You know that."

"Of course." Penny turned to Ken and asked, "Would you like to talk?"

***

After Penny took Ken into her office, Herb got on his cell and called Dave.

"What have we got, Dave?" Herb asked.

"Things are going great, Herb. Anna was a knockout at Kiwanis and Peter had them eating out of his hand at the picnic," Dave replied. "CBS took a straw poll and gives Peter 43% of the vote."

"Good," Herb said, "but still far from enough. Whadaya have lined up for the rest of the day?"

"Benson called an hour ago. He's got Peter scheduled to sign *Peter Squared* at Peg's Book Nook. Figured we'd get the upper hand before Rufus can say anything. Harold called and Barbara Walters is on. Rabbi Pearlman asked for Anna at an old field right outside town. He just bought the land and plans to set up the Jewish Quarter there. He wants to kick off the project by having Anna lay the cornerstone for the new mikva. The symbolism of a clean start for Anderson will be tremendous. We're still working on the rest of the day. I'm waiting to hear from Bufford regarding photo ops at the movie theater, fly fishing tournament and Flo's diner, and from Penny for visits to the nursing home, hospital and cub scout camp out tonight."

"Oh, shit," Herb responded. "I forgot all about her. She's seeing Ken right now. I think they're going to put him away, in the hospital."

"That's good. It'll keep him out of our hair. Make sure you get his laptop. We don't want him writing any text. He could have Peter masturbating in the middle of the street. It's only one day and Peter's still vulnerable for a relapse."

"Don't we all know," Herb chuckled. "Been through that enough times myself...

"Wait," Herb went on. "Penny's coming out. Let me find out what's going on with Ken and I'll get back to you later. Keep up the good work."

"Don't forget to remind Penny to call me when you're done," Dave added.

***

"Herb," Penny called. "Can you join us?"

Herb followed Penny to the back of the clinic and into her office. He saw Ken sitting on a chair in a corner of the room, biting his fingernails, rocking back and forth. Herb took the seat next to him.

"Dr. Bowman is giving Ken some medicine to take. Here are some samples. Can you keep your eye on him until Monday?"

"You're not admitting him!?" Herb asked, shocked and outraged. He looked at Ken who stayed silent as he rocked.

"We can't. His insurance company wouldn't approve the admission. We tried but they say he doesn't meet criterion."

"What bullshit. Damned managed care."

"I agree. But there's nothing we can do. We have to keep him out unless he does something really crazy. Can you keep an eye on him?"

"Not really," Herb protested, "There's a lot to do for Peter's campaign.

"I know. But he's not getting in regardless."

"I'll try my best," Herb said. "That's all I can do."

"I know. Here's our number in case there is an emergency. Otherwise, bring him back Monday at 9:00 and we'll start him in the day program."

"Thanks, Penny," Herb said. "Are you OK with that, Ken?"

Ken, who was now muttering to himself, nodded while he rocked.

Penny shrugged her shoulders while Herb motioned Ken to get up.

"You'll be fine, Ken. Go back to your motel room. Get a good night's rest. I'll buy you a book of cryptogams so you have something to do."

***

Ken sat on the corner of the bed in his room, looking at the book of cryptograms Herb gave him. He opened it and stared blankly at the first puzzle before absent-mindedly letting it slip out of his fingers and fall to the floor. Ken looked down but couldn't muster the energy to pick it up. Ken noticed Howdy Doody lying on the floor where he left him after throwing the lamp. *I should pick him up,* Ken thought.

For the next five minutes, Ken kept repeating to himself, *I should pick him up,* when he heard a knock on the door.

"Hi Ken," Anna said, as she opened the door. It's good to see you again."

Anna and Ken walked hand in hand out of the room.

"Do you like knishes?" Ken asked Anna.

"Yes, very much," she replied.

"There's a vender across the street. They sell potato knishes. Would you like one?"

Anna smiled. "No thanks. They're not Kosher. You know, I'm Hasidic. I only eat Glatt Kosher."

"Oh," Ken replied. "I didn't know the difference. You know, I'm no longer Jewish."

Anna laughed. "I didn't think you were."

Ken and Anna chuckled, the inane laughter of people in love.

Ken asked, "Where can I get you a Glatt Kosher knish?"

"I'd rather get a room," Anna replied.

Anna began to shake as she and Ken walked back into his room.

"I'm scared," Anna said.

"Don't be," Ken replied.

Relaxed by his soothing words, Anna opened her arms and gave Ken a hug. Soon, they were lying in bed, undressed. Ken ran his fingers gently through Anna's hair. He pulled her close and kissed her on the lips. Anna purred, offering her tongue in response. When Anna turned over to offer Ken her rear, expecting him to enter the way her father often did, he gently pushed her back and said, "Lie back. This is for you."

Ken warmly caressed Anna's breasts while she lay on her back. He took her firm nipple into his mouth and sucked it gently, a rolling motion. As Anna began to moan, Ken moved his hands slowly along her abdomen, purposefully delaying his approach to tease her and heighten her desire. By the time he touched her vagina, she was trembling with desire. Anna opened her legs to invite Ken in, but he held back, gently separating the folds of her labia and licking her clitoris with the tip of his tongue. Anna screamed

163

while Ken continued to touch her and lick her, pressing slightly harder as she became wet with passion. Having orgasm after orgasm, Anna begged Ken to enter her, but Ken refused, extending the wait, as his tongue darted in and out of her. Finally, he pulled his head up from her vagina and brought his body over hers, kissing her passionately while his hard organ glided in.

27 A CHANCE ENCOUNTER

At 2:00 p.m., Peter arrived at Peg's Book Nook where several customers were waiting for him to arrive. Dave directed Peter to sit behind a table decorated with *Branstill for Mayor* campaign stickers, buttons and posters, and a sign announcing: **Book Signing Today**. Peter chuckled slightly to himself realizing he would have had to calculate the chair's Graduated Dirt Rating just three days ago, before sitting down. Peter picked up a pen and began signing his name on the inside front covers of the books. As the customers filed by and Peter signed their books intently, he failed to notice Rufus Anderson queue up in line.

"Good to see you, Peter," Rufus slyly said, holding his hand on his copy of *Peter Squared* which he had just placed on the table. Peering squarely into Peter's eyes, he said. "I'm looking forward to our debate."

"Oh ... uh ... hi, Rufus," Peter replied through a forced smile as he stood up to offer his hand.

Rufus rebuked the offer. Peter felt disquietingly ashamed when he realized he was glad to avoid contact, his old fear of dirt starting to come back.

Peter pictured Anna holding him tightly, saying, "All you have to do is decide that you're giving up Ken. You may hurt. You may mourn. It'll be hard. Just make that decision and I'll be by your side."

Don't give in, Peter told himself as he boldly reached out and grabbed Rufus' hand, forcing the handshake.

"May the better man win," Peter said, struggling to sound confident.

Peter reached for his pen, but Rufus whisked the book away and read,

Inside the school, the first voter in line, Peter walked up to the table, signed in, and entered the booth. There, Peter found a full-blown ballot like the sample mailed to him. Waiting for the screen to rise, his naked registrar behind, Peter soon realized that nothing would happen. As he heard the taunts, HA-HA-HA, HE WANTS A GIRL,

NO ONE WANTS YOU, he inadvertently put his hand in his pocket and began rubbing his penis.

"Could you sign the book here?" Rufus asked.

As Peter signed the book, his hand shaking slightly, Rufus added, "Hope you enjoy voting Tuesday."

***

After dedicating the mikva, Anna visited a nursing home where she had the residents in stitches telling old Yiddish tales and singing selections from *Fiddler on the Roof.* She unveiled Peter's plan to insure safety, security, and dignity for all of Anderson's senior citizens with tax incentives for people who visit their parents regularly. She collected a list of nursing home residents who needed transportation to the polls, in posh limousines, courtesy of the Branstill for Mayor Committee.

"The days are numbered when our older citizens must live in fear about how they'll survive. Over the next four years, Mayor Branstill will initiate a five point plan, geared to increase the quality of life for all senior citizens with affordable housing, subsidized utilities, state-of-the-art health care, free transportation and an overhauled public recreational program. These steps are sorely needed after so many years of indifference and neglect by the Anderson dynasty. We expect, once that Peter reveals the details Sunday night during the debate, even Rufus Anderson will be hard put not to give it his full support. After all, we all know Mr. Anderson is planning for his retirement right now, to start four days from today."

***

Ken looked at the book that was lying on the floor. He took a deep breath before reaching down to pick it up. His hand failing to reach the ground, Ken straightened up and took another deep breath before trying again. He reached down, this time his fingers touching the book even though he still failed to get it in his grasp. Ken sat up again and took another deep breath. Finally, he was able to reach down hard and hold himself in a bent position long enough to grab the edge of the cover between his thumb and index finger and bring it up.

Cryptograms, Ken muttered to himself. He slowly got up and moved from the bed to the desk where he put the book down and grabbed a pen from his pocket. Several crumbs popped out along with the pen. Ken looked in his pocket and saw an Oreo cookie he had started the night before. *I should eat,* thought Ken as he fished out the cookie and took a bite. Too tired to keep eating, he put the remaining cookie back in his pocket.

Ken scanned the first puzzle by looking for three letters that might stand for the word, *the*. He found *ʒry* in the middle of the puzzle. As he would typically do, Ken looked to see if there were other instances of *ʒr* representing the *th* combination and if the letter *r* did not reoccur except when it was preceded by *ʒ*. Ken also looked to see if *y* could be found elsewhere in the puzzle, since *e* is the most common letter of the English alphabet. Exhausted and confused, unable to concentrate at all, Ken put his pen down.

Five minutes later, Ken said to himself, *This isn't working*. He stared at the puzzle two minutes more and thought, *I should write*.

Ken went to his suitcase where he found his laptop which he placed on the desk after clearing a space by sweeping the puzzle book to the floor. Once his computer booted up, Ken opened his word processor and began to type:

Peter jerks off. Peter jerks off a lot. Watch Peter jerk off. 72%. You didn't do it right. Anna is a whore. Peter jerked off again. Peter is a jerk off. Peter is afraid of dirt. Peter is …

Shit, thought Ken looking at what he wrote. *This is really bad.*

***

Peter and Anna continued to stump hard the rest of the day. After the book signing, Peter jumped on a platform Dave set up outside the book store.

"My friends," Peter said to several people standing on the street. "I want to thank you for reading my book. Now please, *READ MY LIPS*. Citizens of Anderson. *NO NEW TAXES*.

'The days of tax and spend are over. The years of graft and corruption are a dark stain of the past. The insult of brash nepotism and sinful disregard for civil liberties, individual rights, personal initiative, and human dignity will be gone forever. Let Rufus answer to God and his conscience. Let you, the people of Anderson, cast your vote for progressive ideas, economic growth, high moral values, safe streets, human decency, clean air, and universal health care. Let's finally have a government that's of the people, for the people, and by the people. Thank you. God bless."

Later that evening, Peter joined a panel at the high school where he discussed the burgeoning drug problem facing Anderson. With no statistics to support his assertions, Peter claimed that Mayor Anderson had lost control and that drugs were rampant in the schools and on the streets. Peter outlined a 5-point program that included increased police presence, drug rehabilitation programs, vocational, educational, and recreational services for Anderson's youth.

Anna spent her afternoon at PROJECT HOPE, the women's crisis shelter. She played games with the children while their mothers attended Co-dependency Group. Later, she talked with the women using her best active listening skills. To Anna's surprise, the techniques they taught her at the Day Treatment Program really worked. She spent extra time with one woman who was married to a member of the Anderson clan.

In the evening, Anna started the bon fire at the Cub Scouts camp held behind the elementary school. Several 12-year-old boys giggled when one of them showed his friends his father's copy of *Peter Squared,* opened to a chapter describing Anna's sexual habits.

Exhausted yet exuberant, Anna headed out to meet Peter and Herb for a drink at the Anderson Lounge.

***

Ken looked at his computer again and saw, scrolling across the display, the screen saver he used:

KEN GOLDBERG. GREAT AUTHOR. MAN OF GENIUS. BIG DICK.

He turned to the window and thought, *it's getting dark.* Ken looked at his watch: *8:14 p.m.* Realizing he had been sitting for hours not knowing what he did, Ken pushed the ENTER button and saw the words he wrote reappear.

Awful, he thought as he deleted the file and started writing again,

As Anna came out of the shower, Peter turned his head down, afraid he'd offend her, embarrassed that he had seen her breasts. Peter marveled at their size and began to calculate the circumference of each tit. With the left breast slightly larger than the right, Peter came up with three figures: Right breast, left breast, average breast.

Noticing the semi-circular shape of her mammary glands, he started calculating their volume as well.

Better, Ken thought after rereading his words. Feeling hungry for the first time all day, Ken looked at the cookie in his pocket.

I need real food, Ken thought. He shut down his computer before getting up and walking to the door. On the way out, he picked up Howdy, kissed him, and placed him back on the dresser.

***

The Anderson Lounge is adjacent to the Anderson Room at the Holiday Inn. While eating his dinner, Ken could see his three characters pass by, Herb in the lead, Peter and Anna holding hands close behind.

Damnit!!! thought Ken, his heart racing, his mind swirling, and his face turning red as he reached out and picked up the steak knife on the table.

Hi Peter. I'm Ken. I'm so glad to meet you.

As Peter turns around and offers his hand, Ken plunges the knife deep into Peter's chest.

The threesome took their seats, Herb to the left, Anna in the middle, Peter on the right. Ken thought:

Herb, Anna, and Peter. I just HAP-pened to see them today. Anna spelled backwards is Anna. Peter should not re-PETE his mistakes.

Two men suddenly passed by, one blocking Ken's view of Herb,

Two fictional characters: visible. My old friend, Herb: not visible.

As the man stopped and faced his friend, he shifted his position slightly, ending up in front of Peter. Meanwhile, his friend obscured Ken's view of Herb.

Two men: not visible. One fuckin' whore: visible.

The friend made some quip. The first man leaned back to laugh causing his head to tilt in front of Anna instead of Peter.

Two minor characters: not visible. One dead man: visible.

***

Although he finished his meal, Ken stayed and stewed, waiting for his characters to leave for their rooms. Once gone, Ken got up and moved two feet to the left. He looked at his leftovers to make sure Peter hadn't floated through the air to hide in his gravy. He took eight more steps ahead, six steps to the right, and another ten steps forward, pleased to reach the cashier with a formula of perfect squares ($8^2 + 6^2 = 64 + 36 = 100 = 10^2$). Ken signed his bill and continued, mathematically, to walk back to his room.

***

In his room, Ken turned on the 11:00 p.m. news, where he saw a clip of Peter at the Hasidic-Christian Picnic, speaking from the podium, his shirttails flying out.

Fuckin' slob, thought Ken as he grabbed a copy of *Peter Squared* and opened it to the page where he described Peter's meticulous and compulsive dressing habits. *Damn you!* thought Ken as he tore the page out.

"A dark horse and a long-shot, Branstill has taken this small town by storm giving the Anderson clan its first serious challenge in three-quarters of a century. Now, let's find out who is the man behind the candidate?"

As the documentary went on, Ken heard a cacophony of voices screaming in his head.

"Who's the man!" Ken screamed out loud. "He's a fuckin' jerk! He's a fuckin' jerk who jerks off. A fuckin' jerk who's never fucked, but fuckin'

169

jerks off, always jerkin' off, never fuckin', jerkin', fuckin' fuckin' jerking off."

Ken tore the book to shreds and threw it on the floor. He pulled out his penis and urinated on it. The voices continued to scream, and Ken started smashing his head against the wall.

ONE, TWO, YOU'RE A JEW. THREE, FOUR, YOU'LL WRITE NO MORE. FIVE, SIX, A LITTLE DICK, SEVEN, EIGHT, YOU MASTURBATE. THEY MADE THEIR SELECTION. HE'LL WIN THE ELECTION. 72%. NOW DO IT RIGHT.

28 THE BREAK-IN

"People!" Herb called out. "Let's make this brief. We have lots to do. We picked up some points yesterday, but we're still behind. Dave, how does it look for today?"

"Pretty good," Dave answered. "We've got Peter at schul in the morning. Anna's having breakfast at ..."

"Wait," Herb stopped Dave. "Peter, are you ready for this. You're not Jewish. Do you know how to davan?"

"Practiced all night," Peter smiled as he pictured himself under Anna while she kept screaming *Oh God!*

"OK," Herb said. "But let's be careful. We can't have a hitch. We need the Lubovitch vote. Pearlman! Make sure you help him with his tallis ... Wait!! Where's Pearlman."

"It's Shabbot," Anna answered. "Daddy doesn't work on Saturday. Don't worry. He'll be at schul, and I'm sure he'll help Peter."

"What about the book?" Andrew asked. "Isn't he writing the story now?

"You're right," Herb replied. "Anna, did he say what he's going to do? I hope he wrote today's story before sunset last night."

"I don't know if he did," Anna answered. "But why does that matter? After all, things got better when Ken took a break and Daddy wasn't writing then."

"It got better for you, Anna," Peter replied, shaking his head. "You were out the moment he stopped writing, and didn't come back even after he erased our story. It was much harder for me. I'm a bit afraid he'll try his old tricks again."

"You got the laptop, Herb. Didn't you?" Dave asked.

"Shit!" Herb responded. "I was so upset when he didn't go in, I forgot all about it."

"This is a big problem," Penny added. "According to recent studies, victims of Author Induced Psychosis, particularly the main characters, are quite vulnerable to relapse in the first 48 hours of recovery."

"We can't afford Ken's interference," Herb lamented. "It's too close and there's too little time. Any chance you can get him to write, Anna? Just this once."

"Not a prayer," Anna replied. "He's Ultra-Orthodox."

After several moments of painful silence, Harold leaned forward and said, with a steely look in his eyes, "Then, let's do it."

"Do, what?" Dave asked.

"Turn off the tape," Harold told Peter. "This stays in the room."

***

At 8:00 a.m., Ken woke up. He went to the bathroom and urinated at a 45° angle. He showered with $1/7$ of a bar of soap, and dried the four quadrants of his body with a towel. He went to the closet and picked out, according to schedule, suit, shirt, tie, socks and shoe combination 42619. He walked to the dresser where he picked up the picture of his wife and family. *I love you, Teri,* Ken said softly, calling her by the name he gave her the day he bought the frame at AC Moore.

Ken returned to the desk and removed from the ice bucket an 8 oz container of milk, an 8 oz container of orange juice, and 2 strawberries, bought the day before. He checked his thermometer, 45°, cold enough to be safely consumed. He opened a single serving package of Shredded Wheat and emptied it into a Styrofoam bowl. After cutting the strawberries in equal quarters, he placed the pieces symmetrically around the circumference of the bowl. Wearing surgical gloves, Ken removed a straw from its package and placed it in the orange juice container. Bracing his right hand with his left, Ken carefully poured the milk uniformly on top of the cereal. He mentally halved the bowl five times so he could spoon out $1/32$ of the cereal, which he ate slowly making sure it touched each of the taste zones on his tongue.

After finishing breakfast, Ken went to his computer, adjusted it slightly to keep it equidistant from the edges of the table and turned it on. Soon, he began typing again,

Rabbi Pearlman handed Peter a tallis. Six inches from the edge about 2 feet 3 inches from the end, Peter saw a small stain. Snot, thought Peter as the Jews stood by, waiting for him to put the tallis on.

YOU'RE A JERK, PETER BRANSTILL. WE HATE YOU PETER BRANSTILL. YOU CAN'T EVEN DAVAN. 72%. NOW DO IT RIGHT.

Satisfied with his work, Ken got up and left his room to buy the food he would need for the next twenty-four hours.

***

"Shma Yishroel, Adonoy elohanu, adonoy, ehad," Peter sang out during Saturday morning service.

"That's very good," Rabbi Pearlman told Peter, "for someone who's not a Jew. I think you'll get the Jewish vote."

"Thanks" Peter said.

Soon, Peter was shaking hands with the other congregants, saying, "Good yontiff and Shabbat Shalom," careful not to talk politics on G-d's day.

Strangely, Peter began to feel dirty, cringing each time he took someone else's hand with his. He started working on equations in the back of his head, and began noticing the mathematical qualities of the people he met: their elliptical faces, cylindrical arms, non-perpendicular stances and asymmetrical noses. He noticed odors that emanated from under their arms, and shuddered to think of his penis dipped in Anna's fluids.

What's happening? Peter pondered, feeling like he was falling into a hole. Struggling for a clue, he looked around and saw a stain on his tallis.

Ken, thought Peter as he shook his head. *He's writing again.*

***

"So, whatcha got?" Barney asked Stan Anderson who worked as the weekend clerk at the Holiday Inn during summer break from Nebraska State.

"Don't know," Stan answered sounding a bit nervous. "Got a call from 327. The lady there thought she heard something odd from the next room."

"Like what?" Barney asked.

"Like a burglar?" the clerk answered.

"How would she know what a burglar sounded like?" Barney asked, feeling a bit annoyed.

"I thought the same thing," Stan replied. "But what could I do. I didn't want to go up there alone."

"No," Barney responded. "You did the right thing. Who's got that room by the way."

"That odd feller from New York," Stan replied.

"Odd fella? Odd noise?" Barney shrugged his shoulder. "Who knows what that Yank was doing in his room."

"I know."

"Well, let's go. We better check it out."

Stan and Barney took the elevator while Tex climbed the stairs in case someone tried to get out the back way.

In front of Ken's room, Stan and Barney listened quietly by the door, hearing scurrying sounds within.

"Sounds like a mouse," Stan chuckled.

"Could be a big mouse with a gun, too."

As Tex came out of the stairwell onto the floor, he called out, "Whatcha got ..."

"Sh," Barney said with his finger to his lips.

Tex walked quietly down the hall and joined the group, "Whatcha got?" he whispered this time.

"Someone's in there," Barney replied.

"Should I knock the door in?" Tex asked, eager to charge in.

"No," Barney answered, "We can't just go breaking doors down. Let's knock and see what's up."

When Barney knocked on the door, the sounds suddenly stopped. No one answered.

"That ain't no mouse, " Barney said to Tex. Knocking again he called out, "Police. Open up."

Suddenly there was a rush of feet and some other noises.

"They're opening the window," Stan called out.

"Break it down," Barney said.

"I've got the key!" Stan jumped in, pulling out the master key and placing it in the electronic slot. The door opened, Tex and Barney entered with their guns drawn. Stan shined a flashlight into the room.

Like a deer caught in a headlight, a man stood there, expression shocked, body still with his hands in the air.

Barney shook his head and put his gun down. "Bufford. What the hell are you doing?"

***

"Peter!" Herb called out when he saw Peter walk out of schul. Already feeling better Peter broke into a smile and said, "Things are going great, Herb. Even with Ken's shenanigans."

"We've got problems," Herb responded, cutting Peter off. "Bufford's in jail."

"Shit!" Peter responded. "What do they know."

"Nothing so far. I stepped in as soon as I heard and made sure he asked for an attorney. They can't talk to him without me there. Harold's bringing in a top notch guy from Lincoln. He'll take over as soon as he arrives later today."

"What if he deals? I'm sure the prosecutor's more interested in what he says than putting him away. After all, it's his brother who's running against me."

"He won't," Herb assured Peter. "Don't forget who's paying this lawyer's fee."

A bit wary, Peter said, "This is getting stickier than I like."

"Just keep in mind," Herb reminded him. "You know nothing. Deny, deny, deny."

"How about the laptop," Peter asked. "Did they get it?"

"No," Herb replied. "The clerk put it in the safe when the police didn't seize it. I don't think they knew it's what we wanted."

"What should I do."

"Nothing, right now. Just stay with the campaign. Hit Anderson hard on crime. Use this as an example about why they need you in office. Push tourism. Promise you'll refuel the economy by making Anderson a world class resort once you clean up the streets. The more you're on the offense, the less people will think you're involved."

***

"Mr. Goldberg," Stan called when Ken entered the lobby. "Can you come here a moment?"

Ken turned left, his eyes meeting Stan's. Picturing a straight line to the front desk, Ken noticed a potted plant on the left and a chair to the right, both intruding over the imaginary five foot wide path he would use walking from where he stood to Stan. Ken scanned the lobby until he found an elliptical route that would take him safely to Stan, with no barriers, in exactly sixteen (2^4) ordinary strides.

"I'm sorry to tell you. Someone broke in your room. The police caught one burglar, but the room's pretty messed up. I'm moving you to 439."

"What!" Ken shouted. "Who broke in?"

"We're not completely sure. They caught one local guy, but they're still investigating. They're sure he had an accomplice, maybe one of them agitators that came to town this week. The police should know more soon."

Ken stood still, his eyes glazed.

"Everything's in 439 now. We took special care with your antique doll. I have your computer back here. I didn't want to leave that to the bellman. I sent the maid up. She'll have the room ready for you in a moment."

"I don't need a maid," Ken said in a toneless voice as he reached over and picked up his computer.

"I think you do. The couple that was there last night just checked out.

175

And there aren't any other rooms. With this election going on, the press has pretty much taken things over."

Stan looked up and saw that Ken was simply walking away.

Once upstairs, Ken looked at the maid and said, "Get out of here."

Startled, she responded, "Sorry sir, but I just got here. It'll just take a minute."

"Get out," Ken said again, his voice eerie.

"Whatever you say," the maid answered.

As she tried to wheel her cart away, Ken grabbed it with his hand and in that same measured tone added, "Leave that here."

***

Looking at the room, Ken saw sheets on the floor, a beer can on the bed, several dresser drawers open. He turned to the bathroom where there was water on the floor. One of the towels was smudged with blue mascara. Ken sniffed a few times and was sure he smelled sex in the air. He turned the television on to see what scandal had gone on today. Who was raped? How many children were molested? What prostitute was having another child? Which politician had been caught with his pants down?

Ken thought back to his creation, Peter, a perfect man in an evil world, someone who managed his impulses through a series of rituals, masturbating to women from behind the glass partition, eating the same meals the whole year long, acting on his urges in powers of two. Through *Peter Squared*, Ken gave the world its ideal man. Yet, sadly, like Shelley's Frankenstein and Kubrick's Hal, Ken's creation had spun out of control. *It must be stopped, or it must be destroyed.*

Ken looked at his watch: 11:14 a.m, hours before Pearlman would get back to work. This was his chance to get Peter under control. With no time to waste, Ken picked up the vacuum and cleared a three foot wide path from where he stood to the desk, disinfected the chair, desk and laptop, and began to write,

Having masturbated just five times, Peter was brought before Judge Anderson, charged with jerking off outside powers of two. Herb vigorously argued Peter's case, claiming five's a perfect square in the Base Peter system. The prosecutor scoffed and called his first witness, the well-known expert, Ken Goldberg. Voir dired by the court in psychology, math, and literature, Ken described Peter as clinically sane, yet mathematically disturbed. "Good job, Jimbo," the judge told his brother. "I've heard enough. Guilty as charged. Sixty-four years."

Peter collapsed as Dave gasped, "That's two to the sixth."

29 THE VIRUS

Not yet aware of Bufford's arrest, Anna continued to campaign hard. She joined a group of early risers at Flo's diner. Grinning as she enjoyed Flo's special – eggs, hotcakes, bacon, and toast – Anna revealed Peter's plan to bring world class medical care to Anderson, Nebraska.

"Top doctors, state of the art research, major medical school affiliation: you can count on that with Peter at the helm. Be assured, the days will be gone, when you have to go to Lincoln to get your arteries cleaned out."

Everyone laughed as Anna asked Flo for an extra serving of bacon.

Next, she went to the library to read children stories while promising to stamp out illiteracy. Although no one knew of any children who couldn't read, Anna was convincing in her claim that the schools had declined. Then, Anna joined the Daughters of the American Revolution where she served as a judge for the Annual Flower Show, before visiting the ill at the local hospital and expanding on Peter's health care plans.

***

Peter joined Herb and Harold in Herb's room after throwing out the first ball at a Little League game.

"What's up," Peter asked as he entered the room. "We need to keep this short. I'm meeting the press at the sewage plant in 15 minutes. It's a nightmare what Anderson's done to the environment."

"Cut the crap, Peter," Harold said. "You know we made that up."

"Harold!" Herb responded. "Stop it! He's gotta believe what he says."

"I know," Harold answered. "I'm sorry about what I just said. I'm just so frazzled by this whole damn thing."

"It's OK. Don't worry about me. Just tell me what's happening," Peter replied.

"We think Ken's writing again. And we're not sure what he's going to say."

"I know. He started that crap this morning, putting snot on my tallis. Took me back a moment until I realized what had happened," Peter answered. "I haven't felt anything else since then. Haven't wanted to jerk off or felt dirty in any way. No voices. No calculations. What do you think he's saying."

"We're not sure, but they're trying to get Bufford to talk and they keep threatening him with sentences in powers of two," Herb said. "There's nothing in Nebraska law to support what they're saying."

"How long till sundown?" Peter asked.

"We were thinking the same thing. Let's say long enough to cause problems. We've got to do something now."

"What do you have in mind?" Peter asked.

"The way I figure it," Harold explained, "if we can't get his laptop, we've got to disable it."

"How?" Peter asked.

"Through a virus. The boys at UNC, the ones who put together those campaign ads: they're computer whizzes. When Ken's on line, we send it in an attached file and zap, he's all locked up."

"I think he has Norton's," Peter said.

"And MacAfee, and AOL virus protection, and just about every damn system there is. He's paranoid and knows what he's doing. But these college kids are good."

"Ken's gotta open the file," Herb chimed in.

"He will if it comes from Peter. Just give me your password for peter@lernerandbranstill.com."

***

As he walked to the sewage plant, Peter noticed, 42° to his right, a group standing around what appeared a speaker on a platform. Stepping back slightly so he could see what was happening from a more desirable 45° view, Peter rotated his eyes to the right without moving his head and saw Mayor Anderson speaking to the crowd, his wife by his side. Peter couldn't hear what Rufus was saying as his eyes stayed focused on Mrs. Anderson's bust. A probable C cup, Peter began estimating their MGV (mammary gland volume)...

"You've got mail," Ken heard, interrupting his writing. Ken toggled the screen to look in his mailbox. There, he saw a message from peter@lernerandbranstill.com with the words *I want back* in the subject box.

Ken smiled, *It's about time.*

Ken stopped and wondered if this could be a trick. *No. Peter's not that bright.*

Ken moved the curser to Peter's message and double-clicked. Before it opened up, a message popped up on the screen to warn Ken that files from unknown senders could damage his computer. *It's from Peter,* Ken said to himself. Still, Ken went to the websites for each of his virus protection programs and downloaded their updates. He then used each to scan his computer before returning to Peter's message and opening it up. Ken's screen went blank.

Desperately, Ken hit alt-TAB hoping to toggle back to his word processing program. The display remained blank. He then hit CTRL-ALT-DELETE to reboot his machine. Nothing happened. He hit Escape and Enter, then the space bar sixteen times. No response. He disconnected the power by disengaging the battery before trying to start his laptop again. He began hitting the keys haphazardly, breaking his longstanding practice of engaging the keys with steady, evenly paced strokes. Ken shook the laptop with hopes that his words would fall to the floor. He punched the laptop sharply with a closed fist. He bent the screen backward, snapping it off. He took out a screwdriver and began prying the keys loose. He took out his lighter and tried to set the motherboard on fire. He took out his hammer and began smashing the laptop to bits. He cocked back the hammer and sent it hurling into the mirror on the wall.

With a menacing stare, Ken said to himself, *I'm Ken Goldberg.* He replayed his last thought, *Peter must be stopped, or he must be destroyed.* Ken stood up to see his partial reflection in the remaining broken glass. Taking his hand to his forehead, he saluted his image and repeated the oath he had written years ago.

I, Ken Goldberg, do solemnly swear that I will love my family, honor my country, live with dignity, stay loyal to our traditions, and always use my talents to benefit mankind. As a mathematician, I will never use numbers with malice toward others. As a psychologist, I will help people strive to be sexually chaste. As an author, I will write characters of high moral fiber. I am a soldier in the war against sin and will sacrifice my life to keep my characters pure.

Standing at attention, saluting his image, Ken listened to the voices in the back of his mind.

Onward, Christian soldiers, marching as to war,

With the cross of Jesus going on before.

Christ, the royal Master, leads against the foe;

Forward into battle see his banners go!

Looking at his sorry body reflecting from the fragments of the mirror with the election just two days away, Ken knew he would have to train. He thought back to his days in Viet Nam, a war hero, the last man standing, catching bullets in midair as he fought the Viet Cong.

YOU IDIOT. YOU NEVER WENT. YOU STAYED BEHIND.
4-F. A CERTIFIED PSYCHO. MENTAL MY ASS.

***

Peter skillfully stayed focused on his campaign speech, hiding his worries as he stood before the crowd.

"My friends. We have a nightmare brewing right before our eyes. Why do you think our cancer rate tops the national average? Why do you think our children test so poorly? Why are we seeing an epidemic of respiratory disorders?"

As Peter went on with his unsubstantiated tirade, several well placed plants began coughing on cue. Peter went on to offer members of the audience a 12 point health screen, funded by the *Branstill for Mayor* Committee. As expected, 90% of the participants tested in the very high risk group. After the speech, Peter held a press conference.

The press corps asked for details so Peter expanded on his plan. They sought sources to back his claims so he cited several studies that Herb had just made up. Confident he was home free, Peter invited a final question. From the back of the room, a hand shot up.

"Yes," Peter responded. "You, in the back."

A voice called out, "Bob Woodward. Washington Post. What do you know about the break-in at the Holiday Inn?"

***

Ken stood by the front door of *Al's Video Shop*. On the outside, it looked the way he described it in *Peter Squared*. Ken walked through the door and directly to the counter where he leaned over, cupped his hand, and asked Al, "Can I see the List?"

Puzzled, Al asked, "What list?"

"You know, The List. Porn."

"Pornography!" Al shouted loudly pointing his finger in the direction of a door with the sign, 18 OR OVER, above it. "Over there."

"What about the list?" Ken demanded, remembering how he described John secretly renting porn when he visited this religiously conservative Midwestern town, in *Peter Squared*.

"You mean like under the counter in unmarked boxes?" Al laughed. "Times have changed. We haven't had that in ten years. Just go in that room and get whatever you want."

Shaking with rage, Ken walked to the adult section where he saw everything prominently displayed on the shelves. Holding his head trying to control the pain, Ken thought. *Damn that Peter. Now he's fucking with Peter*

Squared.

Ken quickly grabbed the first 32 tapes he could find and brought them to the counter to check them out.

"Sure you've got enough?" Al quipped.

Lost in his own thoughts, missing Al's sarcasm, Ken said, "No. I want *Taxi Driver*, too."

"Now, that's a damn good movie," Al said as he went down the aisle and fetched Ken a copy of Robert Deniro's classic film.

***

At 6:30 p.m., Herb met Peter and Anna at the movie theater.

"They get a big crowd Saturday night. It's a great place to tout the family values theme," Herb explained. "Give 'em these *Branstill for Mayor* popcorn bags.

"Right now, my favorite family value is staying out of jail. Did you hear about the press conference?"

"Yes," Herb responded. "Dave called me. He's pretty worried"

"He should be," Peter answered. "He's the one who's gonna get caught in the crossfire. Bufford's a local and Harold's gonna protect himself with all his money. Dave's the perfect patsy. I don't like how this feels."

"Worse comes to worst, his psychiatric history could help him," Herb added. "We tell him he did it cause he ran out of his Thorazine."

Peter shrugged his shoulders with a cynical expression on his face.

"On the bright side," Herb went on, "there's been a jump in the polls. People may not really care about the break-in. NBC has you at 48%. We hear there are some Anderson family crossovers, maybe 17% of the clan. We're trying to get one of them to speak out for you."

30 SPECIAL FORCES

At 6:00 am, Ken climaxed the 28th time since coming back to the room with his collection of two to the fifth pornographic tapes. He thought back to Peter who was moaning with pain, crying in Anna's arms, and ready to call it quits with only four masturbations left to go. *What a jerk giving up on the brink of purity.*

In contrast, Ken felt invigorated and refreshed, the best he recalled in years. With each climax, he could sense a cleansing effect as the poisonous semen bled out of his system. *Two more hours and I'm there.* Without needing to masturbate ever again, Ken would have reached transcendence that very few achieve. His thinking clear, his senses sharp, his body pure, he would slay the dragon before drinking the hemlock to pass blissfully into a semen-less state: Not death, but rebirth, the virgin father, for time everlasting.

***

Peter and Anna were the last to enter campaign headquarters at the Holiday Inn Sunday morning. Lacking his usual cheerful smile and with no innuendos about the couple's late entrance, Herb simply said, "Everyone's here. Let's get started."

Peter sat down and noticed a copy of the Sunday Washington Post on the table. "What's this!? He asked.

"Read it," Herb answered.

His eyes starting to bulge, Peter saw a picture of himself standing at yesterday's press conference by a story with the title:

SCANDAL BREAKS OUT IN SMALL TOWN MAYORAL RACE
Prosecutor investigates brother's opponent in third-rate burglary

182

"This looks bad," Peter said.

"It gets worse," Herb replied. "Look at the paper underneath."

Peter looked down to see a copy of the New York Post with the lead story, in tabloid format:

ANDERSON-GATE
Branstill says "no comment" to peep show plumbers

"Shit!" exclaimed Peter. "What can we do?"

"Not much now," Herb answered. "The networks are all covering the story. You still have to deny, but no one's gonna believe you. There's too much doubt, and too little time for answers. And frankly, the answers ain't good."

"It's not fair," Anna pouted. "Peter's the best man and they're just gonna rake him through the mud. It's all Ken Goldberg's fault. First, he makes us crazy. Now, he's still making us crazy."

"I wouldn't blame Ken," Dave chimed in. "He's not doing anything new. We're the ones who decided on this cockamamie break-in plan."

"It wasn't cockamamie," Andrew responded hoping to defend his friend. "We were stuck. There wasn't anything else to do."

"We should have just stayed the course and taken our chances," Anna answered. "Maybe, I should have campaigned with Peter and kept my eye out for signs of Ken's tricks."

"Could've, would've, should've," Harold said, shaking his head. "There's lots of things we could have done, but that doesn't change a thing. Maybe, it wasn't a good plan. Believe me, I wouldn't be where I am today if I kept thinking about the things I did wrong. Mistakes are part of the game. The key is what are we going to do now."

"There's nothing we can do," Anna proclaimed holding up the local paper. "Look!"

PROSECUTOR IMPLICATES BRANSTILL
Outsider Plummets in Polls

"Give me those," Harold said, taking the papers from Anna. After pondering them carefully, he said. "Look. It says 'Third-rate burglary.' What if we could show there wasn't a burglary? It would look pretty bad for Rufus if he used the police for political purposes."

"But there was a burglary," Peter said. "And Bufford's in jail."

"Did Ken press charges?" Harold asked.

"I don't think so," Peter answered.

"It doesn't matter," Herb responded. "I'm a lawyer and I can tell you right now, they don't need a complaint. They caught him in the act."

"Caught in what act?" Harold threw out. "What if Ken invited him over."

"But he didn't," Peter said.

"I know," Harold explained. "But if we can get Ken to say he did, there's no burglary."

"How are we going to do that?" Anna asked.

"Rabbi?" Harold said, turning to Rabbi Pearlman, "Have you started writing yet?"

"Not yet today," the Rabbi answered, his face lighting up. "But I did quite a bit before Shabbat. Wanna hear?"

Without waiting for a response, Rabbi Pearlman retrieved and unfolded some papers from his shirt pocket and began to read,

The crowd started to disperse after Anna laid the cornerstone and Rabbi Pearlman made the blessing. Manny, the caterer, called out to his wife, Myrna, saying, "Wait. Don't go."

Myrna turned around and scornfully said, "Vot. Are you verblantzik. Everyone's going."

"Your monthly," Manny whispered. "It's time for your mikva."

"Mikva? Here. You're crazy. There's no mikva here. I'll have to wait til we get back to New York."

"Please!" Manny pleaded. "It's been too many days and it's Friday night. Please. Just walk to the pool and dab yourself with water."

"It's a puddle, not a pool," Myrna scorned, pointing to the only water she saw in the field.

"But, it's blessed," Manny pleaded again. "Please."

Shaking her head, Myrna stepped over the stone and walked into the field but twisted her ankle before reaching the puddle. Screaming as she fell, Myrna landed face down in the mud. The Yeshiva boys came running back.

As he watched the others help his wife, Manny stood on the side sighing, "Oy vey."

Beaming from ear to ear, Rabbi Pearlman looked up and asked, "Well?"

With everyone looking away, Anna was the first to break the silence by saying, "Good, Daddy, uh ... uh, that's very good."

"I agree," Harold quickly jumped in before adding, "so what else can we do?"

"What about the day program?" Herb asked turning to Penny. "Isn't Ken going to mental health on Monday. Can you get to him there?"

"Sure," Penny beamed. "That's a great idea. It'll be a piece of cake."

"How?" Dave asked. "You'll have five hours. That's not enough time to get him to play ball."

"Sure it is," Penny countered. "We therapists have been playing with people's heads for years."

"No," Anna replied. "You don't do that."

"Sure we do" Penny went on. "How do you think we keep people roped into years of therapy for minor complaints. Ever hear of *flight into health?* You feel better and want to stop, so we instill fear that you'll fall apart if you do. Or, *you're going to feel worse before you feel better.* That keeps you involved even if the therapy's not doing a lick of good. And then there's *repressed memories.* That's when your therapist thinks you were molested by your Daddy because her Daddy fucked her."

"Excellent. That's the way to think," Harold acknowledged. "Any other ideas?"

"What if we got Bufford in the program, too," Herb exclaimed. "We stage a grand reunion between them."

"That's a great idea," Penny beamed. "But, how will you do it? Bufford's still in jail."

"I'll call the judge now and tell him Bufford's insane," Herb replied. "I'll ask for an evaluation in your program Monday morning."

"Amnesiac fugue!" Penny exclaimed. "That'll be Ken's diagnosis."

***

Ahhh, sighed Ken with a blissful grin, climaxing the thirty-second time. Ahead of schedule, he lay in bed, totally cleansed, semen-free, feeling stronger and better than he's felt in years, knowing he'll never have to jerk off again. Soon, the monster would be gone.

0825, Ken said to himself after looking at his watch. Thirty-five minutes until the general arrives.

Ken noticed his book of cryptograms still sitting on the desk. *Why not?* thought Ken as he got out of bed and went to the book with a pencil in his hand.

Swiftly solving five puzzles in less than ten minutes Ken smiled, *You're good.*

Ken turned the page and looked at the sixth cryptogram, writing the letter *e* at the end of a three letter word he was certain was *the.*

Too easy, he thought, *I'll write some of my own.*

Ken put the book down, and picked up a piece of paper, and wrote,

A stitch in time saves nine.
Ken rewrote the saying in code,
    D twlwpf lm wlzq tdeqt mlmq

That's good, Ken thought so he tried it again,
Strike while the iron is hot.
    Orlejw aqebw rqw elgs eo qgr.

Ken thought. *These are too easy, I'll make up some sayings of my own.*

Quickly, Ken wrote:

> Flble vrpb aql
>
> for
>
> Peter must die.

> Vlqhp: Hpl wmcr qmexlg
>
> for
>
> Death: The only answer.

And

> P'r xjq xqmrlsgxim. Jq'z xjp rgzxdmkgxim.
>
> for
>
> I'm the terminator. He's the masturbator.

***

Thump, thump, Ken heard a knock on the door. He looked at his watch: *It's early.*

Ken got up and put his uniform back on, walking by the mirror on his way to the door where he stopped to comb his hair back. He continued until he reached the unlocked door, stood back and called out, "Come in."

The door opened and the General walked in. Ken lifted his hand in a military salute and announced, "Sargent Goldberg, Special Forces, ready for duty, sir."

Herb responded, "How ya doing, Ken?"

***

After service, several congregants came up to Peter and Anna and welcomed them to church. A few shook Peter's hand, but most went to Anna because she was a Jew and the natural object of their evangelical zeal. Peter stayed with small talk following Herb's advice to avoid politics when in the Lord's House. He looked across the room and smiled at Rufus Anderson. *Pretty gutsy,* Peter thought of Herb's decision that he go to the church where the Andersons went. *Maybe, I'll go over and talk to him,* Peter thought, hesitating only because *good yontiff* and *Shabbat shalom* were the only Sabbath greetings he knew. *What the heck,* Peter said to himself as he took a step forward in Rufus' direction before feeling someone's hand tap him on the shoulder.

Seeing Herb as he turned, Peter sighed with relief. "I'm glad you're here. What do Christians say to each other in church?"

"Don't worry about Christians. Let's talk about Ken," Herb replied.

"What about Ken?"

"Come over here so we can talk in private," Herb answered, pulling Peter away. "He's nuts, Peter. Really nuts."

"What do you mean?"

"I went to his room like I said I would. He stood at attention after answering the door, holding a military salute. He called me General and said he's ready for battle. He kept talking about bodily fluids and that the enemy was trying to contaminate our water to get mutated genes in the semen supply. I tell ya, it was right out of *Dr. Strangelove.*"

"Like the movie?" Peter asked.

"Yea. He kept saying we needed to bleed out the poisons. Those who couldn't do it would die"

"Two to the fifth?" Peter mused.

"Right! That's exactly what he said. He kept rambling about immoral fluids, semen emitted, overworked prostates, natural selection, and two to the fifth was needed to survive. He offered me his alphabetized collection of 32 pornographic tapes."

"That's what he wanted from me before Anna brought me to my senses. I was dying at 28."

"Two to the fifth to survive?" Herb pondered.

"So how did he look: drained, on his knees, gasping for air?"

"Not at all," Herb answered. "He looked exceptionally fit but kept rambling on about Mai Lai, the Mekong Delta, Auschwitz, Pol Pot and Cannery Row. I couldn't figure out why he threw that one in."

"Didn't Steinbeck write about the underclass of society," Peter said. "Poverty, prostitutes, factory and farm workers. There's a connection there."

"The one connection I know for sure," Herb replied, "and that's that Ken has really gone mad. He cut his hair in a Mohawk, ridiculous at his age, half bald and out of shape."

"Can we get him in?" Peter asked.

"Absolutely, but do we want to? Remember, he has to clear Bufford or the election is lost. If they take him away, we'll lose our chance."

***

At noon, Ken stopped to watch the news. Flipping between the channels, he watched headline reports of the break-in at the Holiday Inn. Prosecutor Anderson held a press conference where he said he would seek a special prosecutor. By emphasizing the need to recuse himself, he only fueled fears that Peter had a role. Mayor Anderson adeptly dodged the questions he was asked. He even lauded Peter Branstill for the challenge he mounted.

"Let all the world know that democracy's alive and well in Anderson, Nebraska. We welcome the challenge and look forward to a spirited debate. Let's keep this campaign clean in our best Nebraskan tradition. We don't object to a candidate from New York. Just leave your New York tactics on the other side of the Hudson."

Peter meanwhile held a press conference of his own where he was grilled by the press. The news ended with a latest poll. Peter was losing ground.

***

Later that afternoon, Peter stayed with Herb in his hotel room, preparing for the debate. With volumes of documents he had obtained from the library and historical society, Herb drilled Peter with facts about Anderson's history, culture, and economics. By the end of their meeting, Peter felt honored to live in the town where the brave General Lloyd Anderson led his troops to victory in the Battle of Winding Creek, later renamed General Lloyd Anderson Creek. He recognized that Anderson's pig farmers needed real subsidies, not the tired pork barrel politics of the old administration. And, he would take Mayor Anderson to task for failing to foster culture and support the arts. Peter planned to unveil his plans to build the Anderson Museum of Art and attract world class musical talent to town for Anderson's new Philharmonic Symphony Orchestra.

"Just remember," Herb reminded Peter. "Let Anderson talk scandal. You talk issues. If you get pressed for an answer, tell them you believe in the American system and that you're sure that justice will be served. Find a way to give your full faith and confidence in the prosecutor. Tell them you look forward to a new Branstill-Anderson team, joining Jim Anderson in fighting crime.

***

While Peter was dressing for the debate, Herb reached in his pocket and found the cryptograms Ken had given him. *He was really bizarre,* Herb thought, remembering their meeting.

***

"So, how are you doing?" Herb asked.

"Goldberg fine, Sir," Ken responded.

Not sure what to say next, Herb looked around the room and saw Ken's cryptogram book on the desk.

"Been enjoying the cryptograms, Ken?" Herb asked.

"Yes. Sir. Sargent Goldberg has been enjoying the cryptograms, sir." Ken answered.

"Uh. Do you need another book?" Herb asked, not sure what to say.

"No, sir. Sargent Goldberg does not need another book, sir."

Herb stood speechless for a few moments when he realized that Ken was waiting for him to return the salute. Herb saluted Ken who then brought his hand to his side and said, "Permission to speak, sir."

"Uh. Sure, Ken. I mean sure, Sargent Goldberg. Anything you want to say."

"I've infiltrated enemy communications, sir," Ken went on, handing Herb the cryptograms he composed. "We're ready for battle."

"Sure Ken," Herb answered. "Sure."

***

Herb solved the first four quickly: *Strike while the iron is hot, A penny saved is a penny earned, One swallow doesn't make a summer,* and *Two's company three's a crowd,* interrupted when Peter called out,

"Ready to go, Herb?"

"Sure," Herb responded. Not sure what was going on, he stuffed the unsolved cryptograms back in his pocket and accompanied Peter out the door.

***

Peter was brilliant at the debate. Offering clear explanations of Anderson's economic stagnation, Peter outlined proposal after proposal for a better future. The Mayor stumbled over his words throughout the debate, with no new ideas or reasons to reject Peter's plan. In a display of weak me-too-ism, the only points the mayor made were his efforts to implicate Peter in the Holiday Inn break-in and continue his low-handed attacks against Anna and Peter for their sexual behaviors.

Peter proclaimed, "This election is about programs, ideas, and leadership."

Anderson retorted, "It's about family values."

Peter demanded, "We need clean air."

Anderson countered, "We need clean living."

Peter declared, "We'll have safe streets."

Anderson demanded, "Give us safe lodging."

By the end, Peter returned to campaign headquarters beaming and confident. In front of the press, Herb boldly declared victory while Anna hugged Peter and told him how proud she felt. The rabbi gave the benediction while Dave was on the phone working on details for the Barbara Walters interview. Andrew was already gone, visiting Bufford in jail to get him prepared when he saw Ken the next day. With a grin on his face, Harold walked into the room with just breaking news, the latest poll: a dead heat.

"That's great," Peter exclaimed, relieved he had finally caught up. "With tomorrow's interview, I'm sure to win."

"Hm," Herb mused. "I'm not so sure. You're still an outsider against the Anderson machine. We don't really know what they're planning to do. It's just too close to call."

"So where can we find some more votes?" the rabbi asked. "I've been trying to write them into the story, but it would be a lot easier if I could do it in Hebrew."

"Don't do that," Herb reacted with alarm. "We don't need an anti-Semitic backlash. Any other ideas?"

"I've got one," Penny said. "The day patients at the mental health center are all registered to vote. I doubt that any of them actually plan to vote. But if they do, they're all Type Y. You should try to get them."

"How?" Herb asked before picturing Peter's packed schedule. "And when?"

"Tuesday."

"That's election day. You don't campaign then."

"Peter will," Penny countered. "The polls don't open until 3:00. The Andersons have controlled things for years, making sure the voting doesn't start until after the Flag Daze Parade. Have Peter at the program at 2:00. I'll personally walk the patients to the polls at 3:00."

31 THE PROGRAM

On Monday morning at 8:15, Herb arrived at Ken's door to take him to the program. Ken stood by his bed in battle fatigues, ready for inspection, the room spic and span.

"You ready to go, Ken?" Herb asked.

"Yes sir," Sargent Goldberg replied. "Ready to go."

"OK," Herb said as he started out the door.

When Ken failed to follow, Herb added, "Arms right. Forward march!"

Blushing as they went, Herb marched Ken from the Holiday Inn to the Mental Health center.

***

Penny welcomed Ken warmly and brought him straight to day room. There he met Bart, a leader among the patients, who showed Ken around. After introducing him to the others, Bart took Ken to a bulletin board which posted the schedule for today.

"Here's what we're doing," Bart said.

9:00	Community Meeting
10:00	Art group (work with clay)
11:00	Group therapy
Noon	Lunch
1:00	Individual plan
2:00	Music Group
3:00	Wrap-Up

"You're new," Bart added, "So you'll see the psychiatrist at 1:00

today."

***

Penny opened the meeting by introducing the two new members, Ken and Rufus, and offered them an opportunity to say something about themselves. Ken gave only his name, rank and serial number while Rufus told the group he was Ken's old friend.

"We Viet Nam Vets stick together jist like a dang sign sticks to a door it's been nailed to."

Although Ken remained aloof, Rufus followed up on the theme by creating military figures in art group. Placing two soldiers close to each other, he proudly declared, "Ken and me."

By group therapy, Rufus shared stories of their early years as schoolmates together in the Northeast section of Philadelphia. Hoping to sound convincingly Philadelphian, Rufus declared "I like mustard on a pretzel as much as a dang school boy likes to hear that recess bell ring." Meanwhile, Penny explained that Ken suffered Post Traumatic Stress Syndrome and had blocked out all memories of his painful past.

"It's wasn't your fault," Penny carefully explained, "leaving Rufus behind. There was nothing else to do. You were under heavy fire and had to protect the other men. He got out fine, Ken. Your days of guilt are over."

Over lunch, Rufus sat next to Ken grinning ear to ear. "It's like old times, man, in the dang mess hall. I thought I lost ya, man. I love you."

At 1:00, Ken met with Dr. Bowman who adjusted his medications and explained the connection between post-traumatic stress and amnesiac fugue. At 2:00, Chip made music group a tribute to friendship honoring the reunion of Rufus and Ken. Penny called Herb to share the good news,

"He's smiling, Herb. He's starting to believe us. Call a press conference at 3:30 when the program ends. I'm sure Ken will say what we want him to say."

At 3:00, the patients came together for Wrap-Up Group.

"Before everyone leaves, I have a special announcement. Tomorrow is election day. It's a close race between Mayor Anderson, who has done little for the mentally ill, and Peter Branstill, a refreshing new face in local politics. Candidate Branstill has agreed to speak to this group, tomorrow at 2:00. Let's all listen to him, then walk as a group ...

"WHAT!" shouted Ken. "You're bringing that goddamn, two-faced, fucking idiot to talk with this group. No way! He's a fucking jerk and he'll fucking jerk-off all over this crowd. I tell you, he is NOT going to speak."

Familiar with outbursts of anger, Penny assured the patients that the plan was on and that no one person could disrupt it through threats. Then, she turned to Ken inviting him to speak, "Tell us what's bothering you, Ken. What is it about Peter's appearance that makes you so upset?"

"I'll show you," Ken replied, picking up a chair and launching it across the room, hitting a particularly spaced out man on the head.

Penny screamed for help. Margaret, her co-therapist, rushed to call 911, and Zach, an intern, ran across the room in hopes of restraining Ken. Ken punched Zach in the mouth before bolting out the door.

Ken looked back after running to the street. He saw the clinic staff rush out of the building. He heard police sirens wail. Quickly, Ken darted into an alleyway and through the open back door to Bea Anderson's Bakery.

Ken saw a small bathroom near the ovens in the back of the shop. He went inside and locked the door, waiting for the sirens to pass. When things seemed clear, he climbed out the bathroom window, scanned the street, and with no one in sight, darted across making his way to the bowling alley. He quickly entered the Mitzvah Mobile which was parked outside. He tucked his shirt in and ran his fingers through his hair before walking inside.

32 MOLLY'S MOTEL

Herb was meeting with Peter to review some points for tonight's interview when he received a call from Penny on his cell. He thanked her for the call and, with a worried expression on his face, explained the situation to Peter. As they talked, he remembered that he still had Ken's cryptograms in his pocket. Peter, who was quite adept at solving cryptograms, quickly uncovered their hateful and threatening messages.

"You're in real danger, Peter," Herb said. "You can't appear in public until they find Ken and put him away."

"You can't be serious," Peter said. "We've come so far."

"But, you're in danger. He could really hurt you."

"I know, but I still can't stop. I've spent my whole life in fear: cleaning, counting, categorizing, masturbating. What did I get for it? I can't go back. I may not be alive tomorrow. I can't let him kill my spirit today."

Unconvinced, Herb begrudgingly assented, "Let's be careful."

***

Once inside the Mitzvah Mobile, Ken introduced himself as a Jew who wanted to find his roots. The Hasids welcomed him in, donning him with Tallis and Tephillin and leading him in afternoon prayers.

"Sh'ma Yisrael Adonoi Elohanu, Adonoi Ehad," Ken proclaimed. While he had trouble keeping up with the rest of the liturgy, the Yeshiva boys assured him that he could quickly learn. Study and prayers would begin tomorrow morning.

"What about clothes?" Ken asked. "I want to dress like you."

Surprised by the zeal that Ken had quickly expressed, one of the students offered to lend him an outfit until he could buy new clothes of his own. The student briefly left the van to fetch the outfit.

"So what caused you to decide this to do?" another student asked.

"I was reading *Peter Squared,* the book about this guy from out of town who is running for mayor," Ken said, without revealing his identity as author. "He masturbates all the time. I heard that the *Code of Jewish Laws* prohibits that behavior."

"So right you are," the student replied. "You have studied well. It is my pleasure to have you here."

"Now, he's running for mayor. It's like Sodom and Gomorrah. It's just plain wrong and something has to change. I want to live a moral life so I come to you."

"We always welcome a Jew who wants to follow the faith. Here, read this," the man said, handing Peter a copy of the Haftorah.

At that moment, the other student came back with tallis to wear under his shirt, white shirt, dark pants, black overcoat, white socks and black shoes. He also gave Ken a black hat to wear outside. Ken quickly dressed, soon appearing indistinguishable from the Yeshiva boys.

***

Herb ran to the police station with his newly decoded messages. Immediately recognizing the risk, Barney issued an all-points bulletin, then made personal calls to police and sheriffs in the neighboring towns. He and Herb rode in the police car to Ken's room at the Holiday Inn. Barney knocked on the door: No one answered. He knocked harder: Still, no answer. Finally, Barney asked the clerk to open the door. Inside, they found semen and urine sprayed on the floor, Ken's thirty-two pornographic tapes scattered on the floor.

"This is bad," Herb said as he turned to Barney. "They're not alphabetized."

"And look there," Barney adding, pointing to the wall. Written on the wall with shaving cream and feces, Herb read:

Peter Must Die
Peter Jerks Off
Hell is Now

With that, Barney started a door to door search.

***

Before Barney's bulletin went out, Ken was far from the center of town at Molly's Motel. A seedy joint in ill-repair, the sign in front read:

Molly's Motel
Nice rooms
Cable TV

Truckers welcome
Day, week, and hourly rates.

***

Ken paid Molly to stay the whole week, extra funds to borrow her VCR. Inside, he removed his clothes and sat down to watch *Taxi Driver,* paying special attention to the arsenal of weapons Travis Bickle wore. Ken compiled a list of the arms he would need, then rubbed his penis with feces in his hand. *Damn you, Peter,* Ken thought with tears in his eyes. *Two to the fifth, and for what!?*

Ken wiped his hand on the bedspread before putting his clothes back on and walking out the door. He carefully walked down the road frequently turning to look behind before reaching near the railroad tracks, a rickety old building with the sign, *The Sportsman's Paradise.*

The only Hasid in the store, Ken, who was smelling like excrement, walked to the counter where the firearms were displayed. Beau, the son of store owner Red Turner, approached and said,

"Hi, Jew. What do you want?"

"I need a gun," Ken barked back.

"Whatcha hunting? Matzo balls?" Beau laughed. "Or maybe you'd like to go to the crick and ketch some Gefilte fish."

"I need a fucking gun," Ken barked, staring back at Beau.

"You sure smell like ya need one," Beau replied. "So, whatcha hunting? Raccoon, rabbit? This little baby'll do you just fine."

As Beau went to open the display, Ken handed him a list,

"This is what I need."

Beau looked at Ken's list of automatic and semi-automatic weapons, hunting knives, hand grenades, and ammunition belts, and whistled,

"Into big game, ain't you."

Ken gave a piercing stare back at Beau. "This is what I need."

"Come on back to our special showroom," Beau said.

Ken followed Beau through a door to the back of the store where an older man sat.

"Pop. This kike wants some guns."

"What the fuck ya bothering me fer? Show him some guns."

Beau handed his father the list.

"Hm. Now these are some guns. What's going on, Mister," Red said turning to Ken. "We got some A-rabs in town?"

Staring the men down, Ken said, "This is what I need."

"You ain't no fed, are you?" Red asked.

Ken looked through him in response.

"Frisk him, Beau."

196

Beau held his nose and let out an "ugh."

"Frisk him, boy." Red repeated.

As Beau approached Ken, Red reminded him, "Check for wires."

Several minutes later, Beau said, "He's clean. I mean there's nothing there."

"OK," Red said. "Come with me."

Red led Ken out the back door into his truck. Despite his objections, Ken relented and wore a blindfold for the trip. The men rode for an hour, circling around and retracing their tracks, until they reached a campground sporting the sign:

Outward Bound: Where children grow up to be men.

Red guided Ken through the camp and deep into the woods to an old shack. There, he removed Ken's blindfold. In front, Ken saw a wide array of military items: rocket launchers, detonating devices, flak jackets, hand grenades. Red gave Ken some time to absorb the place where he was before he started filling his list. When he finished, Red handed Ken a fishing rod, "Here, compliments of the house. We've got some mighty good fishin' out here, too."

***

With Herb's help, Barney led the search for Ken. Penny came along with the hopes that she could coax him to the hospital with his insurance now authorizing a three day stay. The search brought them to Molly's Motel. Molly confirmed that a man fitting Ken's description had signed in and paid for the week.

"Strange fella. He's wearing this long black coat in the middle a summer. Hardly said nothin'. Gave me the creeps."

Barney showed her a picture of a well-known Rabbi's son's wedding taken from a copy of the Lubovitch Daily News. "Something like this?"

"Yea. Just like that. He's one of them fellas."

Barney then showed her Ken's jacket picture on *Peter Squared*. She pondered that picture before saying, "Can't say it's him. That fella looks halfway normal."

"He's a pro," Barney said turning to Herb. "Dangerous man and a master of disguise."

"Can we see the room?" Barney asked, returning to Molly.

Molly fetched the key to Ken's room and opened the door. She immediately slammed it shut, overwhelmed by the stench.

"What the hell did he do to my room? He ain't staying the rest of the week. And he ain't gettin' his money back."

Barney covered his nose with a handkerchief, then pushed the door open. He flipped the switch, but the light didn't go on, so he reached for his flashlight and shined it in the room. All the light bulbs were gone.

By now, Molly returned with her cleaning cart. "This is gonna be one helluva job," she said.

Barney asked her for light bulbs. He screwed one in the nearest fixture, the light highlighting a room with bedspreads and linens thrown about, the chair overturned, the television smashed, and urine and semen all around. The group slowly entered the room. Penny screamed, "Oh, shit!"

"What is it," Herb asked.

"Shit!" Penny said pointing to a bucket by the bed filled with feces.

By now, Molly had replaced most of the light bulbs.

Herb spoke first noticing the air conditioner.

"Look at this," Herb said. "There's tape over all the vents."

"The electric sockets, too," Penny added.

"Get a gander here," Barney called out. "The toilet's completely taped shut, too."

"That explains the bucket," Herb commented.

"What the fuck ya think's going on?" Barney asked.

"He's paranoid," Penny said. "Every opening to this room is taped shut: The windows, the shower head, the drain in the sink. He's paranoid and extremely dangerous."

Barney noticed that Molly had started cleaning the room.

"Sorry, Molly. You can't do it. I'm gonna rope off the room. It's a crime scene."

"I suppose you'll be back next week to help me clean the dried up stains."

"Let's go," Barney said. "This is serious business."

On their way out, Herb noticed Ken's copy of *Taxi Driver* on the bed. He looked at the label: Al's Video Shop.

"Should we return this?" Herb asked.

Barney took it and looked inside. "It's due by tomorrow morning. I'll drop it off when I get back to town."

"You ever hear of it, Penny?" Herb asked.

"No," she replied.

"Me neither," Herb added. "Mind if I watch it tonight? I've got to unwind."

"OK. Just make sure it's back by morning," Barney said handing Herb the tape.

33 MARTIAL LAW

At the bowling alley, Herb found Peter and Anna in last minute preparations for the Barbara Walters interview.

"We've gotta cancel," Herb implored. "Ken's way off the deep end, paranoid as all get out, and gunning for you. Let's lay low until Barney picks him up."

"No way," Peter answered. "I'm not wimping out. I've done that all my life. You with me, Anna?"

"Absolutely, tiger," Anna replied, reaching out to take his arm.

"But you didn't see what we saw, Peter." Herb went on to describe in intricate detail Ken's room at Molly's Motel.

Peter held his chin in his right hand in a thoughtful pose. "You're right. This is bad. I'm sure I'm at risk. But, I'm going on. That's final."

"OK," Herb said looking at his watch. "We'd better roll."

As Herb went to speak with Dave to check on the plans, Peter leaned over to Anna, "I never thought I'd say this before but it sounds kinky doing it with shit."

"Yuck," Anna cried. "And you can do *that* with someone else."

Anna slapped Peter when she saw him smile, "No you don't."

Dave assured Herb that he had handled all the details. He then called the police station asking Barney to send a deputy over just in case something happened.

Before long, Peter and Anna were sitting with Barbara Walters in a living room setting her crew created in the middle of the bowling alley.

Barbara: Peter Branstill. Up to a week ago, you were an inconspicuous accountant. You had never been in a relationship, never had a girlfriend, never even went out on a date. Now, you are engaged to this lovely woman and are favored to upset the Anderson dynasty and become this town's next mayor. Your name has been thrown around for higher office. How did you do this?

Peter: Barbara. Everything changed for me a few weeks ago when I walked into a bookstore and purchased a copy of *Peter Squared*. I had met Anna earlier that day.

Barbara: And what was in this book that caused such a change in your life?

Peter: I had lived a painful childhood and for years, was unable to achieve the things I wanted in life. Except for my job, I never did anything interesting. My life was a drag. Once I read this book, everything turned around.

Barbara: That's a truly remarkable story, Peter. Are you recommending this book to others, a sort of personal growth Bible?

Peter: Not at all. The thing that differentiates this book from other popular self-improvement tools is that this book truly tells the story of my life. And for that matter, some of Anna's life, too. The book is only helpful if you happen to be one of the characters in it.

Barbara: Truly fascinating, and I agree, *Peter Squared* is not a tonic for everyone. Now, it also appears that there is a darker, seamier side to Peter Branstill that the public doesn't know, one that Peter Branstill, the politician, might want to hide.

Peter: Perhaps, some other politician, Barbara, but not me. I'm ready to answer any question that you have.

Barbara: OK. Well, it says here, Peter, that you masturbate nearly all the time. I think the good people of Anderson want to know, in fact need to know, if elected will you keep jerking off.

Peter (chuckling): No, but if I did, I don't see why that should matter. After all Mayor Anderson has been jerking off the good people of Anderson for years, and it's time for a change.

Barbara: Always the politician.

Peter: True. So let me answer your question seriously. I have been masturbating all my life. I've gone to peep shows. I've bought porn magazines. I've masturbated in the voting booth, under the table while having dinner with my Aunt Cindy, and to visions of horses. It's all there in *Peter Squared*. I'm not going to deny it.

Peter then turned to Anna who was sitting beside him. He placed his hand on her right knee.

Peter: This is a remarkable woman. I thank God every day for her tolerance, patience, and understanding. I have sinned but I am born again.

Barbara: Anna. We understand that you have your own sordid past to account for. While Ken Goldberg described your life less than Peter's in *Peter Squared*, there are still things that may concern the voters of Anderson. Let me read to you this selection.

Longing to "take it up the ass," Anna went off her medication very early and was on the bus by mid-July, looking for a stranger.

In fact, I understand that Mayor Anderson contacted the gentleman that screwed you up the ass in Ohio and brought him to town. As we speak, they are campaigning side by side.

Peter: I'm sorry to break in and certainly don't want to participate in dirty, under-handed tactics. I'm hesitant to even share the rumor I heard. My campaign is based on policies, not gossip and fear. But, I think the citizens of Anderson are bright enough to know that Mayor Anderson did not need to bring this fellow to town to make that point. It's right here in the book. What I want to know is what is the REAL reason Mayor Anderson brought this sodomist and anal sex addict to town.

***

"So whatcha huntin' Jew boy?"

"What the fuck is it to you?" Ken barked back.

"It's a lot the fuck to me, Jew boy. We shoot Jews for sport out here. So lay it on me straight. You ain't duck hunting. What are you gonna do?"

"None of your fucking business," Ken barked back again.

Beau struck Ken across the face with his rifle handle before saying, "You ain't doing nothin' to no one 'cept findin' your way into a deep hole unless ya tell us what yer gonna do."

"Branstill," Ken said. "I'm gonna kill that motherfucker."

"Well, that's a whole lot better. We believe in settling scores like a man out here. Now, that's that goddamn fuckin' New Yorker whose running fer mayor, ain't he?"

Ken stayed silent while nodding his head yes.

"When ya wanna do 'im?"

"Tomorrow, two o'clock."

"Hm," pondered Red. "There's gonna be a whole lotta people there in town. Don't ya think ya should do it later?"

"Two. It's gotta be two."

"Ok Jew boy. Two," Red said, pondering Ken's words.

As Ken left, Beau picked up his rifle and aimed it at Ken. "Lemme shoot that mother fucking Jew, Pa."

Red put his hand on Beau's gun and gently pushed it down. "No. There's something bigger here. Call the fellas. I want them here in fifteen minutes."

***

Herb congratulated Peter and Anna on their starring performances at the end of the show. Benson called it a home run sure that Peter would now have enough votes to win.

"Then, we'll cancel the day program," Herb said. "We don't need it anymore."

"You surprise me, Herb," Peter replied, now a bit disgusted. "You've been in the hospital a lot. Anna says they gave you shock treatments. Look how many times Anna humiliated herself trying to find happiness. Those day patients are you and Anna and me. Even Ken, a respected psychologist and accomplished author, has to go in. Let's give these mentally ill folks some respect and ask for their votes. This is not about winning elections or saving myself. It's about respect, honor and dignity."

As Anna and Peter left to return to their room, Herb's cell phone rang. "Yep," Herb said.

His face drawn with worry, Herb quickly hung up and, at Barney's request, rushed to the station.

***

The men of the *Make America Proud Militia* straggled to the center of camp at Red's call. Standing on a large rock, Red said,

"It's D-Day, boys."

"What?" Beau gasped. "Now?"

"Yep, now."

"When did you get the word?" Beau asked, trembling a bit.

"Don't you recall? You were by my side."

"What?" Beau puzzled.

"The Jew. He's the messenger. Our Supreme Commander, in his infinite wisdom, gave us our orders through a man dressed up like a Jew. It's brilliant, incredible, but it's on. Two o'clock tomorrow. The revolution begins."

"Heil Hitler," the men spontaneously shouted. When the cheers died down, Red outlined the plan. At 1100, they leave camp, their artillery and vehicles draped in American flags and Anderson Flag Daze banners. By noon, they're at the staging area for the parade, just outside town. As last minute entries, they take their place at the end of the parade. Blaring patriotic music, no one suspects a thing. By 1400, cheered by the crowd, they reach the judge's stand. A dignitary, Peter is certain to be there. By 1415, Ken fires, starting the attack by assassinating Peter. Himmler Company fires on the stand and wipes out the entire Anderson clan. The Auschwitz Company secures Town Hall. Gestapo takes the courthouse, Treblinka the telephone office, Dr. Mengele Company the radio station, Eichmann the bowling alley. Goebbels secures the media. We must control all communications out of town. SS: You know what to do. You're special police. Round up the Jews."

202

"Do we expect much resistance?" Clyde asked.

"I don't know. We have our orders, nothing more. If I'm right, we'll have freedom fighters securing small towns all over this land. I promise you, the United States of Nigger Jews will fall."

"Heil Hitler! Heil Hitler! Heil Hitler!"

***

With his penis deep inside her, Peter told Anna, "You're so beautiful."

"Oh Peter, I'm so happy," she sighed as she grabbed him tightly.

In silence, the couple continued to copulate, their eyes shut, climaxing together.

With Anna in his arms, Peter said, "I've been thinking about something ever since Saturday."

"You shouldn't think so much," Anna purred.

Peter smiled at her but went on. "At the schul, Saturday morning, I remembered Bernie's Bar Mitzvah."

"Bernie? Oh yea. I read that in *Peter Squared*. I feel so sorry for you. That must've been awful."

"That's what I mean. It wasn't awful. It wasn't at all the way Ken told it."

"Really?" Anna said in surprise.

"Yes. I had a great time. Got drunk just like all the other kids. Even made out a bit with Shirley."

"Well, your making out days are over, buddy. Unless you want to make out with me."

Peter kissed Anna, then said, "I know. But why did Ken tell it that way?"

"I don't know," Anna said, sitting up in the bed, reluctantly giving up the bliss she was enjoying before.

"What about you, Anna? What about the stuff Ken said about you."

"He didn't really say that much. One chapter and a couple of other things here and there."

"So. Did he tell the truth there?"

"I don't know for sure. I didn't get that far yet. But what he said about anal sex, yes I used to love it."

"That's not what he said. He said you tried it once and it hurt. You were happy that you tried it but so filled with guilt you confessed to a priest because you couldn't wait for Yom Kippur."

"No! That never happened at all. Hand me the book."

Peter reached for the book on the table by his side of the bed, turned it to the chapter, ANNA, and gave it to her. "Here, read it."

As Anna read her chapter, her eyes started to bulge, her expression turned sour.

"Damn him," she shouted. "What a pack of lies."

"Like how," Peter asked.

"First of all, Sol was never mean to me nor did I start cheating on him until after Ken began writing the book. I certainly didn't fuck people on buses and I wouldn't let a pick-up, a total stranger, do me in the ass."

"But you did have anal sex, didn't you?" Peter asked.

"Sure. Most people do, at least once or twice. But, no one shoved a deodorant stick up there or really hurt me. It felt pretty good. And I never did it once I met Sol."

"Before Sol? I don't get that. I thought the Hasidim don't have pre-marital sex."

"They don't. But I wasn't raised a Hasid. My Dad was a Lutheran minister. I never got laid until after I went to college and before I converted."

Anna went on to explain to Peter that she was born in the Midwest. Over her father's objections, she went to New York University where she acted out, drank, smoked pot, and had sex, often with different partners. Her Lutheran guilt got out of hand and she had trouble with her studies. Things changed after she passed the Mitzvah Mobile in Greenwich Village on 8th Street and the Avenue of the Americas. Shortly, she had an Orthodox conversion, becoming very involved with the Lubovitch movement on Eastern Parkway in Brooklyn.

"The Hasids have a love of life, missing in Lutheran stoicism. And I reviled against my father's missionary zeal. The Lubovitchers made it hard for me to convert and wouldn't let me become a Jew until I assured them I really wanted to do it. For awhile, I felt so peaceful."

"What happened?" Peter asked.

"Nothing like what Ken said in the book. A matchmaker fixed me up with Sol. He was a good man, but the sex was boring. You know, they sleep in separate beds and there's no foreplay. Sometimes he'd let me give him a blowjob if it was close to Yom Kippur. I wouldn't dare suggest that he do me in the ass."

"He was pretty abusive, too. Wasn't he?"

"No. That's more shit from Ken. Sol was a good man. Quick on the trigger, he never satisfied me, but he wasn't mean."

"But what about the bus trips? Were they all lies, too?"

"Yes and no. I thought about that stuff all the time, just the way Ken wrote it. But, it was just a fantasy. I had to do something to keep me involved during Sol's rabbit fucks."

"Wow," Peter said. "I'm glad you told me, Anna. There's something I want to tell you, too."

***

Herb arrived at the police station to see Barney quite distraught. "What's wrong?"

"Wait. There's someone who wants to talk with you."

Herb waited until Barney returned with a well-built, fastidiously dressed man, a no nonsense expression on his face.

"Herb. Agent Thomas wants to talk with you."

The man flashed a shield, "Thomas, FBI. I need to ask you some questions."

"Shoot," Herb replied.

"What do you know about Ken Goldberg?"

"He's an author. He wrote the book *Peter Squared*. Peter Branstill is the main character."

"Where did you meet him?"

"Over the net. Peter found the book in Barnes and Noble and sought Ken out when he realized it was about him. They've been communicating by IM the last two weeks. I never met him until Peter ran for mayor and Ken flew in from Philadelphia."

"Philadelphia?" Thomas repeated with surprise. "How do you know he came from Philadelphia?"

"Here," Herb replied. "It's on the book jacket."

"Are you sure this is the man you picked up from the airport?"

"Yes. I mean I think so. He's a little older now, fatter and really out of shape. You can tell he has no taste in clothing and doesn't take care of his health too well. But, it's him. I think so."

Agent Thomas took a deep breath. "We have reason to believe that your IM messages are being intercepted by a right-wing terrorist organization. They are dangerous and dedicated to the overthrow of our government. We believe that your Ken Goldberg, dressed as an Orthodox Jew, covering himself with shit, has entered a camp for a local militia near town with a message to attack Anderson and the Anderson clan. We believe this to be a tightly knit organization that is capable of ordering multiple attacks, here and elsewhere. On reliable sources, we know that eight different Orthodox Jews have entered right wing, White Supremacist, Neo-Nazi camps within the last 24 hours. This cannot be a coincidence. This is a crisis."

"What about Peter?" Herb immediately asked.

"What about Peter?" Thomas replied with some disdain.

"Is he in danger?"

"We're all in danger."

"But he's the target. He's in the most danger. Look!"

Herb gave Agent Thomas the cryptograms that Peter solved.

"Hm. It does threaten him," Thomas said.

"And look at this, too."

Herb gave Agent Thomas a copy of an email he received from Ken's publisher forwarding an email they had just received from Ken.

Ed,

Run another printing of *Peter Squared,* ASAP. Can't explain the details, but by Tuesday, it'll be selling like hotcakes. Regards to your family. Hope all is well. Remember, my wife owns the copyright and gets royalties in case I die. Go to AC Moore. They'll help you find her.

Warmly,

Ken Goldberg

Agent Thomas pondered the letter before offering his response. "Yes. There will be civilian losses, but we can't worry about one man. Ken is going to assassinate Peter at the cost of his own life. And he's right. It will sell books."

"We've gotta warn Peter."

As Herb got up, Thomas called to Barney. "Arrest him!"

"On what charge?" Barney asked.

"You don't need one. The President has declared martial law."

34 CATERING TO THE PEOPLE

"What is it?" Anna asked Peter.

"Did you get to the part where Aunt Cindy changes my name from George to Peter?"

"Yes," Anna giggled. "That was so funny."

Anna suddenly realized that Peter was about to tell her something profound, her mood sobering up to the enormity of the moment.

"I'm sorry," she said. "What about that?"

"That's not true, either."

"It's hard to believe anything in *Peter Squared* anymore," Anna lamented. "So what is true?"

"Filmore. My real name is Filmore Cohen."

"You're Jewish, too!" Anna exclaimed.

"No. My Daddy's daddy was, but we were raised Catholic."

"So Grandpa was Jewish, George, your Dad was not, and you're Filmore Cohen."

"Not exactly," Filmore replied. "My Dad was Filmore, Sr. and I was Filmore, Jr. Dad called me Junior but most people just called me Phil."

"So all this stuff about your Dad being George and Aunt Cindy changing your name because he ate like a dog wasn't true."

"Not at all," Filmore went on. "Dad was quite dignified and urbane, an architect. He always played classical music and read the New York Times, a world class Go player, too."

"So George, I mean Filmore – Filmore, Sr. that is -- your Dad wasn't a slob and didn't eat like a dog?"

"Well, George ate like a dog, but Dad didn't."

"Who was George?" Anna asked.

"Our dog," Phil answered.

"Peter," Anna laughed. "I mean Phil. You're so funny."

Giggling together, Anna and Phil wrapped their arms around each other. Phil gently pushed Anna on her back and began to mount her when Anna held Phil back with her right hand and reached toward the floor with her left. She groped around until she found her purse, retrieving a tube of Vaseline from it.

"Here," she said, handing Filmore the jelly while she pushed him off of her. She turned over propping her head up with her elbows, her knees brought toward her chest, her behind displayed prominently in the air.

***

Tuesday morning, Ken woke up dirtier than before. Looking outside, he saw tanks and transports, soldiers and artillery.

"What the fuck's going on?" Ken demanded.

"We're going to town, soldier," one of the militia men said, not sure if he should salute, not knowing Ken's rank.

"I'm going to knock off that mother fucking Peter Branstill's head. What are you guys doing?"

"We're," said Beau approaching Ken from behind, "going to give you a fucking shower before you get in that transport"

Beau grabbed Ken firmly and, with the help of his comrades, dragged him to the rest rooms where they disrobed him and threw him in the shower. Replacing his Hasidic garb with battle fatigues, they carried his feces stained garments in paper bags until they could throw them into the fire. With nothing else to wear, Ken emerged from the john, fully dressed in battle gear.

"That's better, Jew boy," Beau cried. "Now go into that tent and get yourself armed."

As Ken moved inside where Red had left his Travis Bickle style armaments, Beau returned to his transport to be met by Red.

"What the fuck's the matter with you, boy? This ain't no time to fight amongst ourselves."

"He's a fucking Jew."

"I tell ya, that boy's as Aryan as you and me."

"I hate to tell ya, Pop, but you and I ain't got dicks like that boy's got."

"Whatcha mean."

"He's fucking circumscribed."

"Well, that don't mean nothing. It don't mean he's a Jew for sure."

"Well, I tell ya, this one is. Please Pa. Let me finish him off."

"Tell ya what. Don't do nothing to disrupt the plan. Once the battle starts, if ya want, pick him off."

"Thanks Dad," Beau said, a tear in his eye. "I love ya."

***

Filmore and Anna woke up to the bustling sounds of activity on the streets. Workers were busy assembling bleachers from where the people could watch the parade. Venders erected stands while civic groups decorated the town in red, white, and blue. Anderson dignitaries – Judge Tyrus Anderson, County Clerk Millard Anderson, Tax Collector Jacob Anderson, Public Health Officer Daryl Anderson, Chief of Police Barney Anderson, Town Solicitor James Anderson, Supervisor of Public Works Betsy Anderson, and County Surveyor Emily Williams (Bart Anderson's former wife) -- strutted along the streets with Rufus Anderson, proudly overseeing the preparations insuring that everyone knew where the credit belonged.

Meanwhile, Filmore noticed some children running around.

"Isn't that Joey Anderson," Anna asked.

"I'm not sure," Filmore replied.

"What's he doing?"

"You fucker!" Filmore shouted, starting to run after Joey when he realized that he was tearing down Branstill for Mayor posters.

"Come back," Anna said, grabbing Filmore's coat. "You can't be chasing kids."

"You're right, but look around. They've destroyed all my posters."

"I know, Phil. These guys fight dirty. Let's go back to the Holiday Inn. Herb will be starting the meeting about now. He'll know what to do."

On the way back, Filmore mentioned to Anna. "I've been thinking about all those lies in Ken's book."

"Yes, Phi ... Peter," Anna answered, switching to his old name realizing there were townspeople nearby who might overhear.

"I know why he did it."

"Why?" Anna asked.

"I know Ken. I've met him before. He's not just my author. He's ..."

Realizing they could be overheard, Filmore stopped himself and said. "It's complicated and I don't want everyone to know. We'll talk tonight."

Not willing to be put off, Anna grabbed Filmore's arm and said, "No, Peter. Tell me now."

"I can't. It's too weird. We have an election to win. Tonight. I promise."

"Boo," Anna pouted. "You're no fun. Can't you tell me anything about this?"

"OK," Filmore answered.

Before he could explain, Dave saw the couple and said. "There you are. We're all waiting."

As Dave ushered the couple in, Filmore turned back to Anna and said,

"Seven or eight years ago, three o'clock each day. Think about it."

Dave led the trio briskly through the lobby to the banquet hall where the committee was sitting. As they took their seats, Anna turned to Filmore, her mouth wide open. "OH MY GOD!"

***

Clyde returned from town with streamers and American flags for the men to decorate their tanks, transports, rocket launchers, and heavy artillery in red, white, and blue. Gus, an electrician, wired the vehicles for sound so they could broadcast patriotic tunes before the attack. Billy placed boxes of trinkets with eagles, slogans and flags for the men to throw out to the waiting crowd, before opening fire and seizing the town.

After inspecting the convoy, Red walked to Ken's tent where he had just assembled his personal arsenal in the style of traditional Orthodox prayer gear. Red laughed to see Ken with his gun belt wrapped around his arm, his revolver draped over his forehead. Red reached out to help, but Ken barked back, "I don't need your fucking help."

"You ain't going into battle looking like that soldier. You can't draw your weapons fast enough. Just let me ..."

To Red's surprise, Ken whipped out a revolver and pointed it at him. Lifting his hands high in the air, Red said, "Calm down, soldier. We're in this thing together. If ya can draw a weapon like that, dress anyway you want."

After Red left the tent, Ken stood thinking, for a moment questioning what he was doing, remembering the day that Rabbi Itzhak Rubowski burst in and caught him sitting in the john at the Lubovitch Yeshiva, wearing tallis and Tephillin, reading Playboy Magazine.

Red looked for Beau when he returned to the troops. "You're right, son. Once the battle starts. Shoot him!"

***

After waiting for Herb ten minutes, Filmore realized that something was wrong.

"What should we do?" Filmore quietly asked leaning over to Anna.

"Mayor Branstill. I think you should open this meeting."

Filmore gulped to himself before saying. "People, let's get started. Our campaign is over except for my speech at your program this afternoon? Right, Penny?"

"It's all set. I'm worried that the patients might not come," Penny replied. "I've reminded them all, but let's face it. It's Flag Daze. Anderson's got this town by the balls. With all that free food, I'm afraid they may not come back to hear you speak. I saw a sign in the main square, *Free Food for You if You Come at Two.* I'm afraid Rufus learned about our plan and has taken steps to block us.

"Can we feed them, too?" Filmore inquired. "How about a spread at the program?"

"Can't do it," Benson chimed in. "Ya don't eat inside on gosh dang Flag Day."

"Let's set it up outside, then, in front of the clinic. In fact, let's feed everyone and open the speech to the town."

"Great idea," Andrew proclaimed, the rest of the group except Benson nodding in agreement.

"There ain't no food to give," Benson said. "Anderson's bought out every store. 'Cept for two truckloads of corn I'm taking to market tomorrow, there ain't nothing left. And the bastard bought it up with tax dollars, too. Why we've got less food here than there's water in the whole dang desert."

"What about Gefilte Fish?" Rabbi Pearlman asked. "We've got some."

"Gildy Fish. I don't think so," Benson said. "Folks ain't gonna eat that no more'n you'll find a preacher at a poker game. No one's comin' for corn and gildy fish?"

"Wait," Rabbi Pearlman said. "I'll call Gelberman, the caterer. Maybe he'll have an idea."

While the rabbi left to call Gelberman on his cell, Filmore continued the meeting.

"Does anyone know where Herb is? It's awfully late and not like him."

"No," said Anna.

"Haven't seen him since the Barbara Walters Show," Dave added.

"I'm worried," said Anna.

"Me, too," added Filmore. "If anything, I thought he'd have been here already trying to talk me out of giving the speech."

"I'll pass the police station on my way back to the clinic. Let me stop and ask Barney if he's seen him," Penny said.

"Good," Peter said when Rabbi Pearlman called out and interrupted him.

"Gelberman says he's got lots of food. Just came in from Chicago. It's all Glatt Kosher. He wants to know how many will be there."

"Tell him 20," Penny called out.

"Hell!" Benson interjected. "Let's feed the whole dang town. We need all the votes we can git."

"So what'll it be?" asked the rabbi.

"A thousand, two?"

"Manny," the rabbi said returning to the phone. "Can you manage

2000?"

After a pause, the rabbi cupped the phone and said, "He says it'll be hard. He's got the Feldman Bar Mitzvah this weekend. He can't do it unless the Feldmans are willing to push up the affair, combine the Bar Mitzvah with Flag Daze."

"What would it cost?" Harold quickly asked.

"Manny, what would it cost if Ben Feldman did his Bar Mitzvah today instead of Saturday and we served 2000 guests?"

A couple a minutes later, the Rabbi cupped the phone again and talked with the group. "He's tough. Normally a hundred a plate, but on short notice, $120.00."

"Don't forget tax," Benson said. "Five per cent for the dang Governor."

Filmore dashed out his calculator, "Is the 5 percent on the extra charge, too?"

"It is now," Benson replied. "Maybe you'll run for governor and change the dang thing."

As everyone laughed, Filmore finished his calculation, calling out, "$252,000. Can we afford it?"

"Hell, yes," Harold chimed in. "I would've paid ten times as much for television ads."

"It's a done deal?" Filmore asked.

"Just about," the rabbi said. "I've got to check with the Feldmans, but I'm sure Daniel'll be delighted when he learns that we're paying for his son's Bar Mitzvah."

35 THE PARADE

Mayor Anderson and his entourage walked around town, inspecting the arrangements. Police lines were erected to direct the public to the side to watch the parade. The judge's stand was almost done. Kiosks with free food for Anderson residents, compliments of the city were set up near Anderson for Mayor Headquarters, ready to open at 2:00, when Peter planned to give his last speech.

The Mayor noticed a number of men standing on the tops of buildings. Having never met them before, he called out and waved, "Hey there friends. Welcome to town. You're gonna see a great parade. If you want to vote, let me know. It's a bit late but I've got connections."

The mayor walked on to check the voting booths. As expected, Anderson was written in large, bold letters, Branstill almost too small to read.

ANDERSON

Branstill

The Anderson Butterfly Ballot

On top of Woolworth's, Agent Thomas could see the whole town. Everyone seemed in place where they belonged. He checked his watch --

11:00 a.m. – then looked in the skies, thinking: *Where are those planes?*

***

From deep in the woods at the Outward Bound camp, General Turner signaled his troops to move. Draped in American flags, the caravan was indistinguishable from any other Flag Daze float. As they moved in toward town, the streets became lined with more and more spectators. The children ran close to the tanks. Clyde hoisted two lads on board and let them ride for a minute. Red slapped his son when he raised his rifle as three black children ran to his side.

"Come on, Pa. Lemme pick off them piccaninnies."

"Beau! Later," his father scolded. "You're a soldier. Show some discipline now."

Ken Goldberg rode in the back seat of a jeep at the front of the caravan, two soldiers in the front, one at his side.

"What's a matter, soldier?" one asked as Ken's head jerked back and forth, out of control.

"Nothing to you!" Ken barked back as he whipped out his pistol.

"Sorry," the man said, holding his hands slightly in air. "We're all a bit jumpy."

Holding out his hand, the soldier added. "I'm Traber. What's your name?"

Without answering, Ken returned his pistol to the holster that hung over his forehead.

***

By 11 a.m., the service started. The Lubovitch boys surrounded the pulpit, rocking and chanting, in traditional prayer style. For the next hour, guests kept flowing in from out of town, rushing to make this last minute affair. By noon, in time for Ben's Torah reading, most guests had arrived.

Seated in this makeshift, open air Temple at the front of the bowling alley, Ben sang Torah and Haftorah readings in beautiful tones, a well-prepared student. Daniel stood by his side, proud of his son.

Seated to the right before Ben were the men, many in traditional Lubovitch attire. To the left, there were women in fur coats and stoles, glistening in the hot, Nebraska sun. Fighting the glare that beamed off their fine jewelry, Ben sang on, a flawless performance.

Behind the congregation, the citizens of Anderson stood, farmers and townsfolk, for many the first Bar Mitzvah they'd seen. Meanwhile, Gelberman scurried around to watch his staff put together its finest spread.

***

Sitting by herself in her office at the clinic, Penny kept replaying her conversation with Officer Barney.

"No ma'am. Ain't seen him myself for quite a spell."

"It doesn't make sense, Barney. Herb is Peter's campaign manager. You don't just take off when you're the hub of the wheel."

"Maybe. But maybe not," Barney said. "There's some mighty fine fishin' out here. He coulda gone down to the stream."

"Fishing?" Penny laughed. "He's a New Yorker. Lox on a bagel's about as much fishing as he's ever done."

"Can't tell. This clean Nebraska air can sure change a fella."

"Could we look for him?"

"Can't do it, Penny," Barney replied. "These are Flag Daze. There's gonna be lots a people in town. Need all the police presence we can get. And, I gotta eat, too, you know."

That's not Barney, Penny thought to herself. He always helped whenever she needed him.

***

"Today, you are a man!" the rabbi pronounced as he shook Ben's hand. The congregation stood up to applaud before Gelberman's crew hurried them out of their seats to set up the tables and begin the affair. The musicians began playing traditional Klezmer tunes, the crowd clapping in response. Before long, the tables were set, the food was out, and the party begun.

Dave, Harold and Andrew walked around town with megaphones, inviting everyone to Ben's party. Penny's day patients led the charge followed by a sizable crowd of Andersonians. Seeing the exodus, Mayor Anderson rushed to his microphone and called out,

"The parade is coming! The parade is coming!"

Sure enough, the fractured sounds of the Anderson Junior High School Band could be heard from a distance playing the *Stars and Stripes Forever*.

***

Soon the townspeople crowded around to watch and admire the agility and acrobatics of the Hasidim doing traditional Jewish and Russian dances, puzzled to see men and women dancing apart. The music furiously played on at a frenzied pitch until the musician's took their first break, just as the parade arrived in town, the Junior High School Band turning left on Main

215

Street now in view.

After Ben's guests returned to their tables, Amos Hawkins, the county's best Square Dance caller jumped on the stage, and announced, "What about a square dance?"

The townspeople cheered while the Jews sat in surprise. Meanwhile, Otis Taylor, carrying his fiddle, jumped on the stage and began to play. Andersonians crowded onto the dance floor while Otis played and tapped his feet and Amos called out,

Take your partner, have no fear.
He may be a fella, but ya ain't no queer.
Gals with gals, you can do that too.
You ain't strange, you're just a Jew.

Before long, Jew and Gentile alike crowded the floor, dancing with delight to Otis' calls.

***

"Peter," Penny called after she walked to the bowling alley. "I'm going back to the station. We still haven't found Herb, and there was something very odd about Barney's response."

When Penny realized that Filmore had failed to hear her words, clapping to the music, she called again, "Peter!"

"Oh hi, Penny. Isn't this great? These folks are all going to vote for me. I just hope they don't have too much fun and forget to go to the poll."

"I think we have more important things to worry about."

Still not responding to Penny, Filmore's face lit up. "I've got it, Penny. The Bunny Hop. They do that at Bar Mitzvahs? Why don't we Bunny Hop them down to the polls."

"Not the Hasids," Penny replied.

"How about two lines, one for male bunnies, one for female bunnies."

"Maybe," Penny thought, now shaking her head. "That's not why I came here! We've got to find Herb."

"Any luck with Barney?" Filmore asked.

"That's the point. He acted strangely when I asked him. Something's up. Here, take these keys. You go to the clinic and get ready to give your speech. I'll run over to the police station. Then, I'll round up the patients and bring them over."

"OK," Filmore answered, his tone mournful wishing he could stay at the party.

***

The Junior High School Band had reached the bowling alley, ready to turn right toward the judge's stand just as the Square Dance ended and the Klezmer band returned to the stage. Through the competing tones of Hava Nagila and the Stars and Stripes Forever, Ben's guests began to dance. Soon, the talented Lubovitch boys spun into a dancing frenzy while the crowd of Andersonians split their attention between the party and the parade. The students led Ben to a chair and lifted him high in the air, surrounded by a circle of men. The Yeshiva girls grabbed Mrs. Feldman, who after considerably more coaxing and her husband's offer to use his suspenders to strap her in, allowed them to lift her high in the air, too.

Not far from the festivities, Red and his men brought up the rear of the parade in full combat gear. In tense anticipation, the men stopped throwing out trinkets to the throngs of begging children who were running along. With Ken twitching and Beau waiting to bag his first Jew, Red spied the viewing stand and turned to Clyde who was peering out from inside the lead tank, and signaled him to turn the big guns that way.

***

Penny walked to the police station. With all the officers in the crowd enjoying the parade, no one was there. She jiggled the locked door twice, before looking around, then kicking it hard and breaking in. Hearing the alarm go off, Penny quickly ran through the station until she found Herb sitting in his cell. She grabbed the key hanging by the side and let him out. Before long they were on the street, running as fast as they could just before Barney returned.

"What happened, Herb?!" she asked.

"It's big, Penny. Bigger than you could ever imagine."

"Look!" he shouted pointing to the military vehicles at the end of the parade. Ken was there, sitting in a jeep, in battle fatigues, fully armed in the form of Tephillin.

"Ken!" Penny called.

Quickly, Ken pulled out a revolver, a silencer attached, and shot, "Pfft." Drowned out by patriotic and Jewish music, Penny's screams went unheard as she fell in Herb's arms, dead.

"Pfft," a second shot came, barely missing Herb's head. Letting Penny drop, Herb ran as fast as he could, huffing all the way, dragging his aging body along. With the clinic in sight, 500 feet away, hoping to warn Peter, Herb felt a presence grab him from behind, tackling him to the ground.

"Ow," Herb cried feeling an object crack against his back.

"Why'd you do that," Barney implored as he put his nightstick away.

"We've got to warn Peter," Herb cried. "Ken's in town."

"Look," Barney said, pointing to a formation of fighter jets now high in the sky. "We're ready to fight back. He'll be OK."

***

By now, Red's troops were even with the bowling alley, near the center of town. He watched through binoculars ready to signal the assault on Town Hall. Seeing Mayor Anderson only 50 yards away, Red raised his hand, a ready signal to alert his troops. Before he could lower his hand, to signal to attack, Beau spotted the Bar Mitzvah party, Ben and Mrs. Feldman high in the air.

"Jews!" Beau cried aiming his rifle, catching Mrs. Feldman's fox stole in its cross hairs.

"No!" Red screamed. He lowered his hand trying to grab the rifle. Beau's shot went off, missing Mrs. Feldman, soaring past the crowd, landing on the buffet table, and getting lodged into the brisket. Thinking that Red had signaled the start of the war, his troops began to fire, hitting the judges, town hall, and Mae Anderson's Hallmark Card Shoppe. The sharpshooters fired back from their places on top of the buildings. A low flying military jet zeroed in, strafing Red's men. The brisket slid down the table, sending kugel and kishke flying in all directions.

36 THE FINAL SOLUTION

Ken jumped out of the jeep and ran to the back wall of the bowling alley. Shuffling to his side, rifle in hand, he peeked around the corner and saw the Nebraska National Guard in hand to hand combat with Red's militia. Behind him, he saw two Hasidic Jews fly into the Mitzvah Mobile. Ken dropped to the ground and crawled to the van, a knife in his left hand, the rifle in his right. At the entrance, he quickly sprung into the van, stabbing one Jew, slashing another one's throat. Three more men at the back of the van threw their prayer books at him before getting mowed down in Ken's lethal assault.

Ken rushed to the front, jumping into the driver's seat. Screeching as he stepped on the gas, Ken pulled the vehicle out and headed for the mental health clinic.

While Ben's guests struggled for safety running into the bowling alley, Anna broke away after the van crying, "Phil. He's coming to get you."

***

Ken quickly reached the clinic. His weapons drawn, he moved through the building carefully checking each room in search of Peter.

"I'm back here," Filmore called out. "In the day room. Turn right when you get to the end of the hall. There's no one else here."

A trap, Ken thought. A trained commando with the reflexes of a cat, Ken edged forward, slowly, fully alert. He reached the day room, swiftly kicked the door open, and sprang into the room, aiming his rifle at Peter standing there.

"Ken. Just come in. Let's talk."

Ken stood still, glaring intently.

Noticing that Ken's holster had fallen off his forehead and his gun belt

219

was now draped around his ankles Filmore moved slightly forward saying, "You look awful, Ken. Let me fix those things."

Ken's warning shot over Peter's head caused him to back off and raise his hands.

"Sorry," Filmore said. "I just wanted to help."

"You had your chance to help. You could've stayed to the plot. Why help me now?"

Peter pursed his lips and thought. "I'm in love, Ken. I thought you'd be happy for me."

"In love! With that slut!" Ken shouted. "You read what she does."

Filmore shrugged his shoulders, a pleading you-know-I-already-know look. "She's not really like that. She fucked around in college, but she's pretty straight now. You know her Dad was a Lutheran minister?"

"She's a Jew!" screamed Ken. "A goddamn, fucking (Ken paused to emphasize the difference intended in the second use of his word) fucking Jew. She doesn't love you. You're this year's sin. She'll be fucking someone else next year."

"That's not true," Peter said. "That's your story. I know what really happened. Remember, I know you and her from before."

"You remember having the crap beaten out of you by Aunt Cindy. You remember children taunting you into submission. You remember getting molested at the foster home. And you remember eating snot at camp. That's what you'll goddamn remember."

"Why, Ken? Why would you want me to think those things? I came to you for help. Why the lies?"

Shooting another bullet near Filmore's feet, Ken screamed. "I don't fucking lie. I help people. I bring out repressed memories."

"No you don't, Ken. You create false memories. You trap people with your psychoanalytic bullshit. I'd have been a thousand times better off having ten sessions with Albert Ellis. Three years of your crap did me in."

"You were getting better. We were almost there. The real stuff was right beneath the surface, but you couldn't take it. I've seen this before. Resistance, acting out, flight into health. It's all here," Ken shouted as he pulled out a copy of Freud's *Interpretation of Dreams* from one of his holsters and waved it about.

"Your theories are bullshit, Ken. You could have been a great therapist, but you wouldn't change with the times. Freud was a genius, but for God's sake, it's a hundred years later."

"I made you a man. I gave you an identity," Ken shouted. "And I let you star in my first novel."

"Right," Peter derisively replied. "What a star. You give me a lunatic friend who kills himself while I'm masturbating to death."

"It was something you had to go through."

"It was nothing of the kind," Filmore exclaimed. "I got off so that you could get off."

"You were jerking off before you ever met me."

"Of course I was. My mom died, and I had just broken up with Shirley. I wasn't ready to date so I jerked off every 3 or 4 days instead. I didn't come to you for sexual problems. I needed to work some things out about my mother. You turned my grief into a three-year five-day-a-week ordeal that would have gone on forever if I hadn't dropped out."

"You needed it, Peter. Your masturbation was out of control."

"Quit the bullshit, Ken. You made me masturbate. Remember the sessions. I'd talk about my Mom and you'd ask, 'I wonder why you haven't told me about your sex life yet?' I said that I wasn't in a relationship and you said, 'I wonder why you aren't jerking off?' I couldn't figure out what you were getting at so I said, 'I do, maybe twice a week'. I was hoping to get back to what was bothering me about my Mom but you kept asking me these odd questions: 'I wonder why you aren't masturbating every day?'

"I started to feel like I should so I did. Then, you kept asking me why I was only masturbating once a day? Before long you had me in the peep shows, at the horse races, on the internet, banging away all the time."

"You needed to, Peter. You had to get the poison out of your system. Neurosis comes from semen. If it stays inside too long, you go insane."

"Is that why you jerked off, behind the coach, each session?!" Peter shouted, now enraged.

"I never did that. That was YOUR psychotic transference."

"That's what you wanted me to think. You propped a mirror on your desk so that I could see you beat off while I lay on the couch. Then, you'd challenge my perception whenever I brought it up. I really thought I was going insane."

"You were and you have. Look at you. First, you leave treatment. Now, you leave my book!" Ken shouted firing another shot close to Peter.

"You know why I left treatment, Ken? I'll tell you. It was Anna. I had my session at 2:00. Hers was at 3:00. We'd pass each other in the waiting room, scared to make eye contact. It took time, but we finally talked. We were so goddamned scared of you that we started meeting in the bathroom before her session. Anna told me you jerked off in her sessions just like you did in mine. We figured it out. You worked 8 hours a day, nine to five, seeing eight patients each day, five days a week. Since $8 = 2^3$, you could jerk off all day and stay in powers of two."

"I had to!" Ken screamed. "It was the only way I could help you. I had to keep the poison out of my system."

"The only poison that *I* had to get out of *my* system was you. But then, you fucking put Anna and me in your goddamn novel before we could leave analysis."

"Damn you, Peter. That's a crock. You're fucking ungrateful. This is what I get for all I did for you. Before me, you couldn't even touch your cock, let alone jerk off when you wanted to."

"That's crap, Ken. Sex has never been a problem for me. I've always been able to fuck when I wanted to, or masturbate if I preferred."

Red with rage, Peter reached into his pants, pulled out his penis and began to rub it, glaring at Ken saying, "Watch. I'll do it now."

Ken stood awed as he saw a huge penis emerge from Filmore's pants, twice the size of his own. As Peter stroked it, Ken shouted, "Stop!"

Filmore stroked harder, and Ken dropped to one knee. Peter rubbed his cock, and Ken cocked his weapon.

***

Inured to the mortar falling all around, Anna raced through the streets to the mental health center, the door now locked. She drew back her right forearm and smashed the front window, letting herself in. Dripping with blood, she ran through the clinic screaming, "Phil!"

"Here!" Peter called.

Anna followed the sound, into the day room to see her man standing there, fully erect. Without noticing Ken to the side, Anna broke into a smile and shouted, "Wait! I'll suck you off."

Aware that Filmore was ready to come, Anna flew through the room, entering the sights of Ken's gun, landing on her knees, sliding forward across the floor, stopping 2 feet from Peter's crotch. Peter who was no longer rubbing himself turned his hips toward her face and tried to thrust his organ her way. Anna lurched her head forward hoping to catch his penis with her mouth. Before she could, Peter climaxed and Ken, seeing the white of his orgasm, pulled the trigger.

***

The first shot caught Peter's right shoulder causing black ink to spray against the wall, forming the word, "Mad." The second shot hit Anna, the Hebrew word שׁוּם sent flying through the air. As Ken riddled shot after shot into Peter's and Anna's lifeless bodies, ink squirted everywhere. Soon, the room was filled with declarative sentences and imaginary numbers, dangling participles, quadratic equations. Numbers and letters floated like dust dashing in and out of compound sentences and complicated formula. As the carnage continued, Peter's and Anna's bodies disappeared: ashes to ashes, ink to ink. No longer able to see, Ken listened to the sounds of war outside and the voices laughing in his head.

37 THE LAST NOVEL

Ken looked around and saw some college students laughing four tables away. Behind them, there was a sign, LITERATURE AND FICTION, suspended in the air over several rows of books. Ken lowered his head knowing *Peter Squared* was not on the shelf.

"So what do you say?" Herb asked.

"About what?" Ken replied, jarred from his thoughts.

"About what?!" Herb laughed. "Haven't you heard anything I've said."

"I don't know," Ken shrugged his shoulders. "Why did we have to meet here?"

"Look around," Herb answered pointing to a mural on the wall at the Barnes and Noble café. "Kafka, Hemingway, Faulkner, they're all here. Look, there's Steinbeck. Wasn't he your favorite?"

"When I was a kid, he was. Probably the first great author I ever read. I used to lie around daydreaming that I was him. Then, I'd think, *Who am I kidding? I'm good at math, but I can't write.*"

"But you *can* write and you *are* a writer, Ken," Herb insisted. "You've just got to write."

"I don't know, Herb," Ken said shaking his head. "I just don't know."

"What don't you know? You're already published. *Squared* should have been a bestseller. It just didn't get reviewed. So what? It was your first novel. Keep writing and I promise you, things will change. "

"And what if it's the only book I ever write? Harper Lee stopped with *Mockingbird.* Why can't I be happy with just one novel to my name?"

"You tell me," Herb asked. "Are you happy?"

"Not really," Ken reluctantly admitted.

"Well, I care," Herb went on. "I believe in your work. I believe in you. And if that's not good enough, do it for me. After all, I'm your agent and I don't get paid unless your book sells. It's no longer in the book stores so right now, you can only buy it online. Write a second book, and the first will sell again."

"I know," Ken wistfully replied. "I appreciate all you've done and wish it was worth your while. But it's not in me. I'm a psychologist, not a writer."

"You can still be a psychologist. Just take some time off to write the next book."

"You know I can't do that, Herb," Ken said. "Two kids in college?"

"Then write on the side. That's how you wrote *Squared.* You used to get up at five so you could write before work?"

"I know. I just can't do it."

"Why not?!" Herb demanded. "Tell me one good reason why you can't write another book."

His hand shaking slightly, Ken reached for his cappuccino and sipped it slowly. He put the cup down, looked off to the side, and tapped his fingers on the top of the table before looking back at Herb. "It tears me apart, Herb. You can't imagine what it's like, writing a novel, creating characters, knowing all the time you're describing yourself. It's wrenching and exhausting. It takes an enormous toll. I've thought lots about writing a sequel, with Peter meeting Anna and finally getting laid. I just can't do it. I'm really afraid. I think this time; it could be me, not Peter, who will have gone mad."

ACKNOWLEDGEMENTS

Peter Cubed is a sequel to my first literary novel, *Peter Squared*. I would not have written the book except for the encouragement of Pat Walsh, my editor at MacAdam Cage and my internet, writer friends, Joyce Faulkner and Ace Boggess. I appreciate the help Joyce and Ace gave me reviewing the first draft along with Pierre Tribaudi, my longtime friend and Paulette Lively, an old second grade classmate with whom I reconnected by chance on a flight to Belgium many years ago. They also reviewed the first draft. I appreciate Jenna Sabad for her feedback as someone who had not read *Peter Squared* before reading *Peter Cubed*. As always, I have deep appreciation and love for my wife and long-term ally in everything interesting and off-beat we've opted to do through the course of our lives. Maryka and I set the tone for our relationship years ago when we planned a one-month vacation in the Canadian Rockies but landed in New Mexico on a whim.

ABOUT THE AUTHOR

Ken Goldberg is a clinical psychologist, a graduate of Long Island University, who has specialized in treating the mentally ill in community-based programs. More recently, he has become a leading critic of homework policy and the author of *The Homework Trap: How to Save the Sanity of Parents, Students and Teachers*. Before becoming a psychologist, Dr. Goldberg studied mathematics at Tulane and Columbia Universities. He is a recipient of the Glendy Burke Award, a Woodrow Wilson Fellow, and has studied mathematics at Columbia University on a National Science Foundation Fellowship. Dr. Goldberg has three grown children and lives with his wife outside Philadelphia. *Peter Cubed* is his second literary novel and a sequel to his first literary novel, *Peter Squared*, originally published by MacAdam Cage Publishing in 2000 and re-released in 2012 through Wyndmoor Press.